# Praise for
## TWELVE MONDAYS

"*You grabbed my attention from the beginning and left me wanting to know more.*"  —H. H.


"*Twelve Mondays gives us a peek into life's struggles. Great read where the reality of humanity gets in the way of living. But for God!*"  —Linda J.


"*This story is a wonderful completion of how life happens to us; it takes trauma and defines the root. An amazing unraveling which draws readers to think on a higher level. Well done, I was pleased with the plot, I was most amazed at the descriptive planning. I recommend this book to those who love realities that take us on a journey and guides to know the truth. Profoundly settling, a book definitely for the masses!*"  —author Jamieya B. Johnson


"*I thoroughly enjoyed this eloquently written book, believable and relatable characters. I loved Emma's relationship with her Grandma Rose. The main character's traumas and family dynamic kept me enthralled in her struggles. I will be reading book two.*  —author S. Daniels


"*One of the things I liked about the book was the author's writing style. The story described Emma's life in a fast pace, yet also in a detailed way, from her childhood up to how she came to be in the present. Another thing I appreciated was the realistic take the author took in regard to alcohol addiction, how one copes after a traumatic experience, and how Emma chose or ended up living the life she currently had. Every small event had their own meaning and accumulated to each significant event that occurred in Emma's life. Because of this, there were times when I'd been caught by surprise, not expecting that such small details would come into play in future events. It's obvious that the author planned the story well which made my reading experience enjoyable. In this story, I felt like Emma was human; someone who, despite her wealthy status and upbringing, made reckless mistakes, had flaws, and tried to protect herself in ways that she thought was the most convenient.  —Aubrey L.*

# Also by Laura Gaisie

*Twelve Hearings, Book Two*

*Twelve Days of Terror, Book Three*

# TWELVE MONDAYS

Book 1 of 4

Laura Gaisie

*In loving memory of my grandmother,*

*Essie Lee Colter Caldwell*

# PART I

*CHILDHOOD*

*1991 - 2008*

# ONE

*The Corridor*

MAYBE THEY WERE flashing lights, but how was Emma to know for sure? One minute she's sitting in her Mercedes, wet-faced, and runny-nosed from crying, and the next she's standing against that awful bright light, calling her to attention. She flinched, then shielded heavy eyelids that concealed brown eyes, swollen from tears which made it difficult to see clearly. Feeling detached from her body, Emma tended to her legs, which were weightless but intact. The same with her arms, undamaged, albeit languishing limply at her sides.

The light before her rose and fell; it swelled and then collapsed like a beating heart. Raising an arm over her eyes, the light would decrease. Lowering her hand, the glow increased again. She played peek-a-boo with the rays until frustration replaced her curiosity; and then gratification, realizing a diminished sensitivity to the light. When she was able to see, Emma admired her surroundings.

Pristine-white walls towering above seemed to scold and

admonish, saying, "Wash your hands before touching anything!" Turning her palms up, she checked to make sure there was no residue of dirt—or bloodstains. She twisted a wad of material from her shirt in her fists, a trick she'd learned to do in first grade that calmed her nerves. She was probably dreaming or maybe sleepwalking after crashing on some random person's couch. It was something she'd done before, usually after a night of partying and drinking.

Maybe after crying and binge drinking last night, she had found a late-night party somewhere in North Jersey; that's where she was headed when she left her apartment yesterday. Sighing, Emma thought about her promise to get sober and was disappointed with her apparent relapse. Closing her eyes, she quickly silenced that inner voice that liked to tell her how 'Stupid' she was. That's when the glow returned and resumed its playful exchange, rising and falling again, until her eyes adjusted once more.

She had an urge to explore but looked to the white walls first which seemed to whisper another command, "Clean your feet before taking another step!" This seemingly subliminal request directed her attention to the floor beneath—Gold? Looking again at the spotless walls and back down at the glistening gilded floor, her apprehension was fully realized. Emma suppressed her breathing out of a newfound reverence for the immaculate quarters; the light, still rising and falling, was a reminder to breathe.

Taking in a vigorous amount of air, she discovered a fleeting scent of flowers traipsing through her nostrils. With curiosity overriding trepidation, Emma took her first step forward. There had to be a garden at the end of the corridor.

"Jasmine?" she questioned, inhaling again, then imagined if the walls could answer.

*"Yes, and lavender too!"*

Waiting to hear an audible response, she shook her head.

"Walls don't talk, and that light is not breathing," she mused to herself. "But since we're having this conversation," she said to the walls, "I'd like orange blossoms too!"

It was the Jasmine, primarily, that called for her at the far end of the corridor. Emma knew there had to be a lush garden full of pungent buds, just beyond the walls. Readying for her next step forward, she found that her legs were like cement beams, the soles of her feet as cinder blocks. Though she tried, her legs wouldn't budge. Looking down, expecting to see restraints, she found there was no physical barrier.

"Why are you afraid—just do it!" She questioned, then commanded her body to move.

Refusing movement, Emma slowed her breathing. If she shifted from this spot, she'd wake from a dream, and would be back in her plush Manhattan apartment where her inner demons had first surfaced. As awkward as it was, standing still between these majestic walls that watched for intrusions, made her feel safe; from others and herself. Sighing, Emma imagined that she had outrun every threat and was finally free from harm.

She reminded herself that things were not going well. In fact, everything except her finances was disastrous. She had been betrayed by her boyfriend. Her best friend was refusing to return phone calls, and after quitting her job, Emma lacked direction and motivation. It wasn't like she needed to work, having the trust-fund left behind from Grandma Rose, and the robust portfolio her Dad secured; but like a wise friend once told her, "Idle time wreaks havoc on the mind!" It was her personal goal and unspoken dream that birthed an unremitting quest within. Emma wanted success in the one area that money couldn't guarantee… relationships.

As a child, she struggled with over-talking others, finishing their sentences or changing the topic abruptly. She was always busy, needing to find something to do with her hands, completing school mate's tasks before they had a chance to do it themselves. School teachers loved her, which made her an easy target for bullying. Emma learned the hard way to shut her mouth, take deep breaths, and sit still.

Having no siblings and only a handful of friends, Emma required uninterrupted attention which frustrated her Mother. Her constant rearranging of home décor and incessant talking angered the woman. As an adult, Emma channeled her excessive energy into early morning runs and late-night dancing. A meaningless job served as a day-filler, alongside scheduled dance practices and auditions. On down days, she'd hang out at Central Park, or her favorite deli in Midtown, talking to strangers until they walked away out of annoyance.

Cordial and brief discussions were tolerable if she could shorten details to under a five-minute pitch. She desired meaningful encounters and found some solace in others who met after sunset, defying sleep and morning alarm clocks. That's when Emma first noticed what she named, 'The ugly voice.' It spoke during her quiet, alone moments, and liked to keep a record of her past mistakes and shortcomings. Reminding her no matter how far she ran, the ugly voice would either catch up to her or be there waiting when she arrived. Keeping busy and moving quickly seemed to drown out the noise on days when the accusing voice seemed particularly incessant. Those days tended to find her acting recklessly, spending money on frivolous things and wasting time with random strangers.

Movement from the far end of the corridor drew her back to the wall, and the floor. Whatever it was, it moved faster than her eyes could register.  Several feet away a door came into focus. With slow, deliberate steps, she approached close enough to touch the doorknob, which was dull and unstable, lacking the luster of the rest of the corridor. The impulse to open the door came, then left quickly. Lowering her arm, the urge to stand still was greater. Then, there was the corridor. Where did it lead?

*Beep…Beep…*

Just like the movement, she could not see—and the door—now a sound came from seemingly nowhere. It was faint, but Emma was sure she heard a low, consistent beep. Pressing her ear to the door, she strained to hear if someone was on the other side. With another beep, she gasped and stepped away until her back came to rest against the opposite wall. Shaking her head until the sound was gone, she convinced herself the beeps were imaginary.

She hated her curiosity. Why couldn't she be content with what was here in the room? Interruptions at this point were not an option. There was only one sure decision to be made. Closing her eyes, she wished the door to go away.

A gentle breeze brushed past her face. It was more like a warm wind that signified the presence of another person. Emma, sensing she was no longer alone, opened her eyes and looked around the corridor. A small girl was sitting in a white overstuffed chair waving for her to come near. She had hazel eyes, like Emma's father's, that accented a small oval face with droopy eyelids and the cutest little cupids-bow lips.

"Sit here with me."

Swinging her feet and wiggling pudgy toes, she motioned again. Although her shoulders had been tight and her back stiff, Emma relaxed after seeing the girl motion for her to come and sit.

Drawn by the twinkle of the mysterious girl's eyes, Emma separated herself from the wall and walked over to the chair. This was the movement, and the sound Emma was hearing. As she sat down, she observed the girl's only garment was a crimson red dress.

Bare feet hanging over the edge of the chair seemed to reveal the girl's carefree nature and desire for individuality. She was like a porcelain doll, untouched on a display shelf.

"What's your name?" asked Emma.

"Soon—," she said, then giggled.

"Soon? Soon as your parents get here. Right, you shouldn't talk to strangers," said Emma, nodding her head to show her approval.

"No!" The girl shook her head. She looked at Emma as if she should know better.

"Where's your Mommy?" Emma looked towards the end of the corridor, then to the door, "Is your Mommy here?" She tried to sound calm, so as not to expose her apprehension.

"Yep, Mommy's here," she said, whispering like she had a secret no one else could hear.

*Beep…Beep…*

Emma kept her eyes on the girl, who didn't respond to the faint beeping but moved closer. If this is her home, she was obviously accustomed to tuning the sound out. Climbing in her lap, the little girl touched the tip of Emma's nose. Then one chubby finger trailed the length of her face, from her chin, up her cheeks, across both eyebrows and around Emma's hairline. Emma could feel the girl's rapid heartbeats against her chest. The girl explored further, leaning in and inspecting every facet of Emma's features. Her breath was warm and smelled like sweet milk.

Emma liked the close proximity of the girl, poking her belly button, and tickling her tummy. The girl squealed, enjoying the play. She giggled and then peeled herself out of Emma's arms. Adjusting her dress around her knees, she smiled at Emma. "This is how girl's sit," she said, sitting back in the chair, instructing Emma to do the same.

She seemed to be waiting. Sitting with folded hands in her lap as if she was instructed to sit still and not mess up her dress.

"You shouldn't be here by yourself…I can keep you company," said Emma. "Small children shouldn't be left alone."

Why some people had kids they couldn't properly care for was beyond her understanding.

"Someone should be here with you, anything could happen…" then she thought about what she was saying. "Nothing will happen, I'll stay with you. I need a moment to think anyway, so much going on—not that you'd know anything about that…responsibilities, obligations—then there are other things…."

The girl watched as she continued to ramble.

"Let me wait with you," Emma sighed, then paused to take a breath, the way she had taught herself. The girl reached over to rub her hand, which helped Emma to relax.

"What's your name?" the girl asked.

"Emma-Lynn St. Roman, can you believe it?" She rolled her eyes, remembering how much she hated the name that always sounded like 'Gremlin' when uttered quickly. The boys teased her in elementary school until her Grandmother had the good sense to shorten her name to Emma, dropping Lynn.

"Everyone calls me Emma though," she said.

"Emm…lyn—," the girl practiced saying her name, struggling

with the pronunciation.

"Have you waited long?" Emma asked.

The girl, distracted by her name, made up a catchy rhyme.

"Em-ma, Emm-Lynn…How's it spelled, Emm-Lynn?"

Kicking her feet, the girl exuded happiness, but also hidden anxiety; Emma knew this trait well. While looking her over, she was drawn by a desire to hold her and thought about asking if she wanted to sit on her lap again. Placing a hand on the chair between them, she waited to see if the girl would respond to the offer for intimacy. Her heart quickened when the girl stroked her hand then placed hers inside of Emma's and raised it her face. Her cheeks felt like an apricot, warm from sitting in summer heat; soft, round and slightly fuzzy.

She had a headful of ebony-colored curls, thick like sheep's wool. The girl continued humming as Emma twirled a lock of her hair.

"You are so beautiful!" said Emma.

The little girl smiled, and her diamond shaped eyes stared into Emma's, causing butterflies to stir in Emma's stomach. Her features were oddly familiar, like a face she'd met before. It was more than the color of her eyes that resembled Emma's Dad; the shape of her eyes, the way she held her head, even her laugh.

"Emmlynn, how old are you?" the girl asked.

"Twenty-six," she answered, holding up her fingers.

When the girl began to count her fingers, Emma joined her. They counted in unison from one to twenty-six, then from one to thirty-six, and of course, that led up to one hundred. Counting faster the higher they went in number.

"It's good I made you laugh," the girl said, "you need your family too."

Emma looked away before the girl could see her face, bit her lip, and studied the door. It was best to steer away from this topic. For Emma, family was a sour subject with a bitter root. The girl waited for a reaction; her wisdom seeming to exceed her years. Emma contemplated the door that also demanded a response. Remembering to breathe, she sighed heavier than expected, then took another breath.

Suffering a little discomfort with the girl was more desirable than returning to address what waited. Swallowing the lump in her throat, Emma looked at the girl.

"You're a beautiful child, and smart," she said, "thank you for making me smile."

There was no way she could explain to the girl that family was the reason she was on the run. The ones she loved were gone, and the one she despised were probably still searching for her. Emma was tired of running from her past, and, more than that, the secrets that threatened to expose her truth.

"I'll sit and wait with you," she said, trying to ignore a feeling she knew too well.

Guilt was like an old friend visiting from back home. You wanted to show how you'd grown, your achievements and accomplishments, but couldn't because your friend kept bringing up the way you used to be. How you used to do things. Then by the end of the visit, your friend decides to linger—just until they got on their feet.

Her guilt was reliable, like no other friend she'd known. Greeting her every waking morning and kissing her goodnight at bedtime.

"How long?" was a question Emma often asked herself, expecting her old friend to answer, but it never did.

The problem with houseguests who outstay their welcome is they develop a false sense of privilege and contentment. Eventually, they invite others into your home unannounced. Shame was an unwanted guest. Guilt and shame were like-minded and had a plan together to overthrow Emma's kingdom. They shook hands, not like a greeting, but a tag team.

Emma devised ways to outsmart her guilt; but this new friend was crippling and selfish in nature, intolerable to others and any extracurricular activities. Shame prevented normal functioning of her day. This type of friendship drained an individual, and yet one couldn't imagine why the relationship continued. Her previous attempts to oust shame were futile, but today she would finally have her victory.

"♪Emma-lynn…"

The girl sang her name again, hands bouncing in the air while her feet continued their back and forth rhythm. Emma had to force a smile. Like her Dad, she rarely smiled, guarding her emotions behind a stoic face. Taking a deep breath, she laid back into the seat. For a moment the corridor fell silent. Peace inviting her to rest, she closed her eyes.

*Beep…Beep…*

The beeps were repetitious and ominous, a reminder of how temporal her day could be. The girl's humming was a pleasant distraction, so Emma hummed along with her until the beeps quickened, causing her to sit on the edge of her seat.

"Can you tell me something?" the girl asked.

"Hmm…about me?" Emma answered. When the girl nuzzled against her side, Emma rolled her neck and shoulders, took a deep breath and then relaxed into the chair.

"Well, I have no brothers or sisters, so that makes me an only child—are you an only child too?" Emma asked.

When the girl didn't answer, she continued. She told of the home she grew up in that was cozy but couldn't compare to this mansion the girl lived in with her family. Then of her grandparents' ranch, with lush trees and neighing horses.

"And your friends, what are their names?" the girl asked.

The question struck a chord causing Emma to cringe. Reminding herself of the child's innocence, she adjusted in her seat and forged ahead with memories from elementary school when little boys ate their boogers and chased the girls with sticky fingers. The girls with scuffed leather shoes and uniformed outfits played jump rope and hopscotch. A lot can happen in eighteen years. Her Father was now gone. Why he was taken, and Reba was left, she would never understand. Her Father's older brother lived in Florida. He'd want to see her soon, but he reminded her of Daddy, so she had avoided him. Then there was her Grandpa, though most days he didn't even know his own name. She also knew he'd be a reminder of her Grandmother.

"My Father has a lot of children, and he loves them all," said the girl, with eyes that smiled. "You can stay with us if you want," she said. He had to be a rich man, this Father with many children, living in a place like this—the golden floors.

"Are you waiting for your Daddy?" Emma asked.

"Nope, my Mommy." She shook her head and then crossed her ankles, folded hands resting neatly in her lap.

"Where is she? Did she tell you to wait here alone?" Emma inquired. She balanced her tone and faked a smile.

"I'm not alone." The girl chuckled.

Of course she was not alone, not with Emma sitting beside her.

# TWO

EMANUEL AND REBAKAH Lynn St. Roman married in January of 1989. Emanuel was a man with a stern look that matched his personality. Thick eyebrows and piercing, hazel eyes made him appear intense, which worked to his advantage in his law practice.

Emma wished she had eyes like her Dad's. Instead, she ended up with her Father's skin tone and her Mother's eyes; almond shaped brown eyes, and a long oval face were Reba's contribution. For Emma, it was a constant reminder every time she stared into a mirror of the woman she wanted to forget. Though she couldn't deny it, her light brown eyes were a compliment against her cinnamon colored skin. The small, flat nose, on the other hand, seemed out of place on a face with exaggerated features, like thick eyebrows and a wide-set mouth.

Reba was a giggly, flirtatious woman with butterscotch colored skin and curly hair. She was Emanuel's trophy wife before Emma ever came along. Being a parent changed everything meaning the lovely Mrs. St. Roman now had to cook meals, wear flats instead of heels, and carry diaper bags in exchange for Haute Couture handbags. Nevertheless, she had no interest in parenting. As soon as Emma was old enough, Reba insisted on being called by first name instead of Mom.

Emma entertained the possibility, as she had in the past, that maybe Reba wasn't her birth Mother at all. At least that would explain her actions. Otherwise, the inescapable reality was that she simply didn't care for Emma; ignoring the girl while coming and going as she pleased, with no regard for a child's needs. If that wasn't bad enough, when Emanuel backed Reba into a corner about her lack of motherly affection, she laughed in his face and abandoned them both. Emanuel's Mother soon stepped in, filling the void. Things could've turned out much worse, though they eventually did, but not on her Grandma's watch.

Emma imagined the girl was about four-years old, which would've been the approximate age that Emma began spending weekends with her grandparents in Castle Rock. She remembered their first stop would always be an appointment with Grandma Rose's hair stylist. Not only did she have a slightly darker complexion than her Mother, but Emma also had thick, coarse hair like Grandma Rose. The hairstylist would first wash, then blow-dry her hair until it was light and bouncy when she flipped her neck from side to side. Afterward, she received a mani and pedi before heading to her Grandparents' horse ranch.

Grandma Rose had a way of making everything feel magical. Emma needed only to imagine a desire, and somehow, her wish was granted. One day, she recalled looking at the dreadfully worn out moccasins on her feet, with their defiant tongue, and wished for a new pair of shoes to go with her new white dress. Emma knew what she wanted, a shiny pair of red shoes with tiny dots, barely noticeable. They were in the storefront window and would go perfect.

"What you need is a beautiful pair of red shoes to go with your lovely new dress," said Grandma Rose and winked.

"Bet you're wondering how I knew?" She asked while slicking down Emma's flyaway strands blown out of place from the wind.

Emma was too young to understand then, but now she knew; Grandma Rose had watched as she stared at the shoes in the window, then frowned at the moccasins on her feet.

Those were her fairytale days, like Cinderella's transformation. Grandma Rose was her Fairy Godmother, the SUV was her chariot, and the women at the salon were the mice. One tamed her hair, another fussed over her dress, and the shoe store clerk fitted her with a shiny pair of shoes that winked at her in the midday sun as she trotted back to the SUV.

"Take your time," said Grandma Rose, worrying that her new shoes would scuff on the pavement before they made it home.

Emma slowed her pace to a skip, glanced in a store window, and smiled at her reflection. She was eager for the ride, and all the fuss over her wardrobe made her nervous.

"Now? Can we go now?" Emma was ready after the salon treatment and makeover.

"One more stop, baby," said Grandma Rose, who was trying to concentrate on her next errand.

One stop quickly turned into five, depending on which of Grandma Rose's friends wanted to see the little princess. Emma didn't mind those stops, as the older ladies would slide money into her glitter Pouch Ette; ones and five-dollar bills, coins were rare. After she was a few dollars richer, and her cheeks a little redder from their pinches, Grandma Rose would whisk her away, finally, to the ball that awaited her at the ranch. She had fidgeted with her dress and played with her hair the entire ride. Emma thought back and smiled, remembering her giddiness while sitting in the passenger seat of her Grandmother's black SUV.

There wasn't an actual ball. The fanfare, however, that surrounded her arrival was as grand as any ball she could have attended. Emma rubbed the chair, imagining the feel of the SUV's buff leather seats. She could almost hear the soft hum of its engine as they cruised down the interstate from Denver to Castle Rock. Wind from the sunroof blowing through her freshly styled hair caused brief concern. For a time, she held strands together but eventually gave up and relished the wind in her hair.

The ranch sprawled across 278 acres, land that her Grandpa insisted on having to accommodate his passion for training and boarding horses. He told anyone who listened that he would gladly add another hundred or so acres if his wife wouldn't nag him about it. Emma once overheard him telling Grandma Rose that the property was an "investment worth every dollar to the acre!"

Their two-story, five-bedroom custom house, with a four-stall garage, was a comfortable compromise between the two. Around the holidays when their elder son, Eli Jr., visited from Orlando with his wife and three children, Grandpa liked to tease that he had planned to knock down walls and add extra rooms to accommodate them all. Grandma Rose always reminded him of their agreement, "You rule the land, I reign inside the castle!" The house remained modestly structured.

After his retirement from the military, then Denver County, Grandpa became restless, saying he still had a lot of fight left in him. He was a heavy-handed man but rode his horse gently; speaking softly in its ears, whispering secrets he'd probably told no other soul. He wasn't as kind with his hired help, and it became common for Grandpa to introduce a new worker in spring after the winter's thaw. The horses seemed to outlive hired helpers around the ranch. Emma could smell the grounds before they approached, rocky mountain juniper, pinecones budding on spruce trees, horse manure, and hay.

She peeped her head above the dashboard, then past Grandma Rose's shoulder to see which horses grazed by the fence. On her last visit, Grandpa mentioned that several of the mares were expecting to deliver. 'Baby horses' is what Emma called them.

"There, I see them!" She pointed to an area near the fence.

Three mares stood with their foal; momma horses grazed as colts and fillies hobbled not too far behind.

"Oh, yes, I see the momma horses with their babies!" said her Grandma, without taking her eyes off the driveway. She intentionally slowed the SUV so that Emma could get a better view.

"There are baby horses everywhere!" she yelped. Grandma Rose unlocked the door, freeing Emma from her motorized chariot.

"Don't get yourself dirty, remember we have guests tonight," she reminded. After releasing Emma, she pulled the car into the garage to unload groceries and other items from their shopping.

Emma's Grandpa sat atop his stallion; a handsome Friesian black horse named Misty. The two of them were majestic as they galloped across the field, Grandpa's long legs dangling carefully against Misty's sides. Misty slowed to a trot when they noticed Emma approach.

"Aren't you the prettiest thing I've seen all day," he said, laughing when Emma twirled for him, then turned her hands to the ground and kicked her legs up into a proper cartwheel.

Misty grunted after eyeballing Emma through large, marbled

brown eyes. She wondered what Misty was thinking, and if it minded that her tall Grandpa rode on its back. Maybe someday, when she was much bigger, of course, Misty would allow her to sit up there while high stepping through the fields.

"Thanks, Grandpapa—thank you, Misty," she said, before sprinting across the lawn and up the paved driveway. Grandma Rose waited for her in the kitchen. They would have guests later in the evening, and after Emma pleaded, Grandma Rose said she could help with some meal preparations.

The sweet smell of orange blossoms greeted Emma at the entryway. Last summer, Uncle Eli shipped the two potted mini orange trees from Florida. Grandma Rose placed them in matching stone planters on both sides of the foyer. Grandpa wasn't keen on the idea at first, but even he had to admit the citrusy greeting was invigorating after long hours spent prepping stalls, shoveling horse manure, and bailing hay.

There was enough help on the grounds, but Grandpa wouldn't have it any other way; he wanted his hands dirty, even though Grandma Rose would persist he leave heavy labor for the workers which was the reason for having them around. He often came in the back door, dusty and smelling of musk; unless Grandma Rose was distracted. When the orange blossoms were blooming, he'd attempt entrance through the front door, briefly stopping to sniff upwind like a black bear shuffling through the Rocky Mountains. It was worth the risk; the citrus intermingled with the sweet blooms proved quite exhilarating.

The foyer opened to sprawling hardwood floors that flowed into the great room and dining room. A fireplace dominated the great room and a covered deck wrapped around from the family room to the east side of the house. The kitchen was a baker's delight. There was an 8-burner range, double ovens, slab granite counters, a butcher's block for extra prepping space, black Kitchen Aid appliances, and a butler's pantry.

Grandma Rose would have her personal chef prepare meals when there were five or more, and even then, she preferred to assist with the cooking. Come to think of it, her kitchen staff lasted about the same duration as Grandpa's helpers. Emma plucked a sprig of orange blossom before heading in the opposite direction for her piano lesson. There was no need for thinking about helping in the kitchen if she hadn't completed at least thirty minutes of practice. Grandma Rose gave her that look and nodded her approval.

Placing the orange blossom on top of the Grand piano, she savored the scent that lingered on her fingertips. Positioning her hands: left hand C-E, right hand G-C-E, she prepared for another attempt at Bach's Prelude to the Well in C major.

"Bet you're hungry and thirsty by now," said Grandma Rose.

Thirty minutes had quickly turned into an hour as the world around her faded behind black and white ivories, staff lines, and treble clefs. Emma ignored the interruption.

"C-D, A-D-F," she said aloud.

"Alright then if you prefer—"

Before Grandma Rose finished her sentence, Emma scuttled past her in pursuit of the kitchen.

"Just something to snack on, dinner will be at 6, soon as the guests arrive." she cautioned Emma away from the stove and directed her attention to a plate on the kitchen table. One half of peanut butter and jelly sandwich, cubed cheddar cheese, and a handful of green grapes with a glass of iced tea.

"Mmm, that smells good Grandma!"

She hoped the compliment would gain her a taste of whatever

cooled in the oven.

"Orange-herb roasted chicken," said Grandma Rose. "It should go nicely with the Caesar and Waldorf salad," she added.

Emma smiled; this would be her contribution to their dinner. There were eight guests invited: six adults, and two children around Emma's age.

"I'm going to show my princess how monarchs entertain their guests," said Grandma Rose. "I'll teach you everything I know."

She gathered Emma's hair away from her face then planted a butterfly kiss on her nose.

"Stop all that carrying on," said Grandpa, as he lumbered through the kitchen with a toolbox in hand. Grandma Rose waved a hand in the air. "Pay him no mind - and get that filthy thing out of my kitchen!" He was quick for a big man; with his free hand he grabbed a glass, filled it with lemonade, and was out the door before she could complain.

"Come with me, let me show you what needs to be done," declared Grandma Rose. She instructed Emma to observe as she made an eagle-eye sweep throughout the house. Everything had to be scanned and positioned. First, they checked for spots on the polished hardwood floors, then dusted and readjusted flower arrangements; stared at mirrors to see if there were any streak marks and looked over dishes to make sure they shined. They had a housekeeper, but Grandma Rose wouldn't trust one set of eyes to prepare for company.

When every inch of the house met her expectations, she led Emma upstairs for a wardrobe change. Grandma Rose selected a black sheath dress, and gold sling-back heels, but changed to red pumps when Emma protested; wanting to dress alike, she wore a black tulle dress, with her new red shoes of course. By the time they returned, the guests had arrived.

"Glad you could make it," said Grandma Rose, as she greeted each one individually.

Emma glanced behind the adults and saw the two girls standing side-by-side. She waved in their direction, but neither seemed to acknowledge the greeting; one turned to the other and continued their conversation. When the final guest had arrived, Grandma Rose caught Emma standing alone.

"Come on, this is our time to show everyone who we are," then nudged her toward the two girls.

"My name's Emma, this is my Grandma Rose and my Grandpa. Let me take your coat - you don't have one, that's okay. I hope you like dinner, and afterward, we can play. I have the whole collection of Fairy Garden, or we can play with my Think and Learn pad," said Emma, without stopping for a breath; and she would've kept talking even though one girl turned and laughed.

"My name's Victoria," said the fair-skinned girl with curly black hair.

"And this is Breanna," who only nodded; Victoria was the more outspoken of the two girls.

"Look at the flowers Breanna, they're beautiful. Oh, what was your name, is it Emily?" she asked.

"My name's Emma. This is a Begonia, I water them. We have more plants in the family room, in the kitchen and upstairs. You want to look at my new book? I just got it today, it has flowers on the front…." she continued.

Breanna nodded her head, yes, but Victoria stood in between them and exclaimed, "No, we don't want to see your book, Emily!"

"Emma, my names Emma - Emma Lynn - but call me Emma."

Then she did something unexpected; she approached Victoria

and began spelling her name, so there would be no more confusion.

"E-M-M-A…in case you can't spell!"

She couldn't remember ever feeling this annoyed before. When Victoria laughed again, Emma turned and walked away; bunched a wad of material from her skirt and wrung it tight until she was calm.

Grandma Rose left the adults and headed for the kitchen. Without an excuse, Emma trailed in her footsteps. By the time she entered the kitchen, her breathing was quick and tight, dampness accumulated on her forehead and underarms.

"Perfect timing—take this to your guests," said Grandma Rose. She placed a tray of assorted cookies in Emma's hands and spun her around.

Victoria twisted her lips and narrowed her eyes; scrutinized Emma's tulle skirt, her shoes with the barely noticeable polka dots, then her hair. Then she leaned over and whispered something in Breanna's ear, and laughed. When Emma saw them her jawbones tightened, and her heart hammered against her chest. The tray in her hand felt like a plate of bricks, so she dropped it hard on the table, and retreated to the kitchen.

"Nothing more to do here, for now, let's go entertain," said Grandma Rose, and led her back for another round with Victoria.

Emma considered the roomful of guests and searched for a friendly face to engage. Some looked in her direction, simulated rehashed conversations with smiles tacked on to fake compliments. She skirted the room; found a vase to rearrange, then picked up a napkin from the floor. Wiped a dust ring from beneath a potted plant and checked to see whose cup needed refilling.

She took an extended bathroom break when there was nothing more to busy her hands. When Emma returned to the table, she was relieved to see dinner was served. Grandma Rose had taught her not to talk or smack her jaws while eating; she hoped Victoria was aware of this dinner etiquette.

The meal was going well until she noticed how fast Victoria finished eating; soon as the last bite of roasted chicken was gone, her mouth was open again.

"My Mom said we only came because your Mom's making a donation," she spat at Emma, who stared at her out of confusion.

"Your Mom—over there." She pointed to Grandma Rose as if Emma needed a reminder.

"That's my Grandmother, not my Mom," said Emma, then rolled her eyes.

"I have to be nice to you because Mom said…" Victoria continued. Emma wanted to tell her she should be nice, no matter who said, but she didn't get her chance.

"Um, it's time for dessert!" Breanna interrupted.

Emma picked up their empty plates, steadying them as she made her way to the sink. In the kitchen, she selected three slices of strawberry shortcake and ran back to the table.

"Look what I got for us!" said Emma as she balanced the three plates against her chest.

There were a few short steps before she reached the table, but somehow, she stumbled and went down. The girls' laughter seemed to resonate across the room; mixed with the adults' gasps; for Emma, it sounded like a house of horrors.

"My goodness, baby what happened?" said Grandma Rose as she swooped Emma from the floor and plucked smashed cake pieces from her dress, "This will need to be dry-cleaned, but nothing we can't handle."

When Emma looked in the girl's direction, she locked eyes with Victoria, who stuck out her tongue. Overwhelmed by the attention, she bolted from the room and out the patio door. Sprinting across the lawn in the humid night air, she could hear Grandma Rose calling after her, which only fueled her adrenaline; Emma quickened her steps and didn't stop until her chest heaved from exertion.

It was Grandpa who found her inside the horse stalls. By that time, she had collected a handful of pinecones and named them each.

"Diana, Tess, Jill…"

"What'd you find, Emma?" Grandpa squatted beside her.

"They want to have dinner too Grandpa," she said, then adjusted the cones in a circular arrangement. Grandpa sat silent and waited until she had called all eight of the pinecones by name.

"They're ready for bed." She placed them on top of a haystack.

"Yep, it sure looks that way." He cupped her in his arms. "Let's check on Misty and the others."

By the time they completed rounds to every stall, and it seemed she'd forgotten about her fall, Grandpa carried her back to the house. The guests had moved from the dining to the great room. When Emma spotted Victoria and Breanna, she was surprised by their eagerness to make peace.

"We're sorry," they said in unison.

Victoria gave her a kiss on the cheek, then led her by the hand to a table with puzzles, coloring books, and crayons. Emma noticed if she shut her mouth and smiled, then things were peaceful with the girls. She looked to Breanna, who had evidently learned this lesson. Victoria liked to be the center of attention. Anyone who stole her shine was marked as a threat that needed to be eliminated.

Emma's attempt to control her uneasiness was apparent. Without the need to compete, Victoria's antics stopped; the rest of the evening became quite pleasant.

"That was fun!" Victoria said at the door, then gave Emma

another kiss on the cheek, imitating her Mother who had just done the same to Grandma Rose.

"Princess tell me what happened," asked Grandma Rose when the guests were gone. Then when Emma recapped the events leading to her meltdown, Grandma Rose advised, "Don't work so hard to please people... If they like you, they like you," she shrugged. "And if not, count it as waste."

"Waste like trash…you mean throw them in the garbage?" Emma frowned.

"Yes, that's exactly where I'd put them if they fit." She winked when Emma looked up; Emma loved when Grandma Rose winked at her; it was their own secret language.

"Never mind those girls and little Ms. Victoria doesn't know what she's talking about," Grandma Rose continued. She comforted Emma with a hug, then kissed her on the nose. Emma listened, wishing she had the courage that Grandma Rose possessed; Victoria already had it at five years old.

On Sunday evening, it was time for Emma to return home. She forgot to ask Grandma Rose not to mention the incident with Victoria until it was too late; while in her bedroom, she heard their discussion about her embarrassing altercation.

"I'm just asking that you stop fussing at that child so much, it's ruining her self-esteem!" Grandma cautioned.

"She's got to toughen up," Reba said, defending her parenting skills.

"But she seems more anxious," Grandma Rose huffed.

Emma could hear Reba's grunted response; she didn't like when her mother-in-law interfered.

"I won't raise a weak child, and a girl has got to be even tougher nowadays," Reba groused and thumped a cup on the table to make her point.

"Honey, it won't hurt to hear what Mama has to say," Emma's father pleaded to his wife.

"Just wish you'd encourage her more, is all…praise her for what she does well," said Grandma Rose. When the room grew silent, Emma was surprised at Reba's seeming surrender.

"My Grandbaby," Grandma Rose sucked her teeth. "She's too nervous, and I'm concerned."

When no one else spoke, Emma returned from her bedroom. In the hallway, Reba bypassed her daughter; frowned in her direction, then shut the bedroom door behind her.

"Come give me some goodbye sugar," Grandma instructed. She planted kisses on Emma's cheeks. "Remember what I told you, baby," she stopped and looked her in the eyes. "Everything you need is right here…" she pointed to her chest, "No one can take that away!"

Emma nodded her head but still asked, "what's inside of me?" She knew what Grandma Rose meant but hoped to stall her departure. Reba would be upset when she left; it seemed everything she did, or said, upset her Mother and chased away friends. Grandma Rose was the only person that understood her.

"What if somebody really strong tries to take what I have?" Emma queried.

"Nobody can take Jesus from you baby," Grandma Rose said, shaking her head and squeezing Emma like a stuffed doll.

"Jesus on the inside of you is greater than anyone coming against you—believe that!" She winked, then tickled Emma's tummy, causing her to squeal. Reba grunted from behind her closed bedroom door.

Grandma Rose grabbed Emma's hand and led her to the

kitchen table where her Dad prepared sandwiches. She sat Emma in a chair, then motioned for her son to step outside.

"I know what you're going to say, but I have this under control," he said.

It wasn't a convincing argument, not even to a five-year-old.

"I can't have the fighting or the arguing," he reasoned.

Emma imagined their argument after Grandma Rose had left.

"You need to get your house in order before things fall apart," she commanded.

"Things will get better; I just need to finish law school—"

"Your house must be built on a solid foundation," she scolded. When Emma peeked through the blinds, she saw how her Dad stood with his hands crammed in his pants pocket. His head rolled back as he looked to the sky. He'd heard the lecture many times before, so had Reba; hence, the reason for her earlier escape.

"Balance son, you must have balance in all things."

They were her parting words. Emma heard the footsteps, the engine started, and her Dad was back in the kitchen.

"Let's watch a movie," he suggested.

Curled in a ball beneath his arms, Emma adjusted the blanket he'd wrapped her in. She reached for the bowl of popcorn, then recounted the story of how she had hosted dinner with Grandma Rose; what she wore, who were their guests, and then her run-in with Victoria, who had made fun of her.

"Is that right? Well, that's very interesting," he mused at her enthusiastic style of storytelling.

Engrossed in their conversation, neither noticed when the movie began; or when Reba entered the room, still simmering from the face-off with Grandma Rose. She sat alone in an armchair and pretended not to listen, although Emma noticed whenever she glanced in their direction. The more excited she became, the more Reba cut her eyes and hissed at them.

"Mommy, have some popcorn."

When Emma stood to offer the bowl, the blanket caught her foot, causing her to tumble into Reba's lap.

"Don't you ever sit still?" She grabbed Emma by the arm and forced her back into the chair.

"Let's all calm down, the movies started," said Emanuel, "and look, the horse looks like Misty," he said, trying to change the subject as he ignored Reba's seething glare. Emma frowned at her mother, who picked popcorn from the floor. Then when she saw the noble creature on the screen, her face lit up.

Things were quiet around the house throughout the following week. Hoping to avoid his wife, Emma's Dad worked long hours. On one of those days, two strange men stopped by their house, saying they needed to speak privately with her Mother about an important matter. Afterward, Reba cried often, then demanded that Emanuel spend more time at home.

Once he honored her request, Reba complained of her unhappiness. She needed a hobby, something that would get her out of the house. She wanted to feel like a person again. He had a meaningful career, but all she had was a child that demanded all her attention.

They had reached an agreement; on days when he worked from home, Reba would leave the house and have time to herself. Emma didn't understand their deal, but her Mother did appear happier after having time away from home. When she returned, her behavior was different; she laughed at her own jokes, slurred her words, and talked louder than usual. But things weren't so bad. Emanuel worked long hours, Reba had her private time, and Emma had more time at her

Grandparents' ranch.

One weekend while visiting Grandma Rose, one of the dogs—Tootsie—a chocolate lab, gave birth to a litter of pups. One puppy, a yellow lab, had a difficult time latching on to its mother for milk and seemed to be pushed around by the others. When she said her goodbyes, Emma expressed her concerns, then asked if Grandpa could take special care of the yellow one. For the next two weeks, she'd ask her Dad to call and see how the yellow dog was doing.

"Did he look sad, was he feeding?" she interrupted, before taking the phone from her Father.

"Yes, he's doing fine, but please don't worry. He'll feed when he's hungry," said Grandpa.

"No, he won't do it," she said. "You have to watch him because the other puppies bully him." Her Grandpa felt like her phone calls were turning the rest of his hair gray.

One day, when she came home from school, her Grandmother's SUV was in the driveway. In her bedroom was a small crate on the floor. Inside, the yellow pup yelped.

"He's all yours, now you can watch him all the time," said Grandpa. On the table was a plate of biscuits, left out from breakfast. She had helped Grandma Rose bake them over the weekend and brought a zip lock bag home for her parents to enjoy; this pup's coat reminded her of the color of biscuits.

The yellow dog's name became Biscuit, whether they liked it or not. Reba smiled when she told them.

# THREE

THREE YEARS LATER, Emma and Biscuit had become inseparable. Now in 3rd grade, she struggled to find her place among her peers; but it didn't matter, she and Biscuit were the best of friends. Having him made the days bearable and the weeks memorable; helped her to overlook Reba's frequent absences and her Dad's long workdays.

When Grandma Rose's commitments prevented her from getting to Emma, she hardly missed the time at the ranch. She talked to Biscuit, and he listened. They played together, ate their meals together, and slept in the same bed. Everything centered around Biscuit. Unfortunately, it was a matter of time before Reba gained an interest in the dog as well.

Emma now wished she had known how to deal with someone self-centered and callous. She had labored in love with Biscuit, and as a result, he became more appealing to Reba. It was her mistake to have given in to that first request.

"It takes him a while to settle down when he comes back, I think he misses his bed," said Reba. "I can take care of him while you're gone. I'll make sure he eats, and I'll even talk to him."

Emma remembered a fight between Biscuit and another puppy. Grandpa said it was nothing to worry about, just a dog's way of establishing rank. But she wished to keep him out of harm's way, so she had relented to her Mother's request. How could she have known her decision would foreshadow later events?

Reba would pretend in front of others that Emma was her greatest joy. When no one was around, she spoke only when making a demand, always avoiding eye contact. She would commend Emma on how well she could do her own hair or prepare her own meals, or how good she took care of Biscuit; past that, her words were few. She never said, "I love you!"

Emma watched her Mother's face when Grandma Rose expressed her love. When her Dad used affectionate words, she told him to cut it out. Emma was the recipient of the love that Reba rejected, which caused more problems because she seemed to view love as a weakness.

By the time Emma was ten years old, Reba had become more outspoken about her feelings toward Grandma Rose. She told tales of how everyone in the family made her feel inferior, and how it was Grandma Rose's deliberate plan to get rid of her. When her words fell on unresponsive ears, she resorted to other tactics, like temper tantrums and inconsolable tears.

Reba's belligerence became insufferable, as she continued to express frustration with her husband and child. If she wasn't screaming, she argued with Emma's Dad. Then it was anything, and everything Emma did that set her off. If she swept the floor, it wasn't swept right. When Reba reviewed Emma's homework, it wasn't neat enough. If she asked a question, Emma didn't respond quick enough.

Her crying lasted from late in the night, to midday. Emma

recalled that her father was never home when Reba had her fits. Their home had become a loveless nest. She complained about Emanuel's work schedule; he was never there for her. Emma remembered how she wished there was a way to make her Mom happy, but nothing seemed to help.

One evening while getting ready for bed, she heard sobs coming from the living room. When Emma tiptoed down the hallway, she saw her Mother curled in a ball.

"Why do they hate me?" she hollered to the empty room.

"That woman wants me dead—Grandma Rose wants to get rid of me and take my daughter," she cried into clenched fists.

Emma froze in place, shocked by her Mother's claims. Now she knew the whole scene had been fabricated for her benefit. Had those even been real tears? She thought about it. No, it was just a lot of noise and bad acting.

Reba's behavior had become unpredictable; one minute she gave a compliment, and the next, she needed more space. So Emma crept back to her bedroom, unnoticed. No matter how she behaved, this was her mother, and no one had the right to separate them.

The last visit to her grandparents' house was not enjoyable. She tried everything but couldn't get her mother's words out of her head. 'Grandma Rose wants to get rid of me, she always has!' She wasn't sure what to believe; mystification replaced her common sense. Was this the plan all along? Get rid of Reba so her Grandparents could raise her? If it were true, it would explain the love-hate relationship Reba had with them.

At this age, Emma was unfamiliar with the art of manipulation. What she saw was the image of her Mother, weeping bitterly, over a problem she couldn't control. If she had only talked to Grandma Rose about what she heard, maybe the next few years could have been prevented.

"I want to go home," is what Emma said to Grandma Rose on a Saturday morning.

She had just arrived the evening before, so Grandma Rose tried to console her. After Emma continued this way for several hours, they repacked her overnight bag and drove back to Denver. When they returned, Reba told Emma that she was no longer allowed to visit her grandparents on weekends.

Emma saw the restriction as punishment, maybe because her mother thought she had told them something. Her respite from home was school attendance and depending on the day was often more tormenting than her Mother's isolation. Because of their difference in hair texture, Reba never mastered how to fix Emma's thick tresses, which made the girl an easy target for being teased by other kids.

Victoria now attended the same elementary school and confronted Emma with a vengeance, and a personal score to settle; she never forgot the forced apology at Grandma Rose's dinner. Within a week, Victoria teamed up with two other girls—Vivian and Violet, who branded themselves 'The V's.'

After a few weeks of being their target, Emma remembered the lesson she'd learned from her first encounter with Victoria: Remove the source of negative attention! At school, she'd make a quick dash for the bathroom, take down Reba's failed attempt, and neatly brush her hair in place. When Victoria saw Emma's hair neatly groomed, she passed her by with a scowl and searched for another victim.

At home, she learned to avoid her Mother as much as possible, and Reba was content. Emma didn't like the quiet, but at least there was peace; and she had Biscuit, although when she returned from school, Emma often had to bribe him to leave Reba's side. Her dad noticed how the two interacted with one another, but he was wise; he never interfered with their neutral cohabitation. When Emma accepted things with her Mom were as good as they would ever be, she released expectations that would never be met.

One day when she returned from school, Grandpa and Grandma Rose were at the kitchen table. She remembered that day, vividly; it felt like Christmas. She walked through the front door, headed to the kitchen for a snack, and there was Grandma, back in her rightful place. When Emma went to her, she sniffed the Jasmine perfume on her clothing and touched her manicured fingernails. After their embrace, she listened as her grandparents explained that Reba had moved out.

"Okay, but when can I get my hair done?" asked Emma, seemingly unconcerned with her mother's absence.

"I've already got it scheduled," said Grandma Rose. She assured Emma everything would be fine.

"The Lord is good," she told her granddaughter, with a fist raised high above her head.

It took one full month for Grandma Rose to undo the damage caused by neglect to Emma's hair and wardrobe.

"Let's see if the, who'd you call them girls—the V's? Let's see what they have to say now," Grandma Rose winked.

When Emma arrived at school, glammed and revamped, Victoria had nothing more to say. The bullying stopped immediately. The V's abruptly turned their scoffs to adoration, even offered Emma a seat at their table. She had no interest in popularity, although it felt good not to worry about her looks or other shortcomings. And it was Grandma Rose's idea to host an annual birthday bash for Emma. Each year her Grandmother invited staff, other board members, and a select group of Emma's friends to celebrate her granddaughter's birthday.

"Dream big, invite whomever you want," Grandma Rose suggested. "Whatever you want is what this party will be."

Back then, the only big dreams Emma had was to ride on top of Misty. She told her Grandma - never thinking it could be possible - that everyone who attended her party would get a horse ride. Grandma Rose came up with a practical arrangement; guests would park their cars in a designated area, get inside the waiting horse and carriage, and ride up to the main house. Emma could count her friends on less than five fingers, so she never imagined any more than four guests.

Grandma Rose had sent out thirty invitations, and when Victoria learned of the event, she persuaded Emma to invite a dozen other students. The birthday celebration was held underneath a large tent, complete with catered food, a DJ, and party favors. By the end of her sophomore year, Emma's classmates were accustomed to the annual bash.

Despite the increase in popularity, she continued to struggle with close friendships. Everyone knew their attendance hindered on her acceptance, so they fought for her attention, and often backstabbed one another. She became annoyed with event preparations and saw no point in hosting a party for people who pretended to be her friends. The worst part of it all was having to listen to her classmates' likes and dislikes for weeks; the gathering became less about celebrating Emma, and more to do with entertaining her "pretend friends."

Her Grandmother came up with another idea; it was time Emma learned some work ethics. Grandma Rose was the Executive Director of a non-profit organization she established called PAHST (pronounced past); Parents Against Human and Sex-Trafficking. She had become well-known for her innovative fundraising efforts.

It was her passion, and the organization's mission, to educate the community about human trafficking; PAHST provided support to victims and a speaking platform for survivors. She intended to make Emma her apprentice and had hopes that after her college graduation, they'd work together to expand the mission beyond Denver.

In the meantime, Emma gained valuable knowledge about the underworld of labor and sex trafficking. She studied information on how human trafficking occurred, the role of the buyer, ways traffickers operated, and the unlikely victims. She learned how predators preyed on popular websites, and what she should watch out for; even in her own community.

The more time spent she spent understanding the problem, the more her interest in the mission grew. By the time Emma was fifteen, she had volunteered willingly and distributed the material throughout her school.

# FOUR

IT WAS SUPPOSED to be a typical Saturday morning; first, their salon appointment, a quick trip to the mall, grocery shopping, then back by noon to plan an event that would honor PAHST survivors. Grandma Rose had a brilliant proposal about how to select attendees who'd receive certificates or an award. That day, however, was anything but ordinary.

For starters, both Grandma Rose and Emma overslept, which made them twenty minutes late for their ten o'clock salon appointments. Neither had time to eat the breakfast prepared by the chef. The day was exceptionally humid, which turned their fresh hairdos to frizz. By the time Emma entered the mall, her pressed curls had flopped.

When they returned home, defeated from the morning, Grandma Rose suggested they at least finish the breakfast—spinach and mushroom omelets with waffles. Emma left the table for another glass of orange juice, and by the time she sat back down, Grandpa was kneeling on the floor, calling for Grandma Rose to get up.

At the hospital, they learned that Grandma Rose suffered a stroke. Emma waited for hours, and after some time, a nurse approached with news that the danger had passed. When she asked to see her Grandmother, a woman dressed in a smock led her down the corridor. The hospital room was bright but smelled of antiseptics, and a slight odor of urine. Tubes trailed from machines, then looped around into Grandma Rose. She seemed fragile, lying with her eyes closed. When she extended a hand, Emma approached with teary eyes.

"Be strong, listen to my words," said Grandma Rose. She shushed Emma before giving instructions. She had wanted Emma to focus on graduation from high school, and then "continue the plan exactly how we discussed." Emma nodded her head, though she wasn't sure why they were having the conversation at that moment. "Remember everything I've taught you. I say this because… I'm not sure how long it'll take me to recover."

She wanted Emma to understand that she'd always be there, "just a phone call away," on days when she couldn't get to her. Emma wanted her Grandma to know she appreciated the woman's selfless love, and that she was always concerned with her granddaughter's wellbeing despite her suffering.

When Emma left the hospital, she vowed to stick to their plan. She would make her Grandmother proud, and when she was well again, Grandma Rose would hear of how her granddaughter pitched in during her absence; that was her intentions, even if she failed. If having less time with Grandma Rose had an impact on Emma, there was no way of knowing yet.

Now a junior in high school, she embraced her popularity, which boosted her participation in extra-curricular activities. So, the shift in attention away from PAHST was natural. Emma had a growth spurt which left her with long legs she found useful as captain of the cheer squad. She noticed boys on the football team, and some of them noticed her too. She could've had her pick of just about any boy, but her interest was on one.

Seth was a boy known around school for his athletic prowess on the football field. Even though he had a girlfriend, Emma found herself daydreaming about him in class. When he walked by, she stared at him, and when he scored a touchdown, she screamed the loudest. He would smile in her direction when his girlfriend wasn't around. Then she caught him watching her during algebra class. At an away game, fate gave way to opportunity, and they had their first chance to talk during the bus ride home. After exchanging phone numbers, they often spoke in the following weeks.

Victoria was Seth's rightful girlfriend; Emma should've considered her feelings. "Nope, he's mine now," she said to Biscuit, who tilted his head and raised his ears. Why wasn't she fearful of Victoria's wrath? Maybe it was because she was no longer that timid, awkward girl, who could be bullied by another in her own Grandparents' home.

"The only reason she's nice to me anyway is because I'm more popular than she is now!" Emma explained to Biscuit, but this time, he put his head down and covered it with his paws.

"So, does that mean we can chill sometime?" Seth asked one night. Emma had to take the phone off of mute to respond to his question.

"When and where?" she answered, forgetting every ounce of coyness Grandma Rose had taught her.

At the time, all Emma understood was this was her one shot at happiness. She was content on the varsity cheer squad and excited about having her first boyfriend. It never crossed her mind that this action would be considered a declaration of war. Pondering these things now, she cringed at her incredulous stupidity. The years of peace between her and Victoria caused her to underestimate the true nature of her enemy.

When Victoria learned that she was dumped, and Emma, of all people, was to be her replacement, a dormant volcano erupted. Victoria was an outspoken, in-your-face personality; pretty, but she was known to deliver a smackdown when necessary. A sea of girls parted the way as Victoria approached and cornered Emma in the girls' locker room. She threatened to ruin her, finish her, and then destroy her. Emma, fooled by her own popularity, fueled the flames.

"Suck it up, you lost this one!" she said, with no regrets.

They stood equally in height, so Emma assumed she had a fighting chance. That was the first of many throwdowns between them that year. Rumors were aftershocks to their blowups.

The information gained during their friendlier times transformed into grenades which they hurled at one another. Victoria once confessed that she had a minor struggle with methamphetamine use during her freshman year. An ex-boyfriend introduced her to the nasty habit that led to a six-week detox program over the summer. Emma noticed that Victoria started hanging out with that same boyfriend; so, naturally, she assumed the habit had returned as well. True to form, she blurted it out to everyone that Victoria was on drugs.

For her part, Emma had once shared that her mother abandoned her and her father years ago and had been MIA ever since. Using this information, Victoria fabricated a story around the school campus that Emma was living in a foster home. The rumors spilled over to the hallways leading to arguments, and hair pulling. Seth, caught in the middle, struggled with his grades and his football performance because of the turmoil. Emma was ashamed of herself for the way she behaved back then. It was one of the many things she now lived to regret.

By this time, her Dad had become an established and prosperous criminal attorney. He provided financial security for their home but was still unable to sacrifice any of his time to be present for his daughter on most days. Back then, Emma believed he offered her independence and freedom because she was a responsible young lady. She now understood after all these years that there was some truth to Reba's complaints. He was a workaholic and showed no signs of making himself more available, which was probably why he allowed Reba to take her for that brief period after her first semester in the 11th grade.

That summer leading into her senior year of high school, Emma was mentally and physically drained from the battle she referred to as, World War Victoria. Her attempts to make peace for Seth's sake fell short, and she craved some form of parental support. Something had to give, and having no way to resolve home issues, Emma turned her attention to school and the things that could be controlled. The only solution she could think of was to break things off with Seth, although, she wasn't sure if this decision would change things now because Victoria had moved on to another boy. Their continued feud had more to do with the long-standing animosity between them than with him.

The breakup was not graceful or polite and caused more tension for Emma. She refused all of Seth's phone calls and avoided him at school. He became creative in finding ways to catch up to her, standing around corners and waiting near the girl's bathroom unexpectedly. Emma had to reroute to dodge him. If she had gym class, she went outside the school and around the building to approach from the opposite direction. Lunchtime, she ate off campus to avoid him in the school cafeteria.

He outsmarted her by leaving class a few minutes before the bell rang and caught her when she thought the hallway was clear. "I'm busy!" She pushed past him. He was done with her after that incident. Two weeks later he moved on to Violet, who didn't seem to mind being the third choice, as she was used to playing the second and third position behind the V's. Emma knew now that her treatment of Seth was modeled after her Mother's behavior towards her Father. Without realizing it, she was becoming what she despised the most.

The first year-or-so after moving out of their home, Reba would show up when she pleased or had a need; occasionally, sleeping over, but never past two days. For some crazy reason, Emanuel always allowed her to stay, probably under the guise that it was for Emma's benefit. Reba arrived jolly and full of laughter, telling jokes mostly and tended to divert away from sensitive topics or demonstrations of emotion.

In the beginning, Reba's visits did provide some comfort for them, but morning came quickly, and she was gone before Emma had time to utilize her presence. Reba liked to show concern, initially asking Emma how she was doing but then she'd change the subject when there was a need for a serious conversation that she didn't want to have.

Emma learned that a short "I'm fine," response, was all that was necessary. Reba preferred her as a silent spectator, she told the jokes and expected the laughs in return. Within a month, Emma went from running gleefully into her mother's arms to a brief hug and kiss on the cheek, until finally, Reba avoided any physical contact. By then, Emma simply waved hello before shutting her bedroom door. She had concluded that Reba was using her Father; he would allow it, but she refused to participate any longer.

By the time Emma made it to the end of her high school career, Reba had one bridge left on which she could cross back over and reconcile with her daughter before it was too late. The morning of Emma's graduation, she phoned to extend an invitation for her Mother to attend the ceremony. After the commencement was over, her Father snapped pictures of her in cap and gown. They had just discussed dinner plans when Reba called out to her from the crowd. Not only did she show up late, missing the entire event, but she came with him.

Ogre was the name he went by, the man her Dad had threatened to kill earlier that year if he ever came near his daughter again. They both wore sunglasses, dark enough to conceal their eyes, and were overdressed in long sleeves and pants on a hot June day.

"Hey, look at my baby all grown up!" Reba proclaimed.

Ogre fiddled with his hands, wiped at his face, then he and Reba laughed like two mangy hyenas.

"Ugh, frowning like your Daddy," Reba sucked her teeth.

Her Father glared at Ogre, who heeded the warning and fell silent, leaving Reba to make a donkey out of herself.

"Look at you two," she continued her banter.

Emma saw the tension on Emanuel's face, and she knew the reason for it.

Reba stood defiantly between the two of them, assuming the tension had more to do with jealousy than retribution. When her Father held his silence, Emma spoke up.

"There's nothing left here for you, we're done!"

It was an old threat she had voiced to her Mother earlier that year; Upon graduation from high school, she planned to cut all ties with her Mother for good and continue the work Grandma Rose expected of her. Emma and her Father turned their backs on Reba and Ogre with the intent of moving forward with their lives without her. On the drive home, Emanuel had a moment of clarity.

"I've decided it's time to let go. I'm filing for divorce!" he said.

Refusing to be so easily dismissed, Reba made an appearance at the house later that evening, not at the front door, but tapping on Emma's bedroom window.

# FIVE

## The Corridor

*Beep…Beep…*

T HE PHANTOM SOUND returned, and with it, a warm breeze swept over Emma. She opened her eyes and was startled to see a man standing against the wall. While keeping her eyes on the stranger, she felt around on the cushion for the girl; the seat beside her was empty.

"No need to worry about the girl," he said.

"Who are you?" She asked, getting to her feet, "Are you h—"

*Beep…Beep…*

Emma bit her lip and wrung material from her blouse when the beeps increased. She wished the door would go away. "Not now!" she whispered to the door.

"I see you're awake now, or were you falling asleep?" the

mysterious man asked.

She thought about getting on his case for leaving the girl but was distracted by the flicker of light in his eyes, which reflected off the golden floor.

Emma stood, staring back at the man, who smiled at her until every ounce of concern and anxiety had dissipated. For a moment she was still - like in a dream when your mind tells you to move, but your body refuses. She bit her lip, checking for sensation to confirm whether she was asleep or awake. If there was no pressure, then she could be confident that none of this was really happening.

*Beep…Beep…*

"Do you hear that?" she asked.

He gave no acknowledgment of the sound, nor that he would answer her question. Emma considered his eyes and saw what resembled brilliant sapphire stones. His smile was radiant, diffusing all other facial features. She noticed that he was dressed comfortably in linen slacks and a shirt and wore sandals on his feet.

The beeps were of no concern to him, which was reassuring and made her feel safe.

"I will answer your question but first answer mine. You were falling asleep?" He asked.

It was more of an observation than a question, so she wondered why he waited for an answer. His words were soft, gentle, yet assertive.

"I don't think I was asleep," she said.

"But would you know the difference?" he raised an eyebrow and questioned her further.

She found it interesting how he asked another question without answering her own. Noticing the blank look on her face, he continued.

"When one is falling asleep there is a process the body goes through, a decreased awareness..." he said.

Emma considered that he might be stalling for time. "Drowsiness is involved, you know that feeling you get when you find your sweet spot?" He questioned further, then paused to wait for her agreement; when she didn't answer, he shrugged his shoulders and continued.

"The eyelids get heavy, eye movement slows..."

Amused by his interest in the topic, Emma suppressed an urge to laugh. She didn't want to be rude, as he apparently thought they were having a profound philosophical discussion. Pressing her lips flat, she feigned sincerity.

"Being more relaxed, we're less aware of the events surrounding us," he continued his discourse, hands exaggerating his words. And he was smiling, obviously impressed with himself.

"Muscle activity is reduced, it's a vulnerable position to be in." He was now looking at her, teeth gleaming. She returned the smile, although somewhat confused.

"Now, being asleep..."

She felt a tickle in her stomach, and the sensation made her giggle. After excusing herself for the outburst, Emma felt her shoulders relax, then wondered why she hadn't done that sooner. When she looked at him, he flashed his radiant smile again, "And there you have it, the art of falling asleep!" he announced.

When she sighed her relief, he laughed once more.

"Emma Lynn, there's only one decision to be made," he said.

"Did I tell you my name?" She shifted her feet, then squinted her eyebrows.

Without waiting for his response, she already knew the answer.

He was not your average guy. That smile, the way his eyes sparkled. He was omniscient. Behind those eyes were infinite wisdom.

Emma wasn't sure how she came to know this. It was a feeling in her gut. Even more, He also seemed attuned to her thoughts. Surprisingly, she chose peace over fear. If he were aware of her deepest thoughts, then He would know there was more than a decision that awaited her return. Lives were at stake, and she was probably in serious trouble.

"Peace in the storm!" she willed herself to think instead.

It wasn't that she felt pressured to speak, but she knew his questioning served a purpose. If she could admit her actions here, she would find the courage to move forward. Feeling unequipped for the journey ahead, she refused to take another step, in either direction, until an assurance from within gave her the strength to proceed. There were some missing pieces to the puzzle, as she understood now. That was the real issue.

Emma's life was shattering all around her, and she needed help. So, she allowed herself one decision only—to stand still. Stand until the help she needed came. Then, and not a moment sooner, would she decide what her next move would be. And here he was, the Gentleman. He stood, patiently waiting.

"Having done all you can Emma Lynn, stand!" He said.

She looked down to the gold floor beneath, hoping to conceal her shame. The Gentleman waited until Emma's shoulders relaxed; closing her eyes, she inhaled. When He reached for her hand, she grasped his and allowed Him to lead her back to the comfy chair. Sitting first, He motioned for her to take a seat.

"Tell me something about yourself if you don't mind?" He asked.

The question was harmless, but Emma found it difficult to

answer.

"I'm an only child," she said, after moments of silence.

"Hmm, that must've been difficult," He responded.

Emma shifted in her seat, thinking that 'lonely' more appropriately described the experience.

"It would've been nice to have a buffer!" she replied, quickly realizing that her response revealed more than she wanted to expose just yet.

"I know what it's like to carry a heavy burden," He said.

Emma pressed her lips firmly, forbidding herself to disclose any further information. Stealing a glance in His direction, she found that He was content with the silence between them. He seemed willing to wait for as long as needed for her next move.

"Why are you here?" she finally asked.

He lifted an arm, slowly guided her closer and gave her a gentle hug, like a Father saying, *"I have you, my daughter, you're safe in my arms!"* Taking a deep breath, Emma allowed her head to rest on His shoulder.

"I'm here to help you," He said.

Emma had already concluded Him to be the Helper; it was the reason she let down her guard.

"That is if you want My help?" He asked.

Emma inhaled the Lavender scented air, mixed with a hint of Jasmine.

"I'm glad you're here," she said, after some time of silence. It became apparent to her that this wasn't a chance encounter. This was a summons, and like it or not, at some point, Emma would need to answer some tough questions. Either way, she was pleased with His company.

"What have you accomplished in your 26 years?" He asked.

"How'd you know my age?" She gave Him a suspicious look that caused them both to smirk.

In her relaxed state, Emma found it challenging to recall simple information; Thankfully, He had all the answers. Her mind was as spotless as the bare walls surrounding them. She leaned forward, hoping the change in position would stimulate her mind.

"Hmm…" she tapped a finger against her leg.

He may have been a gentleman, but He sure was a curious one, she thought. Glancing over in His direction, Emma detected His patience. She sighed, then flopped back into the chair.

"How about something you enjoy?" He asked. Finally, an easy question she thought.

"Dancing," she smiled, "I love to dance!"

She was pleased with her answer until He probed further.

"Alright, why do you like dancing?"

Emma perceived His tactics were directed at enlightenment, and the chance to speak without being shushed or ignored.

"I love the freedom of movement," she said with sincerity. "It allows me to express myself in a way that words and emotions fail. It releases me from my cage," Emma beamed, excited by the insight of her response. "I started dancing at the age of 5…well it was gymnastics first, but that didn't stick. Along with piano lessons, but I really love to dance. I just need one chance to prove that I'm good enough."

After the words were spoken, she sulked back into the chair.

"If you do well, will you not be accepted?" He answered, provoking her with questions in the ingenious way He knew how.

"There's no other like me, I'm probably one of the best dancers in the state…it's the producers and the powers-that-be who call the shots!" she blurted, feeling like she was on trial, defending herself unsuccessfully. "No one will give me a fair chance to prove myself," she said, flailing hands about her chest and in the air.

"Emma Lynn!" He said her name sternly, and she knew excuses weren't good enough in His presence. Only the truth would do.

"Why?" was His question.

The answer revealed a reality she wasn't ready to accept. Besides, so what if she showed up late for a few auditions; she was still a talented dancer that deserved a fair shot. Not that it should be a factor, but she had good looks to back up what she lacked in talent. Her age, however, was starting to become an issue, but it was absurd to consider age over talent.

"I'm a better dancer than most," she spoke to her audience of one. "Professionally trained with a natural gift I'm told—"

"Emma Lynn," He spoke her name, tenderly. "If you dance as passionately as you speak, your gift will open doors for you!"

Of course, He was right; The problem wasn't whether she was good enough. The real question to be asked was, "Why was she giving up on herself?" Emma had become unreliable, almost on purpose. Most people her age had set and were accomplishing goals with fewer resources than she had. For the girl with the trust fund and upper-class lifestyle to play the victim would make her look ungrateful. But she was tired of pretending.

The Gentleman offered to help her but failed to mention in what capacity? Unless He could redeem the past and erase events from her timeline, there wasn't much help, Emma thought He could offer. Maybe? No, she couldn't bring herself to ask.

"I'm tired," she announced.

"I'd like to sit here awhile and rest while I'm waiting."

They sat once again in silence. Emma thought about the girl and hoped she wasn't keeping Him from attending to her, but the idea of Him leaving made her sad. She laid her head on His shoulder and imagined herself dancing on top of the golden floor. Humming a tune in her head, Emma envisioned herself there at the far end of the corridor, readying herself in the first position, gracefully, lowering down into a Plié, then lifting into a Relevé…up, higher on her toes into a leap. The dance was more than a vision, she could feel every move, and every turn. Her freedom returned in the dance and inner peace was restored after every jump.

*Beep…Beep...*

Emma's eyes swung open at the sound, adjusting her focus, she stared at the doorknob. The corridor seemed to be cooler, the air, now less fragrant, smelled sterile. Turning, she was relieved to find that the Gentleman was still with her.

"Would you like to take a short walk with me?" He asked.

Emma didn't respond, her body stiffened, immobilized by what awaited behind the door. He stood on His feet and extended a hand in her direction. When she stood up, she was noticeably lighter. Walking with Him, she seemed to be floating with every step. They continued moving down the hallway until coming to what appeared to be an opening to a courtyard. Fragrant scents hung in the air and encircled them as they stepped outdoors.

"Lavandula angustifolia."

Emma tilted her head to the sky. With her eyes closed, she filled her lungs with the essence of the garden.

"Jasminum," she noted, inhaling once more.

Trying to subdue her joy, a hint of a smile teased at the corners of her mouth. Emma looked at the Gentleman.

"Yes," He agreed with her. "They would be among your favorites, correct?" He asked.

"Lavender reminds me of my Dad, and Jasmine was the perfume my Grandma wore," Emma bit her lips to contain her excitement.

"And don't forget Citrus sinensis," He said, then escorted her into a beautiful courtyard filled with Lavender, white Jasmine, red ginger flowers and orange blossoms.

Letting go of His hand, she ran from one bush to another smelling the fragrant blooms and laughing. Throwing herself on the ground, Emma rolled around in the grass until she made herself dizzy. He watched silently, allowing her to enjoy the moment in peace.

# SIX

*The Garden*

A RUSTLING IN the grass causes Emma to look up from the pond. Squinting her eyes, then blinking several times; what she was seeing had to be a result of her wild imagination. There, sitting on the opposite side of the pool was a man that resembled her Father, Emanuel St. Roman. It was impossible, he had been in the grave for at least three years now. And yet the more she squinted his face came into focus - It was him.

Jumping to her feet, Emma began to run but then slowed when guilt surrounded her. She froze in mid-step, then hung her head when shame entered in. Looking away from him, she hoped he didn't know the things the Gentleman knew; things she had done and tried to deny, and the conversation she wanted to avoid. Noticing her inner turmoil, her Father walked over and held Emma in his arms.

"Daddy, please forgive me?" She pleaded with him, as he held onto her as she collapsed to the ground.

"I'm the one who should be asking for your forgiveness!" He said while holding her firmly.

"What are you doing here?" she asked, once her tears were controllable and she was somewhat composed.

"I wanted to see you as soon as I could." He grabbed her by the hand and took her to a settee near the pond. Emma laid her head on his chest. Closing her eyes, she inhaled the fragrance of lavender and spearmint leaves.

"Do you remember our garden back home?" he plucked a lavender head and squeezed the bulb between two fingers.

"Fresh lavender stems in a bowl of water on the kitchen table," Emma smiled.

"Yes, I remember," nodding her head at the memory.

She loved the flowers' sweet fragrance, so pruning the genus Lavandula was one of her coveted chores.

First, her father had taught her how to pronounce the scientific name, then gave an at length lesson about Lavandula angustifolia. This was not only a plant with a beautiful purple color, but it was also a medicinal herb that could be used as an antiseptic and had a culinary purpose. He once showed her how to take a handful of dried out stems and grind them in a coffee grinder to use as an herb.

"Yes, I remember," she said, plucking her own stem and sniffing the sweet aroma.

Emanuel had taught his daughter every detail of gardening, from careful planting in the sunny side of the yard to watering once a week, "Only when necessary, let the soil dry out first," she recalled he would say to her. Tending to their spearmint and lavender garden was something they both enjoyed.

•  •  •  •  •  •  •  •  •  •  •  •  •  •  •  •  •  •  •  •  •  •

Emma was a toddler when she started with him in the garden, but by the time she was in high school, he still found it necessary to remind her of the pruning, and watering schedule of the garden. It had been drilled into her memory by now, but it gave him solace somehow to always instruct her in the specific care of his famed lavender garden.

The hard work paid off, as their garden was once featured in the Home & Garden section of the Denver Post. She remembered his prideful smile while reading the article; Emma was pleased that something she had contributed to gained recognition. They lived in a three-bedroom, two-bathroom house in the upscale neighborhood of Cherry Creek. Their walkway was lined with vibrant shades of purple hedges, a beautiful contrast against the stone, stucco ranch home.

Her dog, Biscuit, was with them then. Emma recalled standing at one end of the yard with large Burr Oak trees towering above.

"One, two, three…GO!" she shouted.

Sprinting across one side of the lawn, through the first set of lavender hedges, across the paved walkway, then cutting through the adjacent bushes, Biscuit was always at her heels. Wind in her teeth, ponytails flying, she ran as fast as her legs would go to the farther end of the yard.

Emma smiled at the image of Biscuit running at her side. It was a race they had ran many times throughout her younger years, and somehow, she'd always won. Biscuit intentionally threw the competition every time, she was sure of it now.

When Reba left their home, she took Biscuit with her. Emma cried for a month straight. She recalled sitting on the porch, hoping for a glimpse of him rounding the corner of the house. He didn't come that week, or the next. Swollen eyes caused her to see mirages of him. Wiping her tears away, she held onto hope that he'd appear out of the bushes until hunger and mosquitos drove her back indoors. Reba knew how much Emma loved Biscuit; he was her best friend.

Sometime after Grandma Rose's fall, phone calls from Reba increased. She was checking in on her daughter, at least that was her excuse. Emma wanted to know how Biscuit was doing and why she had taken him? That's when she believed Reba set her plan in motion. The calls became more frequent, coincidentally when Emma was home alone. She spun a fairytale of the three of them - Emma, Reba, and Biscuit - living in their own apartment. It was her Dad's fault, Reba would say; he made her leave. He worked early mornings and late nights, left them alone, and had made her miserable.

She remembered Reba telling how her Father, and his parents, forbid her from working after she refused a position at PAHST. Emma believed Reba because there was some truth to her story; her Dad kept late hours working full time alongside law school. Hadn't Grandma Rose been grooming Emma too throughout the years to eventually take her awaited position at the organization?

Maybe Reba hadn't abandoned her after all; this was her plan, to set up a place for them to live, and then come back to get her? That's why she'd taken Biscuit first, Reba knew the only way she could coax Emma to leave her Daddy's house was to use Biscuit as bait. The lure worked, halfway through her junior year of high school - during the time of World War Victoria - Emma moved into the two-bedroom apartment on the Eastside with Reba.

It was a low-income housing development on the never talked

about but the all-knowing side of town. The community was quiet, but Emma found the colors dull and depressing. Cement and brick overshadowed sparse trees surrounding the building. There was no garden, besides the flowering succulents lining the roadway. Their third-floor apartment lacked the décor Emma preferred.

There was a small two-seat sofa in the living room with an old tv set on top of a wooden tv stand. Empty cups and cigarette packs adorned the round dining table in the kitchenette. In each bedroom was a twin-sized bed with a dresser in Emma's room.

"This is home now," said Reba.

Her cold stare told Emma to knock off the complaints and make do with what they had. She found Biscuit in her new bedroom, lying in a corner, face between his front legs. His behavior demonstrated how they both felt. Kneeling on the floor, she gave him her face to lick.

"I'm here now, we'll get through this together," she said.

Biscuit managed to give her one doggie-kiss and then put his head back down. She sensed he had experienced and witnessed some shady encounters when his sad, round eyes seemed to say, "It's all bad here!"

It took one full day and two nights for Reba's true intentions to be revealed.

•  •  •  •  •  •  •

## The Garden

"I was relieved when you came home," said Emanuel.

It was a topic they avoided before, never speaking of the day he rescued her from that seedy apartment. It was foolish of Reba to think she could parent alone when she had first failed with the help of her husband and others. Blaming her poor parental skills on an absent husband and over-bearing mother-in-law was part of her delusion. Reba quickly learned there was more to parenting than providing a bed and four walls.

•   •   •   •   •   •   •

It took two weeks for Reba to realize what she viewed as overindulging by Grandma Rose was necessary for a child who was hyperactive and struggled with friendships. Emma required more attention than Reba anticipated. At her father's house, she'd stay up late to talk with him when he returned from work, or Skyped conversations with Grandma Rose, who never fully recovered from her stroke. Reba's apartment had no internet access, and her Dad now lived on the other side of town.

Emma found it difficult to maintain her grades at the school-of-the-arts high school she attended. Grandma Rose had helped her with the application and audition process, encouraging her to believe that she could succeed in a non-traditional school environment. She wanted Emma to focus on her talents in the hopes it would build confidence and foster relationships.

With support from Grandma Rose, her freshmen and sophomore years were effortless. Without them, the pressure reflected in her grades. Though she thrived in dance and movement classes, Emma struggled with her assignments, and academic probation became a looming threat.

Money was tight, and the food was scarce. Reba often complained that the payments Emanuel gave her barely covered household expenses. She hadn't worked in years, so employment opportunities were limited. Reba tried to help with some of her daughter's assignments but usually left the room frustrated, telling Emma to do the best she could. When Grandma Rose gave Emma funds to pay for a personal tutor, she foolishly told Reba, who guilted her into using the cash for other household needs.

"Your Grandma's not here to mollycoddle you, Lynn, put your big girl pants on!"

Lynn was the name Reba chose for her, and Emanuel and his parents loathed. The story was that Reba's Grandmother, Terra Lynn, made an appearance at the hospital on the day of Emma's birth to remind Rebekah Lynn of their family's tradition. All female born children had to be given the same name as a reminder of her life-changing journey across the oceans from Cuba to the United States. Emma had never met her maternal Grandmother, although she was alive and lived somewhere in Louisiana.

Now that it was just the two of them, Reba was free to call her daughter by the intended birth name, Lynn. Rebekah Lynn, however, shunned the use of her full name, preferring the name Reba for herself. Whenever Emma started a sentence with "Mom, can I—"

"What is my name?" Her Mother often corrected.

"What—you know your name," she said, perplexed by the question.

"What did you call me?" Reba laughed as if they were two friends who joked with one another.

"REBA, can I go next door? A friend of mine lives in the building," she remembered saying.

"Of course, girl go ahead." Reba would roll her eyes and wave a hand.

Her behavior would leave Emma with uneasiness in the pit of her stomach. Although her friends were few, Emma knew the difference between a Mother and a girlfriend. What she wanted was a Mom to encourage, love, and yes, sometimes reprimand her.

Reba wanted to play a game that made Emma ashamed of her actions. On some days she empathized with her mother, knowing how she struggled to provide for them. Reba relied on her good looks like an over-utilized credit card, but her crow's feet and wrinkle folds threatened new dating prospects and employment opportunities. Emma sensed their situation could only end one way. Hopefully, Reba would come to her senses, and they could return home together.

Five months later, Biscuit and Emma were miserable; long faces and sad eyes replaced their customary greeting of licks and hugs. She had an indescribable feeling, a somber mood that stayed with her until she was sure something terrible was about to happen. It had been over a week since she'd last heard from her Dad or Grandparents, even though they had agreed to keep in touch through emails and phone calls. After about the tenth day-of-silence, Emma felt an urgency to speak with her Grandma Rose.

It was a Friday evening, and there had been no sign of Reba since Emma returned from school earlier in the day. A note was left on the refrigerator:

**Be back shortly with something to eat, Reba.**

Emma used the opportunity to call Grandma Rose and maybe coax her into meeting at the corner bakery, as they'd successfully met there twice before without Reba suspecting a thing. After sending the coded message, via text:

**Emma: Remember when we ate chocolate croissants and drank spiced cider?**

After four hours passed with no response from Grandma Rose, she sent a message to her Dad, asking if he'd heard from her Grandparents.

**Dad: I'll be by first thing tomorrow to talk to you.**

Emma rubbed her arms, then held her stomach; what she needed was fresh air to calm her nerves.

"Fried chicken and potato wedges, get it while it's hot." Reba was home before she made it out of the apartment. They ate in silence and when Reba teased, "Will you ever learn to eat chicken properly, tear into the flesh like I showed you…" she laughed, but Emma refused to return the smile.

"Well, I suppose you already heard, so no need in pretending it's of some great loss to me." Reba shrugged her shoulders.

"Heard what?" Emma stopped chewing and stared at her Mother.

"Nothing—I thought you heard something in the building about me, is all…" she cleared her throat and giggled.

"You said, 'it's no great loss,' what are you talking about, Reba? If you have something to say, just say it."

She was already on edge, sensing something was wrong. Her emotions quickly escalated, and she knocked her plate on the floor as she stood on her feet.

"Now calm down, Lynn—"

"Don't call me that, my name's Emma - I hate that stupid name you try to push on me, MOM!" she said, hoping for the full-blown fight.

"Alright, Emma…alright. Calm down, baby. It's going to be ok," Reba comforted.

Which only confirmed Emma's suspicions.

There were rare moments when Reba showed her kindness. Hearing her Mother use her proper name and referring to her affectionately was like rubbing aloe on sunburnt skin. Emma's jaw loosened, and her muscles relaxed. It gave her hope that someday, Reba could learn to be her Mother, that somewhere beneath her frown lines and fake laughter was a woman searching for ways to bond with her daughter. This new living arrangement, in time, could prove to be the crux of a deeper relationship between them.

Emma tugged at her sweater and circled around the mess covered floor while Reba fixed her another plate. Not another word had been spoken between them that night. She awoke the next morning to a knock at the front door. His voice was low, but she detected the sadness. It was her Dad, now sitting on the sofa, avoidant eyes met hers as he sniffled.

"I Don't know how to tell you this baby…"

But there was no need to say what she already knew; Grandma Rose had visited her in a night vision.

*Sitting by a pond, someone tapped her on the shoulder. She waved goodbye and smiled, which comforted Emma. Standing tall and proud, she told Emma not to forget what she said, then waved goodbye as she faded in the wind.*

When she awoke, Emma felt the peace of her grandmother's passing.

"Grandma Rose came to tell me goodbye," said Emma to her parents before she broke down.

Emanuel was the first to hold her, then Reba joined in, and they shared a family hug that had been far too long in the making.

"I'm going over to the ranch to check on Pops," said Emanuel; and the miracle occurred when the three of them left the apartment together, in one car.

"Rose Mary was a strong woman…we didn't see eye-to-eye, but she wanted me to be a noblewoman—I couldn't then, but I can try now," said Reba as she buckled her car seat.

# SEVEN

EMMA WALKED THROUGH the front door barely able to use her fingers which were frostbitten. She tapped her shoe on the bare floor, hoping to loosen her unbending toes, frosted from the wintery day. Another round of battling it out with Victoria earlier had her desperate for an escape. Without Grandma Rose, her source of wisdom and advice was gone, and she wished for spring, so she could retreat to her Dad's lavender garden. For now, she still had Biscuit.

There were other voices in the apartment, in the kitchen she saw three strange men, and two women sitting at the table. Reba was at the sink washing spoons.

"Where's Biscuit?" asked Emma.

"You don't know how to say 'Hi' first?" Said a heavy-set Caucasian woman with a raspy voice and ocean-blue eyes.

"That dumb dog is around here somewhere," Reba spat, inciting laughter from her guests.

Emma knew she should be polite. Grandma Rose taught her better than to barge into a house and not greet everyone. She was about to speak, but movement in the corner called for her attention.

"Biscuit!"

She ran to him when he limped toward her, whimpering while he licked her face.

"What happened to him?" she yelled at Reba.

There was no response.

"My Maw would've skinned me 'live for talking to her like that," a black man with freckles and sandy brown hair interjected.

"Reba, what happened to my dog?"

She ignored the parenting advice from the unsavory roundtable.

"Finally, she calls me by my name," teased Reba.

Her veins charged with anger; Emma steadied her trembling hands. Seeing that she was outnumbered she tried breathing slow to calm herself. A fight with Reba now wouldn't end well for her in this setting, but then Biscuit whimpered again which made her forget the stakes. Emma picked up a nearby cup and threw it at the wall. Reba gasped, and someone swore.

"Told you that gal would be nothing but trouble, they only good for one thing," said one of the men.

Her first thought was to get Biscuit and take off. But it was below 30 degrees outside, and 6 feet of snow covered the ground. With no money, she'd have to ask for a ride, bus fare, or hike home to her Dad's house. Emma shivered on the porch, contemplating her route of escape, then a thought occurred; this was their plan all along…chase her out so they'd have a place to party and crash afterward.

She wouldn't give in to their wish, after all, her presence is what secured the low-income housing for Reba; without a dependent child, she wouldn't qualify for the apartment. It was Reba's guests who should leave.

"I'm calling Denver PD in thirty minutes, whoever's not on the lease will have a serious problem," she threatened.

Reba's mouth hung open, and no one else said a word.

"Come Biscuit, I'll take care of you." She guided him to her bedroom.

"She's so uptight… never smiles," she overheard Reba saying.

"Just like her Daddy, that's why I had to go." She heard her mother say before the door slammed shut behind her. Emma had to turn the volume on her radio up to drown out their laughter, then crawled into bed with Biscuit, pulling the covers over their head.

It seemed once Emma relented and was now comfortable addressing Reba by her name, she had utterly lost sight of the mother-daughter relationship. With Grandma Rose out of the way, Reba became bold with her intentions. It was as if she'd been forced to wear a mask all those years and was now living her authentic life, unashamed, and without excuses. Reba's screaming subsided, and her temper-tantrums ceased, but the company increased.

·　·　·　·　·　·　·

## The Garden

"Emma, I was never going to leave you there," said Emanuel, pulling her into his arms. It was all a memory now, but her muscles constricted recalling the days. His expression changed, the way it had the day when she left Reba's apartment for the last time.

·　·　·　·　·　·　·

Something about that day felt off from the moment she awoke at 6:30 am. Emma remembered setting her alarm the night before; so how was it that the alarm had failed to go off? Now, she had overslept and was late for school.

While in the shower, some of the soap slid in her eyes, and no amount of squinting or water flushing soothed the sting. With nothing quick to eat for breakfast, Emma grabbed a yogurt cup from the fridge on her way out of the apartment. After dashing out the door, in less than 20 minutes, she barely made the bus to school. When she found a seat and tore off the lid, a sour smell filled her nostrils; the expiration date was two months past its shelf life. Emma was not impressed with the way her day began, and she hoped things would improve as the school day commenced. All she needed to do was avoid Victoria.

No sooner had Emma sat down in her first-period class, her phone vibrated. She knew cell phones were prohibited once the second bell rang, but the persistent caller made her curious. Hoping to go undetected by the teacher, she glanced at the caller identification; it was Reba. She rejected the call and continued with her studies.

Five minutes later, her cell phone vibrated again, and again… and again. Emma took another chance, snuck a peek at her phone, and saw Reba was still calling. She pushed ignore on the screen, tapped her feet on the floor until her anger cooled.

*Emma: You know I'm in class!*

*Reba: Emergency!!!*

Emma excused herself, saying she needed to use the restroom. When she entered the hallway, her phone buzzed once more.

"Mom—Reba, I'm at school," she whispered.

It could've been a genuine emergency, but Emma was still angry from Reba's antics the previous night; she and her guests slammed the front door, shouted as they came and left. Cigarette and weed smoke permeated the apartment. Their lively music thumped her bedroom walls. Emma fell asleep sometime after 2:30 a.m., with a pillow over her head and earplugs in her ears.

"I'm outside your school, I need you at home," Reba snapped at her before ending the call.

Once in the car, Reba's words were explosive and venomous. Emma was unsure what role she had played in the situation, but knowing surely, she would make an earnest plea to her parents tonight about the living arrangements. She was ready to go back home, and if not home, anywhere but here, far away from Reba and her madness. They seemed to be on a different wavelength and separate planets, and the way Reba drove was a concern. Emma thought about jumping from the car and making a run for it, but if she ran back to her Father's house, how could he help? If he were unable to prevent Reba from taking her in the first place, he probably wouldn't be of much help now.

She sighed deeply as the car pulled into the parking space of the last place she wanted to be. When she entered the apartment, two of the same thugs from the night before were still hanging around as if they owned the place. Reba pulled Emma into the bedroom. Shutting the door behind them, she stroked Emma's hair.

"We're in this together, ok!" she whispered.

Frown lines on her forehead and crinkled nose exposed Emma's thoughts. "What?" said Emma. A knock on the bedroom door caused them both to flinch.

"GIVE US A SEC!" yelled Reba, her breathing escalated.

"Look, I'm your Mom, I'm doing the best I can—"

She frowned when Emma laughed at her.

"—since your Daddy abandoned us!" She avoided eye-contact when she spoke. Clutching herself as if a cold breeze gave her the chills.

"I messed up Emma, we need to stick together," she continued.

Emma saw the desperation in her eyes, and it seemed like the hairs on her arm were standing at attention. Cornered in the room, with the door closed and two thugs waiting in the living room, Emma felt helpless as if a tornado was set to tear through their apartment within moments. What could she possibly do to help Reba out of whatever situation she had put herself into?

"Look, he just wants to talk to you, that's all baby, just talk to him." She spoke in an agitated tone.

As she continued tucking Emma's loose strands behind her ears Reba looked her over one last time, smoothing down her eyebrows, adjusted her blouse and tugged at her jogger pants.

"Quit it!" Emma grunted, then swatted at her mother's hand.

Before she could protest further, Reba ran to the door and flung it open.

"I'm not staying here—" said Emma.

"So, where are we going?" asked one of the thugs. He was a bronzed skin man, with black short cropped hair and a tattoo across his neck that said, 'Amour Puerto Riqueno.' He leaned against the door, and after his inspection of Emma, grabbed Reba by the face and whispered something in her ear.

"Give me something sweet, Ogre!" said Reba.

As he pressed a small object into her waiting hand, Reba kissed him on the cheek. She grabbed the contents hurriedly and never looked back, leaving the stranger alone in the room with Emma.

"You belong to me now, princess!" is what she remembered

him saying last before the commotion rang out from the front room.

## The Garden

It was a terrible moment, even now to recall. Clinging to her father, Emma buried her face into his chest, then inhaled the English Lavender and spearmint from the garden. He squeezed his baby girl tight. Emma was safe here with her Daddy, and she never wanted to leave his side again.

"It was the grace of God that I arrived when I did."

He shook his head, fighting back emotions.

"Your Mother has a lot of demon's, baby, they torment her," he said.

Emma, believing that he was defending Reba, was astonished. After all this time, he still refused to give up on his wife. She wanted to be angry at him, to scream, and tell him to be realistic and see the picture for what it was, for once, just this once. But all she could muster was a defeated sigh.

Peace replaced her anger quickly, a deep peace within that she had never felt before. It ascended from the pit of her stomach and then lifted above her head. First, it was like a canopy over them both, then it wrapped her up like a warm blanket.

"She had been calling non-stop, two weeks straight, morning and night, claiming that you had gotten yourself into a mess you didn't want me to find out about," he said.

Emma listened in shock to events she'd never known before because neither wanted to speak of the incident after that day.

While Emma stood trapped in the bedroom trying to devise a way of escape, Emanuel was at the front door demanding to see his daughter. Reba hurled her profanities, like bombs at the husband she claimed had abandoned her. When Emma realized the other voice outside the bedroom was from her dad, calling out for her, both she and Ogre ran for the door at once.

She was relieved to see her Dad standing toe-to-toe with Reba and the other waiting man. Emanuel meant business that day and wasn't leaving until he had his daughter.  There was a thick piece of steel in his hands, and by the look in his eyes, he had every intention of using it. Grabbing Emma by the arm, he got up in Reba's face.

"She will not be coming back here!"

• • • • • • •

## The Garden

Emma hung her head in shame, as she wondered what her Daddy must've thought happened between her and that man behind closed doors, alone. When she opened her mouth to explain, he spoke up.

"I had a private investigator following Reba," he told her.

"Found out the day before I came for you that she was running around town with some punk, a so-called pimp."

Emma held back words she wanted to speak against Reba.

"People like us can't even begin to understand what it's like for a person like your mom. She was doing the only thing she knew how to do." He stood and admired the scents and colors of the beautiful garden. He leaned over, and snapping off another twig of Lavender handed the stem to his daughter.

Emma remembered that Biscuit was somehow inside the car before her that day. Then when they were home, the first thing she noticed was the sad condition of the prized Lavender garden.

"Our Lavender garden suffered just as much as we did that year, Dad," she reminded him.

"…and poor Biscuit."

He nodded his head in agreement before answering, "With you gone, I lost interest in the garden, unfortunately." He sighed.

"You were always working," she pointed out.

"I had no time for you or the garden," he said sadly then shrugged. "We did make up for lost time for a while there though—didn't we?" he asked.

"If only there had been more time." Emma smiled at him.

Sitting silent for a moment, thinking about the pain Reba had caused them, Emma realized that she had just voiced a complaint similar to her Mother's.

*'You were always working!'*

It had been her argument in the earlier days when Emma was a small girl. Despite his absence or how late he worked, there was no excuse for all that Reba had done and the trauma she had caused her one and only child. Somehow, there had to come a day when Reba would pay for her wrongdoing.

Here, her Daddy sat, defending a woman who caused nothing but heartache and disappointment. And now for some unknown reason, she understood their marriage from Reba's perspective. It all seemed so unfair; there had to be a judge and jury that would hear her case against her Mother, someone who would see the disregard for her safety, the neglect, and the abandonment, and find her guilty as charged. But there was no judge and no jury that Emma could see…only her faithful Daddy, and herself standing as the sole survivors of the wrath of Reba.

# PART II

# THE INCIDENT

*2008 - 2009*

# EIGHT

QUARTER PAST MIDNIGHT Emma was home earlier than she hoped. Upset with her two friends who insisted on going to Seth's graduation party that night. She suspected he had put them both up to solidifying her presence. On the night her peers intended to celebrate their certificate of freedom, her Father had placed the keys in her hands and pronounced that she was the designated driver.

Emma wondered if a secret memo had passed around earlier that day, collecting signatures of all the names committed to sabotaging her evening.

> •Stop Emma from going to nightclub…**Check!**
> •Stop Emma from all illegal practices…**Check!**
> •Stop Emma from any form of enjoyment…**Check!**

The plan was set in motion by their insistence on going to Seth's party, threatening to leave her alone on graduation night, then resorting to pleading and bribery.

"We'll die if we're the only ones not there!" they said.

"My gladiator sandals, they're yours!" was the other friend's proposition.

Emma was exhausted from the day of standing, then sitting, and then standing once more as her exuberant classmates screamed cheers that shook the theatre ceiling. The soles of her feet ached, and her head throbbed. Now in her nightclothes, she relished a cup of iced tea in hand and wanted nothing more than to lie across her bed with a slow tune and snuggle with Biscuit.

She turned the volume to a low setting, hoping to erase the replay of that horrid - dry as dust - rendition of the star-spangled banner from the school choir. Biscuit was not at her side, nor was he in his usual sleeping place beside her dresser, which meant she'd have to track him down because neither of them would get any sleep without the other. She remembered searching underneath her bed that night, and then around the room.

There was a tap at the window, which Emma first believed came from the song playing on the radio. She watched as a slight vibration rattled the window. Emma tapped her fingernails to the beat, then turned to the internet for amusement, hoping it would replace her disappointment from the evening. A pause in the music was long enough for her to confirm another tap at the window. If it was her two friends again scheming for a ride, it wasn't going to end well for them, she thought.

Peeping through the blinds, she saw Biscuit run across the lawn. Then Reba followed behind him - Emma shook her head in disbelief, perplexed by her mother's persistence.

"You don't quit!" she mumbled.

Emma clenched her fists as her breathing stilled, she thought about banging on the window and yelling out some colorful words, maybe confront her. Instead, she watched.

Reba's movements were delayed, clumsy, and predictable. A turtle could've out slicked her. Biscuit made a game out of it, standing still long enough for her to catch up, and then suddenly jumping out of her reach.

"Took my Grandma from me..." Emma whispered, then envisioned lifting a hand to strike her mother.

It wasn't right to hit your parent - she knew it - but she'd seen it in movies. When a person became hysterical or uncontrollable a swift slap across the face restored their sanity. It needed to be a sharp, deliberate, strategically placed whack up against the side of Reba's noggin.

"Chose that punk over me," she ranted.

"Left my Dad..." she slipped her feet into running shoes.

"Now you want Biscuit?"

She grabbed the doorknob and raced through the house.

"It's not happening!"

Reaching the back door, Emma paused to ensure her Dad hadn't heard the commotion because she wanted to confront Reba on her own – after all, this was about her and Biscuit anyway. Emma chose to be with her Dad, so Reba was here to take away what she loved the most. What would she say to him anyway?

"Yep, that's mom running around outside in the dark...No, she didn't come for me. Nope, she still doesn't want you either, it's Biscuit she's after. You know, the dog she despised in the beginning until we fell in love with him, that's what she came for."

No, this was Emma's problem. He could divorce Reba, but she'd always be her mother.

Peering through the door, she saw as Reba went down. Sweaty and breathless, she collapsed on the ground. Biscuit wagged his tail and nipped at her ankles. She waved him away and then put her head down in surrender. In the dim light, it looked like she started to cry. Emma saw her Mother's face; spiral curls framed her gaunt cheeks. Reba could go days without food, but her hair and makeup were always kept up. Emma unlocked the patio door and stepped outside.

"Help me, baby," said Reba.

She reached a hand for her daughter, who took hold and helped her to stand.

"Why are you out here like this?" asked Emma.

Reba looked her daughter in the eyes, thought of an excuse, but then turned away and sobbed.

"You want what you can't have so now you're crying?" asked Emma.

She wasn't sure if it was seeing how her mother fell down- or the tears - but she had softened. The moonlight had framed her face in a way that allowed Emma to see the woman behind the mask.

Reba had an addiction she hid like a secret lovechild; she breastfed it in the darkness until it grew like a well-nourished baby. Its appetite was voracious, throwing temper tantrums when she refused to give in. The weight of its rapid growth caused her bones to ache, and when it needed to be fed, she fought through nausea and a constant runny nose that threatened to reveal her secret; she'd have no peace in her body until relenting to feed her overgrown habit. Her addiction was the real reason she had to finally leave their home, keeping her away from her husband and daughter.

Reba shivered in the night air, then scratched at a rough blotch on her skin. The moonlight revealed bruised and collapsed veins before she could conceal them, and when their eyes met, there was no denying the truth. Looking away, first to the trees, then up to the sky, Emma touched her gently, rubbed her arm, sharing her body heat. Reba smiled, allowing for the closeness, it had been years since they were able to tolerate each other's presence. Emma shut her eyes, inhaled, thinking she'd been too hard on her Mother all this time.

"Listen..." she pulled away. "I need you, come with me?"

Emma rolled her eyes, realizing the moment had passed.

"You can bring Biscuit too," she pleaded.

Emma saw her agitation growing, so she reached for her again, but then stopped when her mother stepped away. Back to the way things were and always would be. Reba's love was held at a distance, far up in giant trees, where wild honeybees kept their hives safe. Her Mother's love was like that honey you'd risk being stung for in the process. Exhausted from the day, Emma threw her hands in the air and then retreated.

This was her graduation day. It was meant to mark her entrance into adulthood, a time when she was expected to forge a path for herself and make responsible choices. There was no time for their love/hate relationship. Tomorrow's first order of business was to decide when and how she'd return to her Grandma Rose's organization. At her Dad's reassurance that he'd shadow her through the transition, Emma agreed to an internship once she selected and registered at a suitable college.

Biscuit's bark caused her to look back; he jumped at Reba, knocking her back on the ground.

"Why do you want Biscuit? He's mine, and Dad's...You left us, so you don't get to have him."

Reba was able to grab hold of his collar this time, and he yelped.

"Leave him alone," said Emma, stepping closer.

The urge returned to slap Reba across the face, but before she knew what was happening, a hand reached from behind her and cuffed a napkin over her nose and mouth. Fumes filled her nostrils and burned her throat, making it difficult to breathe. She beat at the muscular arm around her neck.

"That's enough, Ogre!" Reba shouted.

Emma was helpless, her legs wobbled before she collapsed.

# NINE

THE ROOM WAS dark; stained blue curtains covered a window that had been boarded over with wooden slats. When she went to raise up, Emma found that her hands were tied together, and her nightclothes replaced with a crop-top and skirt. She had been laying on a mattress and box spring, which had no bed frame or headboard.

The floor held onto a mildewed, worn-down carpet that smelled like poor plumbing issues. There was a nightstand beside the bed and a small sink and toilet in a space that was supposed to be the bathroom. Several posters lined one wall with bikini-clad, red-lipped women of different skin tones and sizes.

It took several minutes before Emma was reminded of the incident in her backyard. She had been taken by force. Impulse led her to cry out for help, until she remembered—the hand over her mouth, a napkin filled with fumes, Reba asking for help, and saying how they needed to stick together. Small packages pressed in the center of her Mother's sweaty palms silenced her love-child's hunger.

In her fog, Emma recalled an image of herself tied in the backseat of a moving car. Biscuit had been there, but he was never the target; this was about Reba's debt and Ogre wanted to collect what had been promised him.

Somewhere behind the door, Emma heard the murmurs of her captors. She called for Reba first, and then her anger shifted toward Ogre; screaming threats that he'd receive hard-time and jail cells where he would rot once she was freed. There was no way of knowing if either of them heard her.

Swearing revenge and what she would do to either one of them, Emma wiggled off the bed and tried to yell through the window slats, hoping to draw attention her way. When her vocal cords failed, she turned her violence on the door, kicking hard and praying for strength to knock the hinges loose. She kicked, and kicked, and kicked until her legs grew too heavy to lift.

By the time Emma collapsed, there was silence inside and outside the room. As she strained to listen against the door, Emma thought about her Mother's friends and pictured them blowing smoke through nostrils as they sipped from cups filled with dark liquid. The more they drank, the louder the exchange circled with merriment and wisdom from fools. She imagined their laughter, rejoicing at how they'd finally taught the cherished princess of the fallen Rosemary St. Roman a lesson. She screamed and struck at the door until her body gave in to exhaustion and sleep.

As the first day of her captivity turned to night, the noise level from outside the room increased. Footsteps bypassed her door as some people laughed, and others conversed. The traffic seemed to slow, and someone on the other side of her door jiggled the handle. When it wouldn't open a woman groaned and whimpered as she tried harder to force the locked door. Intuition told Emma the woman was her mother.

"Mom? I know that's you," Emma moved closer.

"Why are you doing this?"

She leaned against the door and listened as the woman sobbed.

"I'm bad off baby, but I'll fix this," Reba whimpered.

Emma pressed her ear against the door. She listened as Reba fumbled with a key ring that fell to the floor.

"Open the door!" Shouted Emma, pulling on the handle.

"I'm sorry—my hands, my nerves…" said Reba.

"We can discuss that later; get me out of here," Emma demanded.

Reba knew once Emma got this agitated, there was no sense in trying to talk.

"I need more time…Ogre—"

And then Reba was gone.

Emma wasn't sure how much time had passed, but she was awakened by a light tap at the door, and then a shadow entered. How she'd gotten from the floor to the bed was unclear. Though foggy and fatigued, she reached for the figure as it approached.

"Help me!" she said, clinging to the person who sat on the bed beside her. A girl stroked Emma's hair until she was calm.

"Here, eat," a tanned brunette instructed.

Not knowing if she was real or imagined, Emma felt her face and hair. She looked young, no older than sixteen.

"What are we doing here, where are we?" Emma looked to the door.

"You should eat," she held a sandwich to Emma's lips.

The bread brushed against a bruise on her lips, causing Emma to swipe at the girl's hand. The food fell on the floor.

"Ewww, that's got to hurt," said the girl.

She leaned over to retrieve a piece of cloth from the nightstand and ran it under water from the small sink.

"They get like that when you fight," she explained.

"Take the pills, you'll feel better." She continued wiping Emma's face.

Someone else had been in the room earlier, Emma remembered now - a shadow that moved in the dark and growled like a beast - he had untied her hands, but not before slapping her hard across the face to show who was in charge.

"Don't cry," said the brunette girl.

She continued to nurse Emma's wound. Afterward, she hand-fed small bites of the sandwich to Emma.

"Just don't fight—"

A sharp tap on the door signaled to the girl that her time was up.

"Take the pills!" the girl said.

She pointed to a small bottle and glass of water on the nightstand before she closed the door behind her. When the lock clicked, Emma's panic resumed. She screamed more threats, but with no results thought her energy should be used toward ways of outsmarting them.

Sooner or later, someone else would come again, when they did, Emma decided to reason as her best strategy. That was it! Kidnapping is a crime; if they weren't aware of the legal system, she would inform them of the terrible offense they were committing in holding someone against their will. The first person through that door, she'd offer them a deal.

"It was all Reba's doing," she practiced saying to the girl.

Of course, they'd want to save themselves, she imagined. Her plan of choice would be to stand behind the door as it opened, attack, and run! There had to be a heavy object in the room she could use, the glass of water? It was plastic. One of the drawers from the nightstand? It could work - swing hard like a bat and run!

Pleased with her plan, Emma sipped the water from the cup. When the pain from her lip and body ached, she decided on one pill, or two, to ease the pain – just once. Fatigue caused her eyes to close. Fighting back her sleep she gave in to a nap that would restore strength needed to execute her plan.

The air was thick and smelled of burnt incense, musty body odor, and booze. As the room grew darker, shadows emerged; she thought it was a dream. The monster had returned and wrestled with Emma in the night. He was stronger than Ogre, hairy and reeked of cigarette smoke and liquor. He tore at her clothes and pinned her to the bed. When he moaned, she reached out during the struggle and sunk her teeth into his flesh, surprised at how the taste of blood incited her.

The monster yelped, retreated, but then returned with a blow to Emma's jaw that knocked the fight out of her; she collapsed. Pleased with his conquest, the monster snarled and whimpered from his injury.

When it was all over, Emma trembled from his attack. The attack was quick and painful - and somehow - she survived. Her head throbbed, and her body throbbed in every way, but Emma had some solace knowing the monster would wear a scar to remind him of the battle not easily won.

She recalled an episode on Wild Planet, where a pride of lions had the scent of a wounded gazelle. Injured and bleeding, it collapsed to the ground; and just when that first lion approached the gazelle sprang to its feet and outsprinted the threat on its life. The brunette warned her against fighting back...but she was wrong, Emma would fight until she was free.

Seconds turned into minutes, then hours had passed.

In a dream, she and Grandma Rose were together attending an event for the PAHST organization. An unidentified guest warned her to keep an eye on the girl; the brunette was there, lurking as Emma distributed materials to attendees.

When Emma awoke, the brunette girl stood at the door.

"Chill, I brought you some clean clothes and snacks."

She tossed clothing items and a small paper bag on the bed.

"Where am I, where's Reba?"

"I'll let him know you're ready to talk."

The girl moved from the door to the sink. Her response was direct and informative, and yet she never answered a question.

"What do they want from me?"

She stood to gauge her distance between the girl and the door.

"You need to chill, play the game," the brunette shrugged.

Emma stepped closer.

"Don't stand in my way," she warned.

The girl took two steps backward, her mouth opened as if to yell or call for help. Emma's reaction was swift, she grabbed the girl and covered her mouth, then dared her to say another word. It was too late. Emma heard footsteps hurrying toward the room, she looked to the girl, hoping to plea with her but the silly girl sneered.

In anger, she rushed the girl, and they fell to the floor; one pulled the other's hair, as the other struggled to gain control. As they tangled, a much larger woman entered the room and separated the two of them. She reached for the brunette with one arm and dragged her from the room.

Emma ran after the woman who shoved her hard with a free hand, that sent her reeling backward. By the time she regained her balance, the woman had shut the door behind them. Emma yanked on the doorknob then kicked, cursing herself because she had been asleep when the girl entered.

Emma stood before the nightstand and trembled from the experience. The brunette wouldn't trust her again after the attack, but someone would have to come in her place. When her headache returned, she considered the pills. Thinking of their benefits and not the side-effects, she tossed a few pills in her mouth, washed her face and laid down on the bed.

Footsteps outside the room caused her to awaken. There was no way to know how long she'd slept, as her earlier search proved there wasn't a clock, radio, or cell phone in the room. She dreamed again, this time not of monsters, but of a big city; a place she'd never been before with skyscrapers taller than the buildings in Denver.

A hand turned the doorknob, and then a man appeared. He was dressed in a custom-made suit and wore polished shoes. His black hair, streaked with gray, was a little long and fell alongside droopy, kind eyes. With slight hesitation, he looked Emma over, then nodded to another standing out of eyesight. As he turned to leave, she noticed an odd tattoo on his forearm, a pattern with an eagle, a serpent, and a thorny vine.

"Am I in Denver? Do you know Reba? She's my Mom, is she here?"

He never looked back, or answered, as the door clicked shut behind him. The signs were clear, and Emma could no longer deny the facts. She'd read enough pamphlets and heard countless testimonies from survivors – this was the heart of a sex trafficking ring.

If Grandma Rose were still alive, Emma would be preparing for college and future career at PAHST. Truth be told, she lost sight of those goals a long time ago. Towards the end of her freshman year, the shift in her interests had already occurred, even before

Grandma Rose fell ill. It was easy to blame her reduced involvement on school obligations, but if she was honest with herself, the distraction resulted from outside influence.

The room was hot and sticky, which caused beads of sweat to form on her forehead. Emma washed her face and then brushed clenched teeth. When she turned off the water faucet, she could smell fried eggs, bacon, and waffles. Emma looked at the door and hoped someone was kind enough to bring her a plate. The brunette wouldn't dare return, but perhaps the other lady would.

If she could remember at least one story of how captured victims escaped, it'd be enough. Emma peered through two wooden slats and was able to see daylight outside. Down below, there was a sidewalk and a roadway; people came and went, into and out of buildings she'd never seen before. There was no sense in yelling because they'd never hear from this distance. Though she wondered how a building with boarded windows could be ignored. With eyes closed, Emma exhaled and slumped to the floor, she wished Biscuit were beside her, and her Dad down the hallway in his bedroom, or his office studying over a case.

This was the lifestyle Reba chose, full of mind-bending drugs, coercive pimps, and doped-up prostitutes. They colonized together in secret rooms like this under the guise of protection. Carpet stains and food crumbs surrounded her, along with laughter and strange noises beyond the walls. Life has a bizarre way of turning the tables and resetting the players. No longer the advocate on how to survive human trafficking, she was now living a story that would need to be told.

Faces of women and men who came to PAHST for redemption reeled in her mind. No one deserved to be abducted, forced to stay, or perform against their will. Unable to recall any useful tip or plans for escape, Emma remembered one thing; every survivor she'd met had gone through the experience and returned home. The goal was to make it back home.

It was an image of Grandma Rose, hands cupped in prayer, that Emma finally settled on.

"Pray…Call on the Lord when you don't know what else to do!"

Her eyes flung open as she heard the words. Pleading for their mercy didn't help. Threats and reasoning failed. Fighting or surrendering hasn't granted her access to roam about like the other girls. What harm could Grandma Rose's advice have?

Desperate and defeated, Emma rolled off her backside and kneeled beside the bed. Imitating the image of her Grandma Rose, she spoke in a low voice.

"God, if you are real, I need your help. I probably don't deserve it—But please get me out of this room. Please!"

It was all she knew to say, to a God she wasn't sure existed. But Emma trusted her Grandma Rose, so if she said there was a God, who sent His son Jesus, Emma put her hope in this God for help.

After her prayer, visions of her Grandma Rose encouraged Emma to bathe, change clothes, and comb her hair for the first time since waking to this nightmare. The clothing items were clean but skimpy, they'd have to do for now. She figured the pickings were the brunette's choices since it was how she dressed on both encounters. Luckily, a thorough search among the pile of mini-skirts and cropped tops turned up one pair of joggers and a simple t-shirt. Satisfied with the outfit, Emma then turned to her face and hair.

Using extra care, she combed through tangled strands, then found comfort in the hair that was a reminder of her Grandmother. Emma hummed a soothing melody as she separated, then braided her hair into two plaits. Observing her reflection in the foggy mirror, it would have to do considering the few options she had been given.

Footsteps outside the room reminded Emma of her surroundings. There was a groan, someone sobbed outside her door.

"Please forgive me, I didn't mean for this to happen," a familiar voice whispered.

"Reba, is that you?" Emma stood still before the mirror, though she already knew the answer. Impulse drove her to the door, but she refrained from banging or screaming threats.

"It doesn't matter now. Let me go, please?" she pleaded.

The response was muffled, then another set of footsteps approached. She heard a slap and scuttled footsteps. Then Reba's threats that caused Emma to step away from the door. A man's voice reasoned with her Mother, saying he understood her confusion, and then they were gone.

"God, if you are real, please help me," she repeated once more.

Emma closed her eyes and focused on the image of her Grandma Rose. Before long, footsteps approached again. The doorknob turned and opened. The well-dressed man stood before her. It was his kind eyes that subdued her, so instead of fighting, Emma watched him.

"You're dressed, good. I will take you out today," he said with a distinct accent.

Standing tall with hands on his hips, he asserted his authority. They stared at one another; him assessing how feral she was, her questioning the level of danger.

"First, you will take these." He tossed the pill bottle at her.

"I'll know when you have," he nodded in her direction and left the room. At this point, she'd do whatever it took to get beyond the rank walls that breathed monsters and noises in the dark. After little consideration, Emma popped several pills and went to the window, imagining herself on the sidewalk, walking and breathing fresh air. This opportunity would give her a chance to run.

"Don't blow it," she said to herself.

Then a series of yawns prompted her to sit down and wait for his return. The well-dressed man pulled Emma close. Her legs were heavy and dragged along the floor, holding onto his arm, she walked feebly. Emma felt groggy, and at first, she thought it was a dream. After their struggle down a flight of stairs, he took her by the hand and guided her through double doors. She paused before taking another step, squinted her eyes because the sunlight was harsh.

"No one will hurt you, or they answer to me," he held his hand out for hers.

"Where…is?" she tried to speak.

They were outside now; sunlight on her skin and the smell of spicy fried foods awakened her senses. When he led her into a Restaurant, they appeared to others as a couple in love; his arms around her waist, her body leaned into his chest. He was going to sit opposite her in the booth but then thought better of it and slid in beside her.

"What would you like to eat?" he asked.

Though she was hungry, Emma wanted to ask where he was from? Were they in his country? Did he now own her? When she failed to respond, he took the initiative and ordered their food.

She wasn't shy about checking him over. She may not be able to speak – because of the pills - but her eyes were focused enough to make out distinguishing marks. She noticed a chip in one of his front teeth, and his hairline came to a point at the center. Judging from his features, she assumed he was Italian, but the accent was German…or, was it French?

When the waitress appeared with a plate of food still sizzling from the grill, Emma abandoned her inspection. It was her first taste of food since - God only knew how long - she'd been trapped in the room. The meal consisted of fried fish, potato salad, and coleslaw. Between bites and sips of iced tea, she observed a woman at the counter who casually glanced in their direction. Remembering her opportunity, Emma cleared her throat and hoped the sound would draw the woman's attention.

"Don't choke, we're not hurrying, everything's fine," he said, handing her the glass of iced tea to wash down another bite.

When the woman looked away, Emma forced a cough.

"So, this is how we're going to do this, hmm?" he said.

His jawbone clenched. When anger replaced the kindness in his eyes, Emma continued to eat, hoping he would relax and trust her again.

"This is the way it works; you behave, you get the best of me," he moved in closer, "or the worst!" he said with a straight face.

The waitress appeared, cleared the dishes, and left their bill. She hardly looked in Emma's direction and gave no consideration to Emma's tears.

Taking the pills turned out to be another terrible decision. She remained drowsy during the outing, and now after shoving food down her throat, Emma was nauseous. She depended on the man more after they left the restaurant. Wrapping his arms around her shoulders, they strolled out of the café and onto the sidewalk.

Emma noticed how the buildings were low, and how narrow the streets were in comparison to the ones in Denver. Music played in the distance, accordions, fiddles, and bass guitars. He said they could sit for a few minutes and listen to the live music before heading back to the room…if she behaved. When Emma nodded, he wiped her face with a tissue before pulling her close again; his attentiveness winning her over.

About a block down, they arrived at a two-story building and entered. It was an empty restaurant that appeared to be in renovation. Leading her through the back door, they stopped so he could pick up a tote bag, then proceeded up the stairs.

"I'll be back, take these," he placed the tote in her arms.

She resisted at first, standing between the door jam, but the look in his eyes reassured her.

"It's better that we do things this way," he said.

Then after convincing her that she was safe as his friend, she stepped through the door and back into the room. His voice was calm as he explained how their meetings would go. Emma wouldn't have to worry about others coming. If she complied, they could continue this way.

"You like these?"

He pulled items out of the tote; two sundresses, sandals, body cream, a bottle of perfume, a book, and two magazines. Emma knew what he wanted; his kind eyes begged for companionship.

"Will you help me?" she asked.

If he agreed to her plan for revenge, then there'd be peace between them. Otherwise, she'd make sure he hated the sight of her. The monster stopped appearing in the night. Emma remained separated from the others, though she could hear them outside the room. She didn't mind so long as they left her alone.

During their outings, he made sure she was stocked enough with supplies and snacks to get her by until their next meeting. His visits were typically every two, sometimes three days. By the second week, their conversations had evolved past expected pleasantries. He was a businessman from Milan, new in town, with little time for extracurricular affairs. He refused to give her a name, so she decided on a name for him, 'Gray,' but he preferred that she'd call him 'Friend.'

By the third week, he agreed to help her, and if he made good on his promise, then she would consider him a friend. Emma hatched a plan that would ensure Reba's wickedness had an end. Because Gray had taken a liking to her, it was easy to groom him, using the same tactics as he had to groom her for companionship. If she could convince him that what they shared was more than friendship, he'd move her out of the room. Freedom would help execute phase two of her plan. Gray proved to be a man of his word, up until their last meeting.

# TEN

THE DAY BEGAN with light rain that increased to monsoon rainfall, matching the tears on Emma's cheeks. Disappointment and regret filled her mind like the pools of water in the street gutters. Gray said the others would leave her alone if she complied with him, so how was it that she had another visitor last night? She tossed several pills into her mouth, then pulled the blankets over her head.

Their last meeting was brief, though she talked more than usual. He disclosed frustration over a search for a white husky. Emma told Gray about Biscuit, then about Reba, and her Dad, who she missed and must be worried sick by now. She talked about her Grandpa's horse, Misty, and her longing desire for friendship. Gray said very little but added that he understood what it was like to be an only child. After convincing her that he was ready to move forward with their plan, he left. That was five days ago.

The building was unusually active that week. More voices outside the room, some laughter, and others arguing over money and time wasted. The more she eavesdropped on the conversations; it became apparent that something was different. She boycotted the day, refused to bathe and eat, and stayed in bed, swallowed in a blanket of misery. With nightfall, the hallway and adjacent rooms came alive.

"I'm about my money."

A couple stood outside the room, engaged in a heated discussion. Then another person shouted that this is the way things go, "You should know this, your peeps invented the game." They spoke low at first, then louder as the argument persisted.

"Let me see her first—" a woman approached the door, it was Reba.

"Take this, on me," said an unidentified man.

A dog barked which caused Emma to toss the blankets off her head for the first time that day. It was Biscuit. In less than two minutes, she threw on the jogging pants, a pair of sneakers, and a hoodie that Gray presented to her on one of his visits. A piece of paper with his phone number written on it, along with a $100 bill, stashed in the back of the bottom drawer.

Their plan was for her to take his phone number, and the money on the day Biscuit was brought to her. Reba had retreated after getting her fix, but Biscuit remained at the door. He scratched and whined and probably wouldn't leave except by force.

The doorknob turned, and a black man entered the room. Biscuit came through the door next, jumped on the bed, and licked her face. The stranger assessed the room, looked her over, and pointed a finger.

"That's not going to work," he said, pointing to Emma's long pants and sweater.

"Leave her alone," Reba entered the room, her fists clenched tight.

Emma exhaled when she saw her mother's face, and without warning, Reba jumped on the man's back. He tossed her hard into the sink, which excited Biscuit. The stranger's back was turned as he wrestled with her mother, who had grabbed the man in a bear hug that defied her size. Both he and Reba yelled profanities. Biscuit growled and then snapped at the man, who hollered from the pain.

During the struggle, the door was left open. Emma waited to see who would come to his rescue - when no one came, she ran from the room…slower than she should have. It was foolish to have taken more of the pills. She fumbled with her legs on the stairs, but then by some miracle, Biscuit was at her side, encouraging her to keep going.

They ran together, with Emma two steps in the lead, like the many times before he'd let her win the race. Down the stairs, through another hall. A woman appeared but quickly moved out of her way. The main entrance was in sight, though a few feet away. Emma heard a pop—and Biscuit yelped. There was no time to check on him, she had to make it out the front door.

Adrenalin pumping, Emma threw herself through the double-doors, and out into the night air. The town was called Breaux Bridge, she'd learned on one of her outings. Past that, she had no other information, and somehow during the commotion, she dropped Gray's phone number and the $100 bill.

She ran down one block, two, then three…faster, she sprinted. First without purpose, but then with an intentional decision to veer off the main road and onto back streets. She traveled behind buildings and then residential homes. By the time she stopped running, Biscuit was nowhere to be found. The pop was the last thing she heard — it had apparently stopped him.

A two-lane road carried her further away from the city. There were no headlights in either direction, so she slowed to catch her breath. Trees lined the roadway, and where the trees ended, storefronts and then grassy fields stretched across the landscape.

Judging by a drop in the temperature, she knew it was well past midnight. There were few cars to worry about, though when headlights approached, she'd duck behind a tree until the road cleared. Her only plan was to keep moving and not stop until she found a police station or squad car.

When the sun rose, fatigue and delirium led her to believe that Biscuit was there. Running ahead of her, this time, he would stop to make sure she kept up. He drove her out of the trenches and onto the open road. On one foot she had a cramp, the other her big toe throbbed. Emma didn't hear the car approach, nor when it stopped. A hand touched her arm, a blue-eyed woman with a broad smile asked if she needed help. Emma nodded.

The woman was quick on her feet. She sat Emma in the passenger seat, and handed her a bottle of water, just before she collapsed. There was a strange band playing on the radio. The trees whizzed by in movement, a bridge, more trees, then a freeway.

*In a dream, Emma was still on the road with Biscuit running beside her, faster than either had run before and this time Biscuit outran her, he ran far ahead out of sight. A car door squeaked, then Biscuit disappeared.*

The driver-side door opened, then closed. The woman skipped around the vehicle and up to the gas pumps. Several hair strands escaped her French braids, mimicking defiance from her unruly eyebrows. Now awake, Emma stole a glimpse of her rescuer and the vehicle. It was an old, faded-yellow Volkswagen van with a worn-down plaid interior that smelled of patchouli oil, and a hint of gasoline fumes.

The middle seat had been removed, and the back seat converted to sleeping quarters. Along the sides were built-in storage space crammed with living items, several crates filled with bottles, hiking boots, and two suitcases. Peace symbols dangled from the rearview mirror, while sun and moon emblems decorated the door panels and roof. The woman approached the passenger side-door and gestured for Emma to roll down the window.

"We'll be on the road for quite a way, might as well empty your tank," she laughed and winked.

Emma nodded, thought about exiting the car, and then decided against it. If her captors found her now, and they had Biscuit as a lure, she'd have no choice but to return. She didn't think going to the police was an option, because they'd only ask why she hadn't left sooner. Didn't she have several opportunities on her outings with Gray to escape? Instead, she chose to stay with him because of her ridiculous plan for the two of them to be together and to get even with Reba.

Then there was Ogre, how could the local authorities stop a man that hid in the shadows and disappeared in the daylight?

"Want anything from inside?" the woman returned to the window. When Emma didn't answer, she patted her shoulder and left. The squeaky driver-side door opened, the woman entered and placed a paper bag in Emma's lap. She turned the key in the ignition, and the van shook as it rattled out of the gas station and onto the highway.

The woman shared that an aunt in Maine had recently been placed in an assisted living facility, so she was tasked with seeing after her home temporarily. Then the woman explained how she preferred a non-traditional lifestyle. "Eating off the land and sleeping in my van," is how she described it. Her goal was to eventually live off the grid. "It'll be good having you around, I'll teach you all I know." Then she handed Emma a small crystal and demonstrated how to draw from its energy. A song came on the radio about tomorrow being a better day. The woman said that the universe confirmed their meeting as divine. Angels rerouted her on a different path that morning, where she encountered Emma.

While driving through Mississippi, and after her rant about an ex-partner living somewhere between New Orleans and Breaux Bridge, the woman formally introduced herself.

"My name's Shelly, it's nice to meet you," she waited to shake her extended hand. "I'm 35 years old, two failed marriages but I'm not bitter. I'm a licensed Doula and an Aromachologist." She paused, seeing Emma's blank expression, and then explained that a Doula is trained to assist in childbirth and provides support to the mother. An Aromachologist works with essential oils that enhance positive effects on human behavior. Emma faced the passenger window and rolled her eyes.

"See those crates in the far corner behind me, there against the window? My very own blend of essential oils and creams."

She further explained how "spirit" led her to a holistic and organic lifestyle.

"Spirit...of God?" Emma raised an eyebrow.

"The universe."

Shelly pointed to the sky, then waved an arm. She said that this spirit connected all living things and looked out for her, and everyone.

"It's what gave the earth, the crystals' healing powers, through meditation one finds their center."

Shelly explained these were her personal beliefs, though she had many friends who thought the same as she did. Talks of universe and crystals were far-out in Emma's opinion, but she was intrigued by the woman's lifestyle. It was the first time she'd known anyone who talked as much as she did and had the confidence to back it up.

As the sky changed from pale blue and yellows to magenta and indigo, then blue-black, Shelly's conversation slowed. She stretched her neck forward, rolled it in a circular motion, then asked, "Do you know how to drive?"

"Yes, but it's been a while."

She was going to add, 'since I was kidnapped by my mom and her boyfriend, sold into a brothel, and the things I had to do!' Instead, she held her tongue; silenced by shame, humbled by the experience. For this reason, she welcomed Shelly's detailed conversation and the long drive, though she couldn't remember when she agreed to accompany Shelly on the trip.

Instead of making her way back to Denver, Emma remained in the van that traveled further away from home, across state lines to lands she'd never seen before. She watched as the world flashed by outside the passenger window, reasoning with herself that a prolonged return home meant avoiding a police investigation...questions her Dad would hear about the details of her abduction. Besides, her absence delayed the confrontation between her father and Ogre, which she was sure would end in violence.

Shelly offered to guide Emma on a path of enlightenment as she sought healing from the experience. It was an attractive offer, at least until things cooled down and it was safe to go home. Shelly watched as Emma contemplated her decision.

"I'll get a hotel room," she said.

Sometime after midnight, they pulled into a hotel in Gadsden.

Shelly placed her cell phone on the dashboard in front of Emma, nodded as if there was an unspoken agreement between the two of them, then exited the van to give her some privacy.

Emma stared at the phone and held her breath. It was now August, and she'd been missing for two months. Calling home wasn't the problem…telling the story was. Biscuit disappeared on the same night, so her Dad would know they were together. Emma dialed the first three numbers, then pressed the 'end call' button.

What happened? He would want to know. Reba was in the backyard, asking for help. Although they'd both agreed earlier that day to divorce themselves from her, Emma wanted a showdown with her Mother. So, she faced off with her alone in the dark. It was the truth, no matter how much of a fool she felt like now for falling into Reba's trap. Emma redialed the same first three numbers.

Why didn't she call out to her Dad for help?

She had been distracted by what she saw in her Mother's eyes, a secret addiction beneath Reba's neatly painted mask. Then before she knew it, Ogre stepped out of the shadows, drugged her, locking her in a room with the groaning walls and monsters that teleported through locked doors.

Where was she now, and is she in a safe place?

Sitting in a beat-up yellow van, somewhere in Alabama, headed to the Gulf of Maine, she imagined herself answering.

Why?

Because Shelly convinced her that the Northern Lights, paired with Venus and the crescent moon in the twilight sky would cleanse her soul.

And who is Shelly?

She would tell him that Shelly was someone who took the time to stop and help. A friend.

Emma's heart raced as she dialed the last four digits. When she heard the pre-recorded voice message, her eyes watered.

"Daddy, I'm alright," was all she said before ending the call. When Emma heard footsteps approach the vehicle, she patted her face dry with a sleeve.

"We rest in style tonight," Shelly opened the door and waved a card. "I haven't slept indoors since leaving Monterey." She tossed the key on the console and found a parking space. Emma expected Shelly to probe about her phone call, but she never did.

In silence, they entered the room and made a full inspection, double beds, a sitting area, microwave, fridge, and a bathroom. Then Shelly left the room and returned with a suitcase.

"We're about the same size, try this on."

She laid an oversized t-shirt on one bed, then offered for Emma to shower first while she cleaned the air by burning Sage.

"Use this," she said, and placed a clear bottle marked, *'SHELL's Calming Body Wash'* on the counter, and another smaller jar labeled *SHELL's body butter.*

Alone in the bathroom, Emma scrutinized the contents of the bottle and jar. Inhaling the notes of patchouli oil and lavender, Emma decided while standing under the running water to embrace her new friend, and all that Maine had to offer. Shelly mentioned earlier that she'd teach Emma how to restore balance in her life and lead her on a path to cleanse her mind, body, and soul.

The room smelled like burnt brush and cinnamon when she returned from showering.

"One for you, I also made a fresh salad."

She handed Emma a steaming mug.

"What kind of meat is this?" She wrinkled her nose when the salad was placed in front of her. Shelly pointed to the words on their matching t-shirts, "Vegan on deck." It was a silly question, but Emma had never tasted a salad this good without roasted, grilled or fried animal flesh. The tea had pleasant natural flavors though Emma noticed there was no sweetener added.

"Are vegans against sugar too?" she asked.

"I'll show you some great recipes for making homemade tea, you'll never miss the sugar," Shelly smiled.

Emma was impressed at how enjoyable a meal could be with just a few simple ingredients. Shelly explained how to incorporate foods like black beans, quinoa, and chia seeds into her diet, replacing junk food with dates, almonds, and fresh fruit. When Emma wrinkled her nose, Shelly discussed the importance of whole foods working synergistically to fuel the body and combat disease. While she talked, Emma finished her second helping of the salad and another cupful of tea.

"You're going to be a great student," she said, then turned off the lights.

Sleep came easy as soon as her head hit the pillow, but not a deep sleep. So, Emma heard Shelly's phone when it rang, and Shelly's attempt to get her attention when she answered the caller.

"A girl used my phone earlier," she said.

Where had she seen her? Emma heard her Dad ask.

"Louisiana, she looked fine. Asked to use my phone, and that was it."

Emma listened intently. She had an urge to grab the phone but resisted, she needed more time. After her mind was clear, then she'd call him back.

She'd left her voice on the answering machine, so he knew she was okay. Now with his return phone call, Emma knew he was safe. When the call ended, she pretended to snore.

"You can always call him back when you're ready," said Shelly.

"Thank you." Emma rolled onto her back and grunted. She was ready to talk, but then her stomach turned and gurgled.

"That would be the fiber and the tea," Shelley called out as Emma made a dash for the bathroom.

"You're welcome," she said.

Emma smiled after she closed the door, acknowledging the symbolism between her urgency to eliminate waste and her decision to break free from the past. Maine was going to give her a fresh perspective on life.

# ELEVEN

COLORS ALONG THE highway change from steel and rusted browns to emerald green with splashes of yellow, red, and orange, that hinted at autumn's approach. Tennessee became Virginia, then Pennsylvania turned to New York, Connecticut, New Hampshire, then Maine. Misty clouds danced above a crystal blue lake. The old van rattled through a tree forest, as pinecones fell to the ground and tree limbs whispered in the wind. A moose stood by the edge of the road, then another behind the first. They each nod solemnly to passing vehicles. The lush land reminded Emma of her Grandparents' ranch in Colorado.

"We'll stop here for groceries," said Shelly.

This time, Emma followed her into the convenience store. No one would be looking for her this far east. Strangers passed by with barely a nod in her direction. Comforted by her autonomy, she walked the aisles, then stopped to thumb through several magazines before finding the wall of lip rouges and eyeshadows.

"Ready when you are!" Shelly waved from the checkout line.

When Emma made her way to the counter, two of the

magazines she had been looking at were on the conveyor belt. She put her head down, then gushed

"I don't have money," she said.

"Don't worry about it, this is on me," said Shelly.

When she saw the lipstick in Emma's hands, she inspected the ingredients, then mumbled before placing the makeup aside. The packaging failed to indicate 'Cruelty-free,' which was the first lecture she'd received during the drive. Shelly regurgitated her stance.

"ANIMALS ARE OUR FRIENDS!" she said.

With bags now loaded in the van, Shelly cranked up what Emma secretly named the 'Veggie Van' and headed for the house they would occupy. Driving through town, then onto a rural road, they drove through more white pines and nodding moose. Shelly explained again to Emma the rights of animals, and how they're not on the planet for humans to abuse.

"We honor mother earth and all her inhabitants…live together in love," said Shelly.

Turning a hard right into a bend in the road as she continued her rant. Emma wanted to interject with details of her Grandparents ranch with majestic Misty, and sprinting deer.

"Why can't humans respect the rights of all life?" Shelly continued.

She overcorrected a bend in the road, which caused items in the back of the van to fall. Her knuckles clenched the steering wheel before she pressed down on the gas.

"Think you can take from me and get away with it," she continued.

The 'veggie van' crossed the double yellow line without signaling, then sped around a slower-moving car. Emma held her breath when a logging truck turned into the lane before them. The van lurched to a stop on the opposite side of the road.

"What's your problem? I told you I didn't have any money," said Emma.

A freed apple from the tipped over grocery bag rolled forward as Shelly reached without looking, snatched the runaway fruit, and took a bite out of it.

"One second…my sugar's low."

She devoured the apple in four quick bites. When she asked for the mason jar behind the passenger seat, Emma scrunched her nose at the contents of old fruit and half eaten apple cores.

"We'll make homemade vinegar with this," said Shelly.

Then proceeded to drive the van out of the ditch when the road cleared. It wasn't much further, but they drove in silence. Then when Emma was just about over being polite, they pulled into a hidden driveway surrounded by vast timber woods. A small brown cottage with a large wooden deck came into view. A sparkling lake flowed behind the house.

Emma and Shelly exited the van, stretched their limbs, and sniffed the fresh pine air. When they entered the house, the smell of spoiled, or rotten eggs caused them to flinch and hold their breath. Shelly left the front door open and raised a window nearest the front door.

"I'll put the groceries away, open the bedroom windows for me, please," said Shelly.

The kitchen had knotty pine cabinets, a small four-burner stove, and an extension kitchen table. The living room interior had wood-grain walls and a sofa with camouflage upholstery. Further inspection revealed the camouflage to be a print with moose, flying birds, and brown bears. And if that wasn't enough, there were a matching recliner and moose mountings on the wall. More moose images decorated the drapes. A fireplace was in the corner, about a 32-inch television, a basket of knitting yarn on the floor, and a bookcase with four rows of books, mystery mostly, some romance and several self-help books.

The wood-grain paneling stretched throughout the house, which consisted of two small bedrooms and one bathroom. Both bedrooms had a queen-size bed. One room had a quilt with trees on the duvet and drapes, and the other had bears and fish decor, while stuffed moose toys dangled from tacks in the ceiling.

"You got to be kidding!" Emma frowned, knowing this would be the room she'd be forced to sleep in.

In the bathroom across the hallway, were more moose decorations with fish on the shower curtains and towels. After the bedroom windows were opened, Emma retreated to the living room and sat on the sofa. When the pungent odor of rotten eggs made her nauseous, she stepped outside to breathe.

The air outdoors was wispy and fresh with timber wood and pine. A large bird perched in a nearby tree squawked, then took flight across the lawn and out over the lake. Emma followed the bird's path until she could see no further than the water's edge. The ground was covered with pine needles, and other areas carpeted with pinecones.

"Brains are like pinecones," she remembered her Grandpa once told her. He had explained how the center of the brain was shaped like a pinecone, and even got its name, pineal gland, from this similarity. Finding a grassy spot, Emma sat down, admired the lake, and then gathered a mound of pinecones to count. For fun, she thought about naming each one like she used to do on the ranch.

"It's a beautiful day for a dip," said Shelly.

She approached from behind.

"Come in with me." She had taken off her shoes, but seeing

that Emma wouldn't stand, she sat down.

"You don't talk much," she said, then gathered her own mound of pinecones, peeled back the scales and popped out its seeds. Emma wondered if the seeds would be used for food or maybe a body butter ingredient.

"There are a lot of people who would disagree with your observation," Emma laughed. "I've got a lot on my mind, and some decisions to make," she said and shrugged.

"You're like this seed…"

Shelly placed one between her fingers and held it up between them.

"Everything this seed needs to become a pine tree is in here, it's full of potential," she explained. "But with the scales removed, it's vulnerable and anything can happen," she said, tossing the seed back into the pile.

"I need a little time to figure things out…you don't mind if I hang around for a bit?" asked Emma.

"Same here, that's why this situation will be perfect for us, being here together, we've both been through such injustices," Shelly said.

"I don't think a breakup compares to being kidnapped and…"

Emma was sure Shelly didn't understand what she'd just survived. She couldn't say the word…rape, but maybe she could whisper it. If only she could have her revenge, she thought. She wouldn't be able to identify the hairy monster with the raspy snarl because she had been asleep mostly, and drugged.

Emma couldn't blame anyone but herself for the pills. The brunette girl merely suggested, and they were left on the nightstand. She took them of her own choosing, by the handful, which was the reason she couldn't fight back when the time came to run. Her judgment was off because she chose to be sedated, and in her confusion, she lost the phone number, and the money…which slowed Biscuit down too because he always ran at her pace—and now he was gone.

She wanted to return for him, but the other half knew she had to keep moving forward. If she ever saw Reba again—but arresting Ogre or Reba wouldn't replace what she'd lost. If she were able to contact Gray, their plan would provide the retribution she sought. Emma smashed the neat pile of pinecones with her fist until the crushed scales exposed a bare core.

"That meltdown I had earlier, it was because of my ex. He despised my love for mother earth and didn't respect my lifestyle," said Shelly.

"We were married five years, had bought a house in Monterey, then started a business—Bikes & Pita's, another of my ideas—we rented bikes to tourists and sold pita sandwiches to locals." She continued, picking seeds from Emma's pulverized pinecones.

Shelly shared how she had started to observe a trend towards vegetarian pitas from consumers, and that is what began her wholistic journey. Her spouse didn't appreciate the change, saying that she was becoming a hippie, and was losing touch with reality.

"He left early for work that morning, and by the time I arrived at noon, the doors were closed…I didn't know his clothes were gone until I returned from the bank. He had the nerve to leave divorce papers dangling from a clothes hanger," Shelly said, smacking her lips.

"Were you able to locate him in Louisiana?" asked Emma, thinking it was a devastating story. No one deserved to be dumped that way.

"I sure did, him and his fiancé too, and their newborn son. And he had always said he never wanted kids," she shrugged. "At least not with me." The pinecone pile grew as they talked; Emma collected while Shelly plucked the pine seeds.

"My Mom is a drug addict. She had her boyfriend kidnap me a few months back from Denver."

Emma realized she had spoken the words aloud when Shelly stopped messing with the seed pile and gave her full attention. "I've been locked in a room since June, and…" Emma shivered. She wanted to tell Shelly about her plan for revenge, but she pinched lips instead. "It's getting cold out," she rubbed her arms for warmth.

"Fate!" Shelly yelled.

"Fate brought us together, and there's no going back—for either of us."

She lifted her head to the setting sun and chanted some indistinguishable words before leaping from the ground, and in a few long-legged strides, dove into the lake.

Emma stood, walked closer, and waited for Shelly to resurface. Judging from her form, she appeared to be an excellent swimmer, so there was no need to panic. A few seconds later, Shelly emerged weighted down from her drenched clothing, she smiled. There was something in her hand, it flipped then twisted.

"It's salmon, the land receives you, Emma!" she yelled and waved, holding the fish up by the tail.

Maybe it was because they had bonded over their stories, but Shelly had agreed to allow Emma to cook the fish; outside on the pit, and Emma would have to clean and prepare it herself. She would've dived into the lake herself if it meant she could eat fish that night, or any other day, thought Emma. Shelly prepared the rest of the meal; baked sweet potatoes, pea and carrot soba noodles with tofu, and homemade fermented tea.

The first week went by with Emma as student and Shelly as her teacher. Books were strewn throughout the cabin on essential oils, veganism, and holistic anatomy. It was at breakfast during the second week while Emma ate another bowl of steel-cut oats and dried berries as she imagined chopping off one of Shelly's limbs for the meat.

Emma heaved at the thought of gnawing on human flesh, then placed a hand over her mouth and barely made it to the trash can before the oats came back up.

"I need meat," she cried.

Before she could return to her seat, Shelly had retrieved two sets of fishing rods from a closet. Emma's cheeks flushed, embarrassed by her animalistic desires.

Shelly didn't mind Emma eating fish, but if she wanted it, she'd have to catch her own—which led to the fishing lessons. The cabin was complete with fishing gear, so the excuse of not having money to buy equipment was useless. At first, she passed on the idea of learning to fish, but by the second week of eating edamame, portabella mushrooms, and tofu as meat replacements, Emma begged for the lessons.

She didn't catch any fish that morning, but by afternoon, Shelly did. Then by the next day's lesson, Emma caught her first fish.

"AHHJAHHNUU!" Shelly wailed her delight, before she jumped in the water the same as she had done on their first day by the lake. This time when she emerged, it was a small quartz rock in her hand.

"The land wants you to have this," she said.

# TWELVE

OCTOBER ARRIVED WITH subfreezing temperatures and icicles. At first, the mornings were cold, then the evenings got colder. Finally, the days and nights, along with Sebec Lake, froze over. Emma stayed in bed and slept more than she should. Shelly didn't seem to mind, as she continued to bring steel-cut oats, and ginger tea in the mornings; but by lunchtime would suggest they ate together at the kitchen table. Afterward, Emma promptly returned to her room, where she slept until early the next day.

Shelly must have grown bored, as she announced on a Thursday afternoon that some friends would arrive towards evening to watch the Northern lights. She would need help with house chores and laundry in preparation for company. Emma used the opportunity to bathe since she had avoided doing so for countless days. When she loosened her hair from the two plaits, she was surprised by the amount of new growth.

Then as she undressed and faced the mirror, a rounded face and pudgy belly reflected back to her. Despite eliminating meat from her diet, she'd managed to put on at least ten pounds.

"I'm fat!" she said, loud enough for Shelly to hear.

"That's what eating and sleeping all day will do for you," Shelly replied.

The sun had set, but the cabin glowed from burnt embers in the fireplace. Shelly had spritzed the rooms with her own blend of cinnamon oil and sage, making the air inside as invigorating as the outdoors. When Emma heard tires approach in the driveway, she called to After running out the front door, she returned moments later with two men and three women.

"I was only expecting three of you, but it's cool we'll make this work," she said, her voice high-pitched and exaggerated.

They each carried a bag filled with items from their stop in town. After setting the groceries on the kitchen table, they took turns introducing themselves, first with a handshake followed by an embrace.

One said, "Love," with his handshake.

Another said, "Tranquility," after his hug.

Then one of the women said, "Fire," after shaking Emma's hand. Still, another said "Wrath," after her embrace.

The last said, "Liberty," and handed Emma a sage bundle.

In the kitchen, the group ate together and filled their wine glasses. The conversation centered on the upcoming meteor showers, and how travel from Florida to Maine had to be precise enough not to miss the light show in the Northern sky. After one of the men went outside to prepare a fire, they all congregated around the firepit. Laughter mixed with chatter spread throughout the crowd. When Emma was handed something to smoke, she refused, then passed it on to a woman sitting beside her.

By the time one of the men pressed play on the portable radio, heat from the fire, mixed with fumes from whatever it was they were smoking caused Emma's head to spin. The more they drank and smoked, the louder the conversation became. Emma clutched her coat and wrung it tight in her hand. She stood to leave, suspecting no one would notice her departure. But before she could retreat, one of the women reached out, pulled her close, and began to dance. Round and round she swung as their singing escalated.

Not wanting to appear anti-social, Emma danced and pretended to sing along to lyrics she'd never heard before. Then one of the men reached for her waist and spun her around in his arms. When he let go of her, another person turned her around; that's when her head and stomach fell out of sync. If she could stop spinning for two seconds, she would tell them goodnight, but when the music lulled, food chunks flew out of her mouth and landed at one of the women's feet.

The woman was pleasant and helped Emma to the bathroom where they both cleaned themselves. When she insisted that this wouldn't ruin their party, Emma graciously said goodnight and proceeded to lock herself in the bedroom. It wasn't that her head was spinning from alcohol, her stomach churned from something else, maybe the food they'd brought.

When she awoke, daylight teased at her bedroom blinds, and a plate with dry toast, sliced oranges, and coffee was at her bedside. The expressions from Shelly and one of the women spoke their concerns.

"Please eat something," said Shelly.

"Are you feeling better? You slept for like a whole day yesterday," said the woman, her eyes searched Emma's for confirmation.

"Yes, it was too much spinning with the wine," said Emma. "It was my first time drinking," she blushed.

"You slept all of yesterday, I thought you were—well, maybe poisoned or something." Shelly raised an eyebrow.

"No, like I said before, I need rest and time to think," Emma insisted.

"I could use a shower and something to eat—but otherwise I'm fine."

She took a bite of the toast, hoping the explanation would take turn the attention away from her.

When she left the room to shower, she heard their discussion from inside the bathroom. Shelly worried if she'd had any of the "other stuff." One of the women said she was sure Emma hadn't touched any of it. In the shower, Emma rubbed her pudgy stomach and tried to calculate the timing of her last menstrual cycle.

By the time she joined them later, a plate of grilled fish was placed in her hands. Another of the women showed Emma the stock of fish they'd stored in the freezer for her.

"You can have it whenever you like," said Shelly.

When she shrugged her shoulders, Emma imagined Shelly's guilt, believing her forced diet change had caused her mysterious illness.

One of the men approached and presented a gift, a crystal necklace with small colored crystals for leaves and twisted wire shaped into a tree.

"This will center your energy," he said, then placed the chain around her neck. When Emma thanked them for the gift, but mainly the fish, they encircled her into a group hug.

The circle of friends stayed through the weekend and left early on a Tuesday morning. Emma gave each one a goodbye kiss, then Shelly escorted them outside. Afterward, there was another round of farewells, and then someone suggested a group picture, which led to more conversations and more hugs.

In all, it took about forty minutes for them to load into their vehicle and pull out of the driveway. When they were gone, Emma remembered their smiles as they admired the Aurora Borealis. She wondered what it must be like to have friends who'd travel thousands of miles to spend time with her.

Several days later, Shelly was surprised to see Emma spending more time with her and less time secluded in the bedroom. Emma learned some of the eclectic music that Shelly liked to play, and they danced around the cabin as a foot of snow blanketed the ground outside.

The next morning, the newscaster announced that blizzard-like conditions were expected for the coming weekend. Shelly said they would need to prepare for the change in weather and restock household supplies and groceries.

Shelly showed Emma to the closet where winter coats, sweaters, and thermals were stored.

"Try them on first, you've gained a few pounds," she said. It was something Emma already admitted, but still hearing Shelly mention it was hurtful.

"It's the food you feed me, what're you trying to do, fatten me up for the kill?" Emma complained as she grabbed an oversized sweater.

"You're safe with vegans, is all I'm saying," Shelly teased as Emma disappeared into the bathroom to try on a few clothing items.

Hardly anything fit, and after three trips back to the closet, Emma decided that what she held in her hands would have to do. Holding her breath, she yanked, then stretched until the seam popped on the fleece bottoms she tried squeezing into. "This doesn't fit either, sorry about the tear," she said, tossing the failed outfits aside.

"Stay here, I'll run into town, shouldn't take me too long," Shelly responded.

Emma pouted when she heard the van's car door squeak open and shut, then waved goodbye as it clunked onto the ice-covered road and out of sight. It was useless to protest; without proper clothing, Emma would've frozen even if she stayed in the car.

The tree limbs above, now covered in ice, shivered and caused more snow to fall on the snowdrifts at its trunk. As Emma turned to go inside, movement down by the lake caught her attention; a moose with its calf made their way from the water's edge. She locked eyes with the moose, who intuitively looked to its calf, before heading off into the woods.

When evening came, Shelly had not returned from her trip into town. The conditions were icy, but the roads would be salted and shoveled enough for safe passage, so Emma figured there was no need to panic. Instead, taking advantage of the solitude, she ran bathwater and changed the radio to a pop music station.

Adding some of Shelly's oil blend - and a little bit of coconut milk to moisten her skin - she stepped into the scented bathwater. Despite her quirkiness, Emma had to admit that Shelly had a natural talent with scents and oils.

With eyes closed, she inhaled the fragrance, enjoying the warm water and music she preferred. It was probably no more than ten to fifteen minutes before her eyelids shut. She dreamed of him:

*The dark shadow of a man, the one from Breaux Bridge. Hidden underneath a full beard, he had a toothless grin to go with his hairy face, and arms. Then her friend Gray appeared, he wanted to know why*

*hadn't she called yet, like she promised and if she'd
plan to return?*

Emma awoke abruptly to tepid and crude bathwater. After drying, then putting on her pajamas, she cleaned the tub and wiped the droplets of water from the floor. Next, she checked the driveway to see if the yellow van was parked—Shelly hadn't returned—so, she decided to turn in for the night. The chanting is what woke her.

"Ahhjahhnu…ahhjahhnuu…ahh…jahhh…"

Shelly's voice echoed in the stillness of the night.

It was dark outside, and when Emma went to check, the time was nearing 2 a.m. She went to Shelly's room and found the bed empty. Then after searching the rest of the cabin, went to the window and peered outside. The van was parked, Shelly must've chosen to sleep where she felt most comfortable.

When a light flickered in the opposite direction, Emma looked beyond the deck. There was Shelly, dancing under the moonlight in her undergarments while holding a candle in one hand.

"What was it they gave her—she'll freeze!" Emma whispered as she watched from the window. Cold smoke trailed from Shelly's mouth as she continued her chant.

"Better not come near me with that hocus-pocus foolery," Emma shook her head, then shut her bedroom door and crawled back in bed.

When morning came, the sound of the bedroom door opening stirred her awake. Shelly stood over her and mumbled something indistinguishable. Then she tossed a small package on the bed and sat with her legs entwined like pretzels on the floor.

"Can't you see I'm sleeping, what is it?" Emma mumbled

"Take the test!" she demanded.

Her puffy eyes were wild from a sleepless night.

"I'm not leaving this room until you do."

By the look in Shelly's eyes, she wasn't going to budge until Emma obeyed her command. Inside was a box with the words, Pregnancy Test, written in bold letters.

"You shouldn't have wasted your money."

At first, she was offended, but then she remembered Breaux Bridge.

"We both already know what the result will be," said Emma, before she threw the blankets over her head.

"I can take care of you, remember I'm a Doula," she said, "this is part of our destiny." Shelly unfolded her legs and kneeled close to the bed.

"You've said all that before," Emma snapped, "so stop being dramatic." She wanted to tell Shelly to mind her own business, but that's hard to do when you're sleeping in someone else's bed, eating the food they purchased. Emma took the pregnancy test with her to the bathroom and shut the door in Shelly's face.

When she returned to the bedroom, Emma tossed the stick at the foot of the bed. She never looked for the results, there was no need to. Her weight gain, sleeping more than usual - even the moose with its calf - had already told her the test would be positive. As Emma pulled on one of the Parka's in the closet and stepped outside for some fresh air, Shelly's delighted scream filled the cabin. For a moment, she thought about jumping into the lake and sinking to the bottom, but the lake was nearly frozen over, so the idea was impossible.

Once she assessed the damage and contemplated her next move - without Shelly's input - Emma went back inside. Standing before the mirror, she observed her chubby stomach. It had been five months now since Breaux Bridge, and Emma hadn't had a menstrual cycle since July. Sure, she thought of it then, but her survival superseded all other concerns.

Besides, naivety led her to believe stress was the cause of the missed cycles, and there was no way a pregnancy could endure the trauma she'd experienced; this baby wouldn't survive.

Shelly would be devastated with the outcome, but after delivering the still-born baby, it would be time to go home.

But what if the spawn of darkness survived?

Emma was sure about one thing—she'd have no part in raising such a dark seed. Shelly could keep the baby and add it to her list of things the universe gave her.

"This is great news!" exclaimed Shelly, who met her in the living room.

"No, it's not, but it will be," Emma shrugged, then turned on the television. Shelly gave her a peculiar look, grabbed the remote, and switched the tv set off. "How can you think any part of this is good?" Emma asked, standing on her feet.

It was Shelly this time who shrugged, "It's an innocent life—" Before she could add how the universe gifted her the child, Emma sidestepped her and retreated to her room.

As time progressed, Shelly made frequent trips into town to prepare for the delivery. On one of her trips, she met a neighbor who happened to be a retired Ob/GYN. He was an elderly Greek man who favored Einstein; his eyes teared without reason, and his hands shook when there was no greeter.

How Shelly was able to convince the man to do a home visit was a mystery. If he was in his right mind, very little research would reveal that his eighteen-year-old pregnant patient had gone missing in June and was now hiding out with a sage-burning Doula down by

Sebec Lake.

There was no way Emma could protest the examination; it was February, and her protruding belly was now poking and pinching her insides.

"The spawn wants out!" she demanded, showing Shelly the movement from within her stomach. She meant it as a joke, but Shelly didn't find any humor in her words, nor did she appreciate the negative reference to such a beautiful gift. Gently stroking Emma's stomach, she sang melodies until Emma, and the baby relaxed.

The doctor steadied his hand long enough to check her cervix and measure her stomach. Then he announced that Emma was approximately 28 weeks pregnant. After confirming a heartbeat with his stethoscope, he declared the "baby is healthy and growing on schedule for birthing!"

Emma's vision of jumping in the lake returned; this time she imagined sliding through one of the drilled holes left from the ice fishers.

"Seven months, two more to go—I can't wait to deliver her or him." Shelly clapped her hands together with delight.

Emma stretched her mouth to fake a smile for the doctor who watched her closely.

"Have you thought of any names yet?" he asked, while packing away his equipment.

"Only one name comes to mind… Spawn!" mumbled Emma.

This time Shelly popped her on the backside.

"Ignore her, it's just a little joke between us," she said, then escorted him to the front door.

Emma stood back and contemplated the argument she knew they'd have once he was gone. Shelly's outlet for anger was usually cleansing the air with burnt sage while mumbling to herself. When she returned from seeing the doctor off, Emma handed her the sage bundle; Shelly glared at her, then took the burning sage and began cleansing the air.

Four hours passed without conversation - Emma tried - but Shelly ignored the attempts. Finally, before dinner was served the silent treatment ended.

"Don't you ever call that baby a spawn again!" she demanded.

"Agreed," said Emma flatly, hoping to avoid an argument.

Besides, peace came easy knowing she had a plan in place; deliver the baby and leave it with Shelly.

Emma's room had been converted into a home birthing station, complete with an inflatable tub. Shelly left in the mornings and returned midday with packages filled with supplies for a newborn. Because she had one pair of pants and an oversized shirt, Emma didn't feel presentable to venture out into the public. When Shelly offered to purchase maternity clothes, Emma politely declined. And when she returned with a crib, Emma put her foot down to block the entrance to her bedroom.

"Don't even think about it, that goes in your room!"

"Fine by me, I don't mind baby duty," said Shelly.

Emma watched while Shelly struggled with the crib assembly. Frustrated by the task and refusing to be defeated, she worked until her fingers stiffened and caused a screw to fall and roll out of sight.

"Thank the universe for giving us this baby," she declared, then waved the screwdriver in the air, "and expanding our family—take that you abusive men that take and don't want to give back!"

She hopped up from the floor and kicked a leg in the air. Emma didn't hide her laughter, as she watched Shelly dance and kick to an imaginary tune. When her frustration subsided, she collapsed back down to the floor.

"Don't worry about the birth," she said, labored speech from the impromptu dance. "I've studied midwifery also. If the Doctor doesn't get here in time, I can handle things,"

Emma's eyebrows raised. She fought the urge to tell Shelly of how she had hoped for the worse—agreeing to the home delivery was for obvious reasons; Shelly wanted the baby to have a natural introduction to life, and Emma wanted no trace of having been pregnant or giving birth.

"I'm not worried, if everything goes well, you'll have a baby," said Emma.

"We'll have a celebration after, invite our friends again," Shelly said without missing a beat.

At night, Emma had dreams of her abusers, but instead of herself locked in the room, Reba lay on the frameless bed.

> *A needle hung from Reba's arm, and a mysterious elderly woman stood at the foot of the bed, scolding and forbidding her movement. Then in a second dream, the older woman approached to strike at Emma, who was now lying in Reba's place. She flinched just before the blow landed.*

When she awoke, she lay on a sweat-drenched pillowcase. After the third night of similar bad dreams, Shelly offered to watch over her until Emma was sleeping peacefully. With a glowing sage bundle in hand, she chanted words meant to cleanse the room. When Emma asked about the ritual, Shelly told her how she'd been crying out in her sleep for the past few nights.

"It will help your anxiety," said Shelly.

She came near the bed and handed Emma a small pouch then instructed she put it in her pillowcase. Emma sniffed the vanilla-scented sachet and decided it was harmless, so she placed it underneath her pillow.

"The nightmares are about my Mother, she's in trouble!" cried Emma.

"Shhh, don't stress yourself," she comforted, standing near the door with the burning sage.

"I don't know what to do…maybe she's in that room, I'm the only one that knows—"

"Shhh," Shelly shushed her again, "there's nothing you can do about it now, would you like to go back to those people that take, take, take?" she asked and stepped closer to the bed.

"I could make an anonymous call to the police," said Emma, seeing the furrow in her friend's brow.

"I don't need to remind you that the baby you're carrying - and you - belong to them," Shelly stood over her with arms crossed.

Emma reminded her that the call would be anonymous, but Shelly kept shaking her head.

"Take, take, take," she repeated, as she waved the sage higher in the air.

"I won't do anything stupid—It was just a thought," explained Emma. It was only because of her current condition that she allowed Shelly to play this head game.

"This is our family now," Shelly's shoulders relaxed a bit.

"THE UNIVERSE—" they murmured in unison.

Shelly gave her that knowing look before she left the room. When she was gone, Emma pulled the blankets off; and for the second time since this tragedy, she knelt on the side of her bed and said a prayer… "God, please forgive me, save my mother." was all she knew to say. She climbed back in bed, squeezed her pillow, falling into a sound sleep while inhaling the vanilla satchel.

# THIRTEEN

DAYS QUICKLY TURNED into weeks. With swollen feet and a huge belly, Emma waddled like a penguin through the cabin that now resembled a nursery. She didn't smile much, though Shelly tried her best to lift Emma's spirits; food at her request, magazines, ice cream if she wanted.

After seeing how agreeable Shelly had become, Emma purposed to make her requests intentional. Focusing on her needs after the birth; traveling expenses and clothes. Emma began to ask for money, $5 and $10 here and there.

In her mind, she envisioned having the baby in the morning and then taking off later in the night when Shelly was on baby duty. With the money, Emma would catch a bus anywhere, then contact her Dad the first chance she could. It wouldn't be wise to call from the cabin, because the baby needed to remain a secret. Besides, after giving birth, the baby would belong to Shelly - and even though she believed Emma was bluffing - her decision was final. Shelly would name the baby, raise it as her own, and could also adopt it if she desired.

"I've never been pregnant," Shelly shared one afternoon when the Doctor returned for another examination.

"Are you lesbian?" he asked her directly.

"No," She told him. It was due to scarring in her fallopian tubes that she couldn't conceive.

"This is your baby," said Emma, after the Doctor had gone.

"You can't hand off a baby like an item," she protested.

"I'm leaving it with you!" Emma yelled, then stormed off. Shelly handed her another fragrant satchel, told her to settle down and breathe.

"Well then adopt it, either way, it's yours—you said so yourself, it's fate." Emma inhaled the scented pouch as Shelly sat her in a recliner, massaging her swollen feet.

"You have enough here, with me out of the way, and your friends to help, you can teach the kid to dance in the moonlight, counting stars... the whole Jupiter aligning with Mars thingy," Emma murmured. She noticed a smile on Shelly's face as she fell asleep.

The day before Emma went into labor was an abnormal warm day for March. It was a Friday, so there was more traffic on the lake then on weekdays. The high noon sun melted fresh snow off the tree limbs, and the ground impacted with ice and snow was firm. Emma walked along the bank and mulled over her plan once more. After the delivery, she would have Shelly take it away; the rest would be easy. Acknowledging her need to rest after the birth, Shelly was sure to give her space. That's when she'd leave with her backpack and the $350.00, she collected over the last two months.

Shelly earned a decent income with online sales of Shell's Oils and Butters and was generous enough to share some of the proceeds with Emma. The body butter and vanilla satchel were her favorites;

she planned to tuck them both in her backpack for the journey. From her research, Emma discovered she could catch a flight in Bangor to New York. Once there, she could figure out a way to contact her dad – then this nightmare would end.

Pleased with her plan, Emma looked over the span of the lake, now a frozen highway of solid ice used for snowmobiling and ice fishing. On the opposite bank stood a single moose, it nodded to the wind - to the trees - then over in Emma's direction; they both knew it was time for her to move on. She waved back, wanting to say a proper farewell to the moose.

When she returned to the cabin, Shelly's guests had arrived. "We celebrate childbirth and motherhood tonight," said one of the women, as she placed a harvest crown made of leaves, acorns and small plastic berries on top of Emma and Shelly's head.

"There'll be a brilliant show of lights," said another, as they unloaded grocery bags and more gifts for the baby.

Emma smiled when she spied the variety of food choices. The men and one of the women unpacked ice fishing equipment and headed down the trail towards the lake. Shelly stayed back with the woman who crowned them and prepared side dishes and vegan courses. Emma's contribution was to sweep the floors and tidy the cabin.

"If she's okay with the idea, I'd prefer our baby to be Vegan," said Shelly.

"It's your baby," said Emma. She said with her back turned away from them as she swept the kitchen floor.

"What do you mean?" the other woman asked. She looked from Emma to Shelly. Emma stopped near the doorway to listen to their conversation before she placed the broom in a corner and sat with them at the table.

"It's nothing, she rambles sometimes," said Shelly.

"She's adopting the baby; either way, it's her baby," said Emma.

The woman cupped her mouth with her hands as Shelly grabbed her chest and held her breath.

"It's your gift," said the woman, "for all you've gone through." She wiped tears from Shelly's face.

"I'm honored," said Shelly, "thank you!" she reached for Emma's hand.

"I'll be leaving after your baby is born," said Emma.

"Nonsense!" said the woman.

"This is your home," Shelly argued.

Emma shook her head.

"I'll come back to visit, but you should bond with the baby," she said, and when she finished speaking, the baby kicked in her stomach, causing Emma to flinch.

"You promise to come back?" asked Shelly as the woman massaged Emma's back and Shelly kneaded her feet.

"Yes," Emma nodded, knowing it'd be against her will if she ever saw Shelly or the baby again.

It was 2 a.m. when her contractions began, at first like cramps, and then increased to the point where she clenched the mattress and yelled for Shelly. One of the men came first, followed by another, then every living being within the cabin filled her room. Between contractions, Emma stood up and was going to push everyone out except Shelly. That's when her water broke.

The men retreated when they saw the puddle, as the women advanced to pass the men and prepare the birthing tub.

"I'm a nurse," said one of the men, as he made his way back into the room. By the time Emma was in the water, the delivery had become a team effort...some gave high-fives and decided on names.

"Clover!" said one.

"Cassia!" said another.

"Fin!" someone yelled across the room.

"I like Winter," said the nurse. "And what about you two?" he turned to Shelly and Emma. Emma wanted to scream in his face, tell him to shut-his face. All she could manage was a grunt.

"I'm right here," said Shelly, helping her to concentrate on the breathing, while another woman rubbed her belly and waved a satchel of cinnamon and vanilla oil under her nose. Several contractions later, the baby squeezed out of her body and into the water.

"She's beautiful," Shelly cooed, intercepting the nurse's handoff to Emma.

"We need to clear everyone out now," he said.

Everyone cleared the room, except the woman who was aware of the adoption. Emma remembered how her body ached, and her head throbbed, as she was helped from the tub to the bed.

"Please let me sleep," said Emma, realizing that her plan to flee quickly after the delivery was absurd.

"Are you ready to nurse the baby?" asked the nurse. "She needs your milk."

"Emma will pump her milk," said Shelly, then nodded to the woman should tell the others their plans for the baby. She escorted the nurse out of the room and closed the door behind them.

"Would you like to hold her—she's beautiful," said Shelly.

Emma pulled the blankets over her head then turned to face the window.

"I'll let you rest, please pump, I'll be back in 30 minutes."

Finally, Emma was left alone, and she slept for the rest of the evening. Whenever someone entered her room, she asked them to leave, saying she was exhausted.

Their guests cleared out by Monday. When they were alone, Emma looked at the sleeping baby. "You'll be safe here," she whispered while stroking her soft cheek.

"Told you, she's beautiful," said Shelly, when she saw Emma standing at the crib.

"Take care of her, I'm leaving tomorrow," she said.

"But where will you go?" asked Shelly.

Still unsure of how to execute her travels, Emma decided on the place she knew would eventually connect her to Denver. "New York first," she said.

"I'll take you. I have a friend there who can expedite the adoption," said Shelly. Emma shrugged, saying, "Either way, I'm leaving tomorrow— nothing personal, it's just time for me to go."

Shelly nodded her head, "I'll tell her to be expecting us."

A week went by, and there was no more mention of their travel to New York. With each day that passed, it was a struggle for Emma to avoid interaction with the baby – who didn't cry much, so it was easy to enter a room not knowing the baby lay in the bassinet. Other times, Shelly would have her in the living room, or kitchen to feed. Finally, on that following Wednesday, she announced they had an appointment in New York the next morning. Emma's heart raced when she heard the news.

That night she remembered having a mixture of emotions which ranged from excitement to gloom. During her many hours of rest she couldn't help but assess the bizarre behavior of her friend. She had concerns for Shelly's ability to care for a newborn. She even considered asking Shelly if she preferred to take the baby to child welfare services. Finally, she convinced herself that this was the better choice, she wanted to believe the child would settle Shelly, give her something to believe in again.

"I understand why you have to go," said Shelly, once they were loaded into her van, and she shut her squeaky driver-side door.

"Come back when you're ready," she continued.

Emma stared out the window at the lake and cabin as they pulled away.

It was about an eight-hour drive to New York. The road stretched wide; tree lines thinned to open skies as they traveled from Maine through toll booths, under concrete overpasses, and steel bridges. Cars and trucks approached, then bypassed; some exited, and others continued along the same path.

Emma silently coached herself to stick with the plan and not give in to her worries or concerns. There was no way she could take the baby with her. To ensure that she didn't grow soft, she avoided looking at Shelly or the baby during the ride. Finally, a swell of traffic merged in various directions, honking horns and skyscrapers announced their entrance into Manhattan.

The meeting in Central Park was a sketchy deal. Another one of Shelly's friends happened to have a friend who was an adoption attorney. It all made perfect sense and then made no sense whatsoever, but then that was the way things had been for the past year.

Fighting off her nerves and ignoring her intuition, Emma signed off on the documents and shoved the paperwork in the attorney's hands.

"What's this beautiful baby's name?" the attorney asked as Emma walked away and sat at a nearby bench. She watched as a jogger ran with a headset over his ears, and then a biker rode past. The traffic increased as strangers strolled, ran, and talked. Some sat down and had a conversation nearby.

Taking in the surrounding atmosphere, Emma imagined herself living amongst the many people passing her by. She wondered what it would be like to catch a train, or maybe see a Broadway play?

"We'll be waiting in the room when you're ready," Shelly said.

As she approached the bench, the baby cooed when Shelly nuzzled her nose. When they were far enough out of site, Emma fell in behind a group of runners and ran until the wind could no longer hold back her tears. Then when her body ached from the unexpected sprint, she crashed on a nearby bench, heaving, and sobbing.

"Everything's going to be alright," said a guy who sat nearby. "Here's some sunshine—I'm Chen," he said.

She reached for his extended hand, and instead of a handshake, he passed her a small bundle. Emma shook her head and refused his offer.

"I don't touch that stuff, I could use a drink, though."

Outside of the park, the stream of traffic increased. People of all types filled the sidewalks and hurried off to various destinations. Everyone seemed to be in a rush; some laughed together as they walked, others focused straight ahead, yet they all knew how to keep step in what could easily be mistaken for a stampede. Tightly knit in gridlock, the street honked and screeched with cars and taxi drivers.

"It's easier to walk," Chen yelled over a car horns blare.

Emma frowned as she tried to mimic his footsteps. There was a rhythm to the streets that he and the others were attuned to. They walked for about two blocks then entered a pub. Chen led her to a booth and ordered.

"To Life!" she said, tapping his glass and then tossing the drink in her mouth. She forced a smile, then prepared herself to except the new life she would create for herself. Maybe it was the 'keep up or be trampled' induction from the walk, but her adrenaline was high, and the shots were not slowing her down.

She told her new friend stories of Denver and the wannabe's who thought they ruled her high school. Then she imitated several of the more popular girls and mocked how their induction into New York City would end. Before long, several others joined them, and by midnight, Chen invited everyone to his apartment not too far from the pub.

"You're welcome to join us," he offered, gauging her comfort level with the group as she sat engrossed in a story of a girl who sat nearby.

"Sure, the night is young!" she answered.

The girl was upset. She cried. Then before a tear left her cheek, she laughed through clenched teeth, telling how she'd have her revenge.

"You missed a line," said one of the others.

"Urgh!" she beat the table with her fist, then exclaimed, "One more time!"

This girl was an actress, and Emma's new circle of friends were actors and dancers who were recently cast in a play.

Emma liked watching as each took turns taking on another identity when in character.

"What else do you do other than acting?" she asked the girl.

"How long have you lived here?" she asked a guy from Utah while he was in the middle of his story.

"Sorry to cut you off, I'm very curious!" she apologized.

He said it was no problem, but she noticed how he quickly switched seats with another actor. Two girls stood, and in the corner of the room, they practiced a choreographed routine. The movements were complicated, but because she'd danced before Emma knew she could mimic their steps. Imagining herself alongside the two girls, she watched – fascinated - then joined in.

"Not bad, you can dance with us anytime," they said.

That was how the desire to become a professional dancer was birthed. Dancing, she figured, would be less complicated than acting because she already had some training. There was no talking when dancing, which meant she wouldn't annoy anyone.

By 4:00 a.m., the crowd in her new friend's apartment thinned, and Emma contemplated finding her way to the hotel with Shelly.

"Crash anywhere you'd like," said Chen.

Emma squeezed into a spot on the sofa, amongst notebooks and crumpled pages, then curled in a ball and dozed off. When she woke, another group of strangers had entered the apartment. This time, they were singers yodeling vocal exercises, and musicians, who strummed on their guitars.

"You won't get much sleep here now, I'm afraid," said Chen.

He reached in his jacket to hand her his cell phone. The date on the screen said, April 28th.

"Today's my birthday!" she announced, not knowing whether to be happy or sad.

"Cool!" said one.

"This one's for you!" said another and played a chord on his guitar.

Emma excused herself and went into the bedroom to make the call she could no longer delay. The phone rang several times before the answering machine came on. When the singing increased in the other room, she decided against trying the number again.

"I'll be back later," she told Chen.

With fresh air on her face, and steaming java in hand, Emma made her way back to the park where she'd last seen Shelly. If she could find the exact location where they separated, then she could remember the name of the hotel. Maybe Shelly's friend would be kind enough to offer her a place to crash until she got on her feet. Otherwise, she would have to sleep on a park bench that evening.

Central Park was just as complicated as the surrounding streets; a maze of twists and turns. One bench was just as good as another, but then not so good when it wasn't where you needed to be. Frustrated, Emma took a seat beside an elderly man, who wasted no time in striking up a conversation with her.

"You're a beautiful girl, just like my daughter," he said, "Though I haven't seen her in years, she went off to college back in 1982—Florida State, then met a boy down there, that was that." He wiped his nose with his handkerchief.

"Sorry to hear that," said Emma, pretending to show interest.

"Parents worry about their children, no matter how old they are," he said.

"All we ask for is a phone call if you're too busy for a visit," he continued.

When Emma looked in his direction, he waved an accusing finger at her.

"A phone call if nothing else!"

"I tried to call home today, besides I don't have a phone," she explained. He reached into his jacket and handed Emma his phone.

"Daddy, it's me!" she said, relieved to hear his voice.

"I'm coming to get you, no matter how far you are," he said.

"It's my dad, he's going to come for me," she whispered.

The man smiled with gratification.

"A lot has happened— Reba took me," she blurted, and was going to tell him everything figuring it'd be much easier to do over the phone.

"We'll talk about that later, where are you?" he interrupted.

"In New York...I have a few dollars, I'll get a hotel room tonight," she said.

"Guess I'll stop being an old goat myself and call my daughter back," he said, when Emma gave him his cell phone. He gathered his paper-bag, stuck his phone inside and walked away.

# FOURTEEN

*The Garden*

EMMA REACHED HER hand into the still pond and disrupted the water. With her head propped up on the ledge, she closed her eyes and inhaled orange blossoms in the wind. It was peaceful enough to take a nap, but she resisted, fearing to awaken from a dream. Checking her reflection in the water, she admired her eyes, observed her mouth, and hair.

A ripple drifted by, then another, and finally a sprig of flowers - delicate white orange blossoms - reminding her of how her Grandmother made flower crowns out of the orange blossoms during summer.

"Grandma Rose!" she shouted and lunged from sitting to standing.

Emma was sure of it now; she was either having a supernatural encounter, a vivid hallucination, or at the least, a dream. With one full breath, she made it around the pond.

"Oh, my princess," said Grandma Rose, opening her arms just in time to embrace Emma.

"It's so good to see you, my baby!" she repeated.

At first, Emma couldn't speak past her sobbing. Then she mumbled inaudibly how this was all a dream she didn't want to wake from.

"Don't wake me, don't wake me!" she repeated over again, shaking her head back and forth.

"This is what you've been missing, let Grandma see her princess!" Grandma Rose squeezed Emma close to her bosom.

Pausing to look her Grandmother over, Emma touched her face and then her thick, coarse hair. She closed her eyes as Grandma Rose did the same. Leading her by the hand, they sat on a wooden bench. There was enough space for four people, but it didn't matter, Emma sat on her Grandmother's lap.

"You've grown quite a bit since the last time we've done this," she laughed.

For a moment they sat in silence, holding onto each other, smiling from the inside-out. Grandma Rose was right; it had been eleven years since they'd seen each other last.

"I miss you!" said Emma and squeezed tighter.

"Can't I stay here with you?" she asked, knowing it was impossible, but hoping the moment wouldn't come to an end. Here, she could be with the people who mattered the most in her life. They understood her and loved her unconditionally.

Then it was that door to consider, waiting for her return in the corridor – and the beeping - that beckoned for an answer. Perhaps it was just her alarm clock on the other side of consciousness. Either way, Emma refused to leave now, because there was nothing more valuable in her apartment, or in life, then what was here.

She'd already quit her job, and even she had to admit her dream of wanting to dance in a Broadway play was fading.

Every passion she once held dwindled like embers growing cold in the night. She lacked the discipline needed to accomplish anything past what she wanted at the moment.

"There's plenty of time for that yet baby," said Grandma Rose, kissing her forehead and then her cheek. Emma squeezed tighter until Grandma Rose bellowed with laughter.

"Things can't be that bad," said Grandma Rose.

She patted the bench, instructing that Emma sit beside her so they could talk face-to-face.

"Are you in trouble?" she asked.

Like the door she wished to avoid, Grandma Rose asked a question she wanted to ignore. Shame choked the truth from being spoken, so the question hung in the air like a hot-air balloon. She looked up to the sky, wishing it would drift up and away, far beyond the clouds.

There was no need to look because she could feel her grandmother's stare searching her over with an eagle's eye vision. Grandma Rose had a way of getting to the root of a matter, and she was not the type to be easily dismissed. Knowing a confession was imminent, Emma's throat tightened as she contemplated how much to reveal.

For a fleeting moment, she thought about running, but that would be foolish. Where would she run to? If this was all a dream, she could create a different outcome. Emma forced herself to imagine Grandma Rose to have a sudden interest in the Orange Blossoms, but her Grandmother continued to stare. She tried to imagine the little girl wandering into the garden with them, and they would talk about how beautiful her eyes were together. Grandma

Rose didn't budge.

Emma thought about Grandma Rose's accomplishments, the organization she'd left behind, her legacy. The blueprint to her success was entrusted to Emma, who had rejected it all; mostly because it meant going back to Colorado, where she imagined Reba would be waiting for her return. Then there was that now fading dream of being a dancer, that no one, not even herself, took seriously.

"Emma," called Grandma Rose, "You're all worked up over nothing. Did you forget what I taught you?" she asked.

Emma remembered Grandma Rose whispering in her ear, *"The secret to my success is prayer!"* Then, she'd wink, *"Call on Jesus when you don't know what to pray!"*

Emma nodded her head.

"You told me to pray!"

"You remembered!" said Grandma Rose, beaming. She clapped her hands together, then threw her head back and lifted her open palms up to the sky.

Emma looked at the courtyard entrance, her eyes landing on a cluster of flowers.

"Orange blossoms are in full bloom," she said, hoping to shift the topic.

"What a relief to hear you remembered to pray," said Grandma Rose. With a sigh, she clutched a hand to her chest. How Emma wished she could allow her to believe the lie.

"No, I haven't prayed lately." Emma's eyes began to well from her tears, she closed them, now hoping this was a dream. Otherwise, she'd just disappointed the most important person in her life.

"I understand now," Grandma Rose cleared her throat.

Emma looked from the sky to the garden, the pool, and then

the door. When she could take the silence no longer, she faced her Grandmother, who to her surprise was smiling. They laughed together, but Emma's laughter wasn't from happiness. If she smiled harder and laughed longer, maybe she wouldn't have to face what she knew was coming.

"I haven't had time for anything, everything I try to do ends up being a mess," she said.

"What keeps you so busy that you don't have time to pray?" asked Grandma Rose, who was concerned by now. Emma knew there was no getting around a full confession.

"A lot has changed since you left, it seems I go from one bad situation to the next," she said.

"Things have happened— it makes me very upset to think about," She frowned, not wanting to go into details.

"I'm listening," said Grandma Rose.

Emma shrugged her shoulders and sighed. The plan was to graduate high school and then college—that's it. She wasn't expected to solve any of life's greatest mysteries, just go to college. Grandma Rose didn't care if she attended a junior college or a university. Money wasn't a barrier

Emma left the bench and paced around in circles. Grandma Rose, watching, picked up the sprig of flowers, and touched the petals.

"Remember how hard it was the first time we tried making flower crowns? Took us three tries before we finally got it right!" said Grandma Rose, while gathering more sprigs to make a crown. Then placed it on her head so it wouldn't fall over. Emma came back to her side and adjusted the crown more securely.

"Let's make another," she said, reaching for her Grandmother's hand.

Grandma Rose gave her that look, there was no fooling her; this was the woman that talked to Jesus and rebuked Santa Claus. She knew the truth, and when someone was trying to avoid it.

"Emma, do you remember that night? What a show, your poor mother just didn't know any better," she shrugged.

"What about Reba?" Emma frowned and sat back down.

"Your Mother," she corrected.

Emma forgot that Grandma Rose hadn't known that Reba preferred to be called by first name, or that Reba was the source of all Emma's troubles.

"That night when you said you wanted to go home—I knew it wasn't going to end well," she said matter-of-factly. "The Good Lord had already warned me in a dream," Grandma Rose said. Emma was reminded of how Grandma Rose always spoke of the 'Good Lord' as if she had known Him personally.

"By the time we got there, your Mother was beyond control and reasoning…If we hadn't shown up when we did, Reba would've had your Dad thrown in jail far longer than a few days!" she said.

Emma had to think, but then remembered that night; for her, it was just another one of Reba's tantrums. When she didn't see her Dad the next day, or that week, she figured it was business as usual.

"Oh yes, your Daddy went to jail for four days behind that awful fight they had that night—you don't remember?" Grandma Rose continued. Emma shook her head no, but what she remembered was being alone with Reba for far longer than she wanted to be.

"Your Mother said he slapped her…they handcuffed him, and she told me not to even think of coming near her house, or her child, again," Grandma Rose said. She blew air and then waved a hand. Emma blinked and then shook her head. All this time, she thought her Grandmother was upset with her for wanting to go home early, never imagining Reba had something to do with her absence.

"I gave them space because your Dad asked me to," she patted Emma on her leg. "They were trying to make it work without any interference," she went on.

Grandma Rose stayed away at her son's request, giving him the benefit of the doubt. He wanted his wife to feel secure in the marriage and be the mother she wanted to be, Grandma Rose explained. Emma wondered if she knew how miserably Reba had failed at both.

"I stayed away because the good Lord assured me that everything was going to be alright—and it was," she said. Placing her hands over her heart, she spoke silent words underneath her breath.

"Drinking and using drugs, it's what Reba was taught to do from the ones that called themselves her family," she said.

Emma marched back and forth as Grandma Rose recounted the story, then pouted when her Grandmother patted the seat instructing for Emma to calm down.

"You've experienced a lot of loss and suffering; I wish I could've spared you," she said. "but what your mother had to endure is a pain on a whole different level," continued Grandma Rose.

Emma listened without interruption, realizing a message her Dad, and now Grandma Rose wanted her to comprehend. If she could see past her anger, maybe then she could figure out what they both wanted her to understand.

"I've come to know that compassion soothes the pain and patience will produce understanding," Grandma Rose said. Emma nodded her agreement, not because she identified with Reba's pain, but because she had experienced compassion and patience for herself.

"If you hang out with a person long enough, you'll come to understand what drives them forward or keeps them stuck," said Grandma Rose, while wiping a tear from Emma's eye. One or two drops escaped from her eyelid, then a steady trickle, until there were huge droplets that seemed enough to fill a bucket. She had sprung a leak, and if she could find the source, she would stop these worthless tears. When her tears slowed down, she felt lighter, relieved that her anger had lifted.

Grandma Rose found a sturdy piece of twig and gathered some orange blossoms. Neither said a word until the flower crown was completed. Inspecting her work, she then placed it on Emma's head.

"I went to New York to get away from Reba, then I met some people, and I fell in love with the city…and dancing, I thought I could combine the two and dance for a living," Emma confessed. Grandma Rose listened, nodding that Emma should continue.

"I blew it—flaked on a big audition, and now nobody wants to give me another chance!" she said.

"You're a good dancer, what could've possibly gone wrong?" She asked.

Grandma Rose knew of Emma's potential because she paid for the dance, gymnastics, and piano lessons. She had been there for most, if not all, her recitals.

"Did you see the man?" Emma looked away.

Her Grandmother raised an eyebrow and then folded her arms. Emma caught herself looking at the entryway, hoping for a diversion, but the courtyard was quiet, even the beeps went silent. Grandma Rose would need to brace herself before hearing what her little princess had been up to since her passing.

# PART III

# *YOUNG ADULTHOOD*

*2009 - 2016*

# FIFTEEN

A SOFT BUT STEADY rain had begun around 4 a.m., just about the time Emma left the bar and followed the crowd to Chen's apartment. Another night with the aspiring artists had left her with $150.00 to survive on until her Dad arrived. She worried about her looks, the extra ten pounds she gained during her stay in Maine, and the other thing.

What she needed was a warm shower and a place to sleep for at least six uninterrupted hours. A decent hotel would cost $149.00, and a low-budget room around fifty bucks. Chen would have let her stay another night; the problem was he had the same open-door policy for anyone he knew. Sleeping there would be at her own risk, in whatever spot she could squeeze into and how much noise she was able to tolerate. If she could stand the noise and tight quarters, then maybe she could at least get 20 minutes of sleep.

Replaying the conversation with her Dad over again, Emma zipped her parka, threw the hood over her head, and made her way down the block in search of the first room she could afford. A quiet room would give her space to prepare for the dreaded conversation of the days since they'd seen each other last.

It was her birthday, her Dad had reminded her, and she told him that was the reason for the call. He was relieved and wanted to know where she was. When Emma mentioned she needed to tell him something, he insisted that the conversation be put on hold until they were face-to-face. Now the anticipation of seeing him for the first time in a year, then having to tell him about the night Reba and Ogre kidnapped her and the journey she went on after that was dreadful.

If she could tell the story without admitting that she was pregnant, it was almost bearable, but Emma felt guilty about withholding the whole truth. He would want to know about the baby. The last thing she wanted was for him to search for a baby she never wanted to see again. Her only recourse was to act like it never happened and move forward from today.

All that mattered now was seeing her Father, and with any luck, she could talk him into supporting her decision to stay in New York. Maybe if she enrolled in school? If not, she would have to find a job to make ends meet on her own. Either way, returning to Denver was not an option.

By the time Emma located a decent hotel, her shoes squished, and her clothing clung to her limbs like plastic wrap from the moisture. Preoccupied with thoughts of showing her Father around Central Park and Times Square, she didn't notice the puddles of water left in her steps. She did catch the glare from a housekeeping attendant as he rolled his bucket and mop to erase her soggy trail.

The room cost $80.00 and had nothing more than two beds and a bathroom, but it was clean. Emma checked into the room, then phoned her Dad to give him the name of the hotel and room number. He informed her that his flight would land at 9:15 that evening, but not to worry because he would find her. When she hung up the phone, Emma jumped from one bed to the other and danced around the room until she caught a glimpse of herself in the mirror.

The leggings and an oversized shirt were reminders of her stay at Sebec Lake. The shirt was now tied in a knot, her best attempt at trying to fit-in with the artsy crowd. The bags underneath her eyes from lack of sleep were noticeable, and her hair was frizzy from the rain and tangled from being uncombed. If her Dad saw her like this, he would worry more than necessary and refuse her request to stay in New York. Emma remembered seeing a thrift store a few blocks down; with the leftover money, she hoped to find something presentable there.

She scored at the thrift shop. After making her purchase, Emma hurried back to the room and showered. Then she changed her clothes. Combing her hair into a neat bun, she was pleased there were still several hours to spare before her Dad's arrival. The only thing left to do was to get rid of the bags underneath her eyes, and the remedy for that was sleep. Laying across one of the beds, she took a much-needed nap.

When Emma woke up later in the evening, she panicked at first thinking she'd overslept. Then her worry about the impending conversation returned. She imagined again how her Dad would hug her, and then she would cry. He'd sit her down and ask her to tell him everything. She would give him the condensed version of events; she left Louisiana and came straight to New York, that's when she called. She cringed when she considered the timeline between her first call home and the final call earlier today.

There was a knock at the door when Emma realized she'd fallen back to sleep again. Without hesitation, she ran to the door and flung it open. A young guy holding two steamy square boxes grinned.

"Your pizza?" he asked.

"No, it's not mine," she said, trying not to lick her lips. In her excitement, she had forgotten to eat.

"You sure? Room 12, it says right here..." he showed her a slip.

"Sorry, I didn't order anything," she said, but this time when she caught a whiff of the pizza, she licked her lips.

"Hmm, well it's paid for, and this is the correct hotel and room number—so it's all yours," he said, handing her the two pizzas.

Emma wanted to protest, but he walked away so fast. When she closed the door, she thought about eating one slice – just one. If someone came looking for their pizza, she could offer her last 10 bucks as payment. Hopefully, they'd be understanding.

Thirty minutes later, and another knock came at the door. Emma looked at the box and remembered the slices she ate. She grabbed what was left and braced herself before opening the door.

"Thank God, my prayers have been answered," were the first words out of his mouth. "My baby girl!" his voice seemed to reverberate off the walls.

After inspecting the room, he announced they would be staying elsewhere. The room was "okay," but he had better arrangements suited for their reunion. Emma and her Father entered a waiting car that drove them farther away from central park. Because of the traffic, their ride was longer than expected, but it gave them a chance to talk.

Reba had been in contact with him and spun a story of how she'd taken their daughter to meet her family in Louisiana. She didn't ask his permission because he would've said no. Initially, her call was to request that he give them some space. By August she phoned saying Emma left after they had an argument, and she should be showing up at home soon. When Emma never arrived was when he first became concerned.

"I called once, and hung up when the answering machine came on," she said, remembering the day Shelly picked her up on the side of the road.

"You probably thought she was going to make you come back," he said.

"That woman always wanted you to herself," he went on.

Emma frowned, and then realized he didn't know the Reba she knew. Then she realized the story was so believable it provided a way to avoid her own confession, so Emma went along with Reba's version.

Her Father's idea of New York was in Soho where the streets were slightly less crowded, and the shopping more luxurious. It was at dinner the following night when her Dad gave her the best news she'd heard in a long time.

"Well, you left so unexpectedly, I didn't have a chance to tell you about the trust fund," he said, handing her an envelope with some legal documents to review. Emma was relieved that he was the first to introduce the topic because her pockets were empty. Then it was the discussion of how to convince him to fund her stay in New York. If he could agree to six months...a year would be better, she could find a job while waiting to get accepted into a school.

"Dad, what is this?" she asked eyeballing a large figure on a statement balance. "This is a lot of money," she said.

There was an initial six-figure payout, that would be followed by monthly payments of a little over $10,000.00 each, and then a final payout at the age of 40 that would make her a comfortably wealthy woman. Grandma Rose had named her as the sole beneficiary of a hefty insurance policy.

He then handed Emma her purse that was left behind the night she was taken, with her cell phone inside and the five thousand dollars given her as a graduation gift that day.

"Why live like a pauper when you're a princess?" he grinned.

While spending the last year running from Reba and trying to conceal what happened, Emma forgot about the life she'd left behind where money wasn't an obstacle. Shock kept her from going straight home once she left Breaux Bridge, but by the time she made it to that hotel room with Shelly, Emma knew she was pregnant even though she tried to wish it away.

He stayed with her in Soho for two weeks before they had the first discussion about her plans. It was during breakfast he broached the conversation.

"Shall it be tomorrow?" he asked after a sip of coffee.

"I was hoping we could spend the day in Manhattan tomorrow," she said.

"About the flight?" he said, directing her attention to his laptop screen.

"But you can't leave without seeing a show first," she whined and pushed the list of current plays before him. When he showed more interest in the schedule, she sat at the computer and began an apartment search.

"You'll need a two-bedroom at the least. I want to be comfortable when I visit," he said after he took control of the search engine.

"I wouldn't have it any other way, Daddy," she said, squeezing his neck and jumping up and down on her toes. When he called a college friend in the area, he was given a referral to a trusted realtor.

To both their surprise, the real estate agent, Tamar McNeil, was a young woman in her early twenties, she proudly informed them after he asked.

"And don't let the age fool you, I make dreams happen," she declared. Tamar kept a professional demeanor at each apartment showing while Emma and her Dad fought about anything they could disagree on.

"This won't do for me!" He turned up his nose at one unit.

"And just how often do you plan on visiting?" Emma fussed back at him. She wanted large walk-in closets, which were hard to find in the city. He was disappointed when Emma said a flat out "No," to living on the outskirts of town.

"I need to be closer to Central Park, that's where the actions at," she said. "I want to audition for some of those plays you see on that flyer."

The apartment they finally agreed on was perfect in Emma's opinion. The location was incredible, situated in the vicinity of Central Park where she could venture out whenever she wanted, whether for a walk or jog, a restaurant or shopping. There was an abundance of activities for a young person, not to mention the bustling nightlife.

Tamar pointed out that some of New York's finest cuisines were only a stroll away, and the C Express and B trains were just a block down. Her unit had high ceilings and oversized windows, perfect for people-watching over a morning cup of coffee. The kitchen was large and had white oyster tiles and granite countertops. The living space had Ebony hardwood floors, room enough for a large couch or a small sectional; and to her delight, the bedroom had sufficient closet space.

After closing on the sale, it was her Fathers suggestion that they repay Tamar for her patience. Emma phoned with the invitation to which she gladly accepted with a recommendation where they should meet; a local wine bar that served food as well.

After they toasted their spirited drinks and ordered their meal, her Dad disclosed that his primary concern about Emma's stay in the big city was her age. Tamar shared that she had been on her own since the age of 16, and at the age of 18, she became a licensed real estate agent working for a broker. Now 21 years old, two years older than Emma, Tamar had her own apartment and was holding down a full-time job.

She shared her struggles while being raised in the foster care system and how she came to work and live in Manhattan. Growing up "alone" wasn't an ideal situation, but it made her a survivor.

"Well, if you can make it here, so can my Princess," said her dad, holding up his glass to toast.

The day before his scheduled departure, her Father made a final pitch for Emma to forget about the big city and return home.

"Daddy, what about the apartment we just bought?" She reminded him.

"It can be rented," he said so quickly Emma knew he'd already thought the plan through.

"I'm just a phone call or flight away…and besides I'm not ready to deal with Reba, so please don't tell her you've seen or heard from me," she pleaded.

"Will you ever come back—"

"I want to be far away from Reba," Emma protested.

When he looked her in the eyes, he understood her plea, then said no more.

"What about that Mercedes coupe you were eyeballing?" He raised an eyebrow. His lip curled upwards, a slight smile growing from the corners of his mouth. She thought he was making another argument – so she frowned.

Emma had dropped every hint she could think of the previous

year for her birthday; she had posted flyers on the refrigerator, and finally in desperation, arranged a visit to the dealer showroom. The most she got out of that visit was a test drive.

"I'll need transportation when I'm in town," he teased.

Emma's eyes lit up when she realized he was serious about purchasing the Mercedes.

# SIXTEEN

TAMAR, WHO ENDED up becoming the first real friend Emma ever had, later revealed how much she looked forward to those meetings with Emma and her father. Tamar walked with her head in the air and wore determination as an overcoat. Confidence dripped from her heels, leaving its imprint in her footsteps. She had flawless dark skin that accentuated glossy veneers and her signature matte lipstick.

Sometimes she wore wigs for versatility, but mostly she wore her natural hair shoulder length and would toss her head in such a way that her bob-cut would whip the air. Careful consideration went into her presentation, this was her brand, and it was what made Tamar unforgettable. Little had been handed to her in life. She worked hard and always had a purpose in mind.

Emma liked to watch the deliberate plan and execution of Tamar's wardrobe and makeup; down to the way she spoke. This intentional presentation fascinated Emma. This was not her Grandma Rose's elegant evening attire or her Mother's eclectic hobo skirts with bangles. Instead, Tamar was a young lady she could identify with. And Emma tried to secretly emulate her mannerisms.

"If you're going to wear couture, you need to commit to the style," Tamar fussed at Emma who took her wardrobe for granted.

"YOU own the garment, now show everyone who YOU are," she coached. Those were the early days when Tamar and Emma were inseparable.

Tamar was now married to Beaumont, a med-school student. Though she initially had her doubts, Emma had to admit that her friend was happy, and that was her only concern. Tamar reassured Emma that she was part of their family. However, they both had to admit that things were different now.

Children thrive when they are nurtured at home, with parents that make them feel safe and wanted. Tamar was deprived of that opportunity as a child but now was able to offer all the love she had to her new family. Emma resented the change in their friendship but refused to allow her needs to stand in the way of her friends' happiness. She was the sister Emma never had, and a sister should be there to support the other at all costs.

For the majority of their eight-year friendship there's had been an understanding of respect and admiration, but lately things were a bit strained. Emma tried to remember good times shared with Tamar. They both loved to dance; there was a time they'd dance well into the night and early morning to just about whatever song played. It became customary for them to meet around 6 p.m. on Fridays at Emma's apartment. After sharing laughs and a few drinks, they picked out their outfits and would hit the streets.

It seemed like a good time for them both then, at least Emma believed they were having fun. After all, Tamar was there with her in the beginning, drinking and laughing- she even brought most of the bottles – and never refused an invitation to party.

From Emma's perspective, they had a sisterly bond that came easy and was mutual. They laughed at each other's jokes, cried when the other was sad, got mad at the other when a call went unanswered, and after no more than two days apart, were back together like nothing happened.

Emma remembered the days when Tamar would arrive at her apartment with a tote bag full of groceries, which meant it was their culinary night. Inspired by a movie where a girl decided to recreate all of Julia Child's French recipes, Tamar's interest in cooking was birthed. She found a blog on gourmet cooking and decided they should traverse through the various recipes together.

Whatever Tamar's taste-buds craved on Wednesday night dictated the menu for Friday evening. One week, they prepared a simple homemade pizza, the following week was beef stew, and the wee after was a Sous Vide pork tenderloin. Initially, Emma declined shopping duty, which is why Tamar wound up bringing the groceries herself. In the end, however, Emma had to admit the food was delectable and the conversation was even dripping with flavor.

They had come to be known in a circle of night-goers as the Irish Sisters, because they shared the same birthday, though born in different years. Typically, meal prep consisted of discussions of each other's hopes and dreams; Emma wanted to make it as a Broadway dancer, and Tamar wished to build a real estate empire. The spicier part of the conversation would be saved after the table was set, and steaming plates sat before them. The regulars who also frequented their same nightspots were served up au jus.

It was over a Cavatelli pasta with mushrooms, kale, and soft-boiled eggs meal that Tamar mentioned the rooftop party on 48th Street that upcoming Saturday. Emma hesitated at the mention, but hearing "Ladies in free before 6 p.m.," changed her mind. She failed to ask what the theme was, mostly because she didn't care for rooftop events, and figured she'd only make a brief appearance anyway.

As it turned out, the party had a reggae theme. An amateur band covered top hits from Bob Marley to Sean Paul. Emma wasn't having the best of times. It wasn't that she didn't care for the music, but she found it difficult to incorporate her unique style of dance with the Caribbean beats.

When she had enough of the DJ's fake Rastafarian accent, Emma sauntered over to the group where Tamar had been, giving her their secret code for readiness to leave. When Tamar paid her no attention, she noticed the chemistry between her friend and a tall gentleman with locks and a neatly lined beard that framed his strong jawbone.

"Beaumont is my name, but they call me Beau, sweet ting," he said with an accent more believable than the disc jockeys.

"Nice to meet you, Beau," Emma said, returning the greeting.

"I was just telling your friend—" he started.

"Sister," she corrected him.

"My apology, your sister. I just transferred to NYU from Université d'État d'Haïti," he said, flashing a broad smile.

Emma remained straight-faced, observing the way he stared into Tamar's eyes and how she gushed back into his. Emma squinted her eyes, and gave the secret code once more, slower this time - a hand against your face like you're unbothered, then turn and look to the entrance. Tamar saw her friend's cue but chose to ignore it.

"Beau, finish telling me about your travels to Europe," said Tamar. It was her way of saying, 'This catch is mine, and I'm not throwing it back.' But Emma gave her another cross look, then mouthed the words, "You're falling for this line?" Emma knew any attempt past this one would be useless.

As she suspected, Tamar ended the evening enraptured by Beaumont and his 'sweet tings.' Emma eventually gravitated to a different crowd, with a drink in hand, and continued drinking until her movements slowed down enough to imitate the reggae beats; or maybe it was until she no longer cared what music was playing to what moves she danced.

During the next week, Tamar's calls centered on what Beau said… and who Beau knew…then what Beau wanted to do; Tamar had been struck by cupid's Beau-and-arrow. And Emma learned everything she ever wanted to know within three short phone calls about her friend's new love interest. He was from Haiti, lived in London for a year, visited Australia once, and now Beau was coming over for dinner at Tamar's apartment on Friday—which meant she needed to cancel their weekly gourmet meal night.

Tamar swiftly went to work crafting her best attempt at a Haitian meal: rice and beans with stewed chicken, boiled plantains, and hard dough bread.

"Wow, that's a heavy meal," Emma pointed out, knowing her friend preferred no more than two starches per day.

"Yes, it is, I've already thought this through, I'll only eat the Chicken and plantain," she promised.

"Well, you better put on your loose-fitting green dress, eating that way," Emma warned. "And be prepared for three extra laps around the park," she teased before the beep came through on Tamar's phone. Emma sucked her teeth when Tamar clicked over to answer the incoming call.

"Girl let me call you back—" said Tamar, when she returned.

"IT'S BEAU," they said simultaneously. Tamar chuckled, but

Emma sighed as their call disconnected.

Several weeks passed with fewer conversations between her and Tamar. When Tamar did call, it was to give more Beau updates. So, Emma was surprised on Wednesday when Tamar sent a text message and asked if they could have pasta on Friday for their gourmet night recipe. She wasn't in the mood for pasta, but craving time with her friend, Emma agreed. On Friday, Tamar's smile entered the apartment before her body, and the sparkle in her eyes was unlike one Emma had seen before.

It was over the meal prep for their penne pasta with Genovese sauce that Tamar blurted out her first announcement that signified a change on the horizon.

"So, about that show in Jones Beach," she said while her back was turned cleaning out a saucepot. Emma continued to slice four pounds of red onions without looking up. The art to receiving disappointing news was to act casual, detach your emotions.

"I had something else planned anyway." Emma shrugged off the news. "Don't worry about it, Gianna asked if she could go." It was a lie, but Tamar wouldn't call to confirm the story.

"Or…you can go with me and Beau?" Tamar offered.

Maybe it was the way Emma whacked the blade of her knife against the cutting board, or perhaps Tamar had intended on inviting Emma all along, who's to say for sure. All Emma could think of was here was another pasta meal that ended with bad news.

'I hate pasta,' thought Emma, as she continued to butcher the onions. Then when the bag was emptied, she moved to the tomatoes… 'And I hate men named Beau.'

When the tomatoes were hacked, she reached for a bunch of carrots. Then when the vegetables were all chopped, there was nothing left to do but simmer the ingredients and digest the news.

Emma grabbed the bottle of wine Tamar brought meant for the penne pasta, and Tamar reached for two glasses. They sat at the kitchen table and drank the bottle in unaccustomed silence.

"I want you to come with us," Tamar insisted after their silence grew awkward. Emma knew she felt guilty, and had it not been for her own battles with guilt, she would've made Tamar feel like a rotten friend for canceling. Not wanting to be the third wheel, and knowing Tamar the way she did, Emma refused.

"My dad was thinking about coming out that weekend anyway, I'll let him know I'm free after all. You and Beau have a good time," she said. And when Tamar gave her that suspicious look, Emma said, "Seriously, you know how he is about his princess." After Tamar was convinced that Emma was okay, they finished their meal with both pretending not to notice the shift in their relationship.

There were no further canceled plans, nor did she have to come up with more lies to shield her disappointment, because all of Tamar's dates were now with Beau, and their friendship reduced to phone calls.

# SEVENTEEN

THE DAY OF the show at Jones Beach, Emma decided to spend pampering herself. Expecting a short trip to the natural market downtown, she threw on a pair of faded jeans, a sweater, and a baseball cap. Once there, she splurged on orange essential oils, lavender Epsom bath soak, vintage-linen candles, and detox products for her skin and hair. Then for a light snack, she picked up a triple cream Brie, purple grapes, and soda crackers.

Feeling content with her choice, Emma made her purchase and left the market. If it wasn't for the liquor store two doors down that caught her eye, she would've never met the man that helped change her destiny. Entering the store, she followed a perceived path toward the wine selections with tunnel vision. There was a man in the aisle preoccupied with labels along the shelves. He wore a dark suit and had on a soft blue colored tie. Emma stole a quick glance, then adjusted her baseball cap and sweater. It was too late to turn around.

Looking in her direction, he flashed a warm smile.

"Hello," he said.

Emma thought about grabbing the first bottle within reach and leaving before any other handsome men crossed her path. She wasn't usually attracted to men in suits, but this one called her to attention; he smelled clean, like maybe a citrus-scented soap. Summing him up she guessed his height to be about 6 feet, at least. He was neatly groomed and wore his hair cropped short, with a trimmed beard and mustache. His suit hung perfectly around his solid frame. Emma could tell by his stance that he was physically fit.

Hoping to get a better smell of the air around him, she moved closer and then pretended to have an interest in a bottle nearby. Avoiding eye contact, Emma reached for a selection close enough to lean in for another sniff.

"If you had me over for dinner which wine would you like?" he asked casually.

She hesitated longer than necessary, with thoughts of how Tamar would respond in this situation. If she could channel some of her wit, then she'd say something like, "How about you surprise me when you show up tonight," or, "I have the wine, you just show up." But Emma wasn't that bold.

"It helps to know what's being served," was her reply.

"So, what will it be?" he awaited her response.

If she had an expectation of meeting someone before leaving home earlier, she would've prepared better...chosen a different outfit, practiced clever responses, and flirtatious replies.

"Would you like to get dinner, or lunch sometime?" he asked when she gave no reply.

"Sure," she answered, wondering what it was he saw in her of interest.

After they exchanged phone numbers, he told her to expect a call in a day or so. Orion was the name he gave her; he called on a Monday and asked if they could meet for lunch on Thursday, or dinner on Friday? He was polite, but a 'straight to the point' type of guy, he seemed to know what he wanted. ⌒

His days were filled with college and full-time employment, but he would still like to know her—if she didn't mind, that is? Emma agreed to dinner on a Friday evening. Which led to another date that following Thursday, and another the week after that…and then again on Friday. Now she understood how Tamar went from a chance meeting with Beaumont to canceling their Jones Beach concert.

Orion was usually inaccessible on Saturdays and Sundays due to time-honored commitments near his home in Harlem. Three months passed with his excuses for not being available on weekends. Then Emma began to question the predictable pattern. She called his bluff after a discussion with Tamar revealed some upsetting truths.

"Does he come on set days?" she probed.

"Yes, Thursday and Friday."

"Mm-hmm, have you met any of his friends?" she questioned.

"No, we like to be alone."

"Mm-hmm, and where does he live, or work for that matter?"

All Emma knew was that Orion went to NYU and volunteered his time at a community center on weekends.

"Have I taught you nothing, or haven't you been paying attention?" Tamar laughed.

After their conversation, Emma had a list of questions of her own. If he had intentions of playing games, then it was time to teach him some of her rules. She would start with his cell phone. They were having dinner at a restaurant in town when his cellular phone was inadvertently left at the table while he retrieved condiments and napkins. So, she picked it up and somehow began scrolling through his contacts.

"Whatever happened to respect others privacy?" he asked upon his return. Emma had his phone in hand as she scrolled through the contact list.

"I'm looking for wifey, my girl or maybe babe," she answered.

"Eat your food before it gets cold," said Orion.

He never reached for the phone, so she was satisfied for the time being. By the time they returned to her apartment, Orion had told her to ask every question she had, and he was going to answer truthfully. Emma shared how a recent conversation with a close friend led her to question the predictable routine of their dates.

Where was the rest of him? Where was his family, or friends…where was home? That was the night he decided it was time to show her what living in his world was like. Orion introduced Emma to a different side of the city, one where people sacrificed their time to volunteer at community centers and people's kitchens.

On Saturday mornings he met with a group of kids at a community center in Harlem and coached a basketball league. From there he helped at a teen center on the other side of town where he mentored and counseled at-risk youth. After an early dinner, Orion then caught the train back into town to study at the NYU law library.

"You must sleep all day on Sundays," said Emma, by the time he dropped her off that evening.

"People's kitchen in the morning, church with my Pops after— would you like to come?" he asked with raised eyebrows.

"No thank you," she shuddered at the thought of having to rise early after the day she'd just experienced.

Orion had the determination of two people. His drive reminded Emma of the times she volunteered at her Grandmother's non-profit, the satisfaction felt by giving back to the community and being of service. Motivated by his ambition, and some to do with his urging, Emma decided it was time to get a job. She needed something to do with her time during the week when everyone else she knew was working. After a casual mention to her Father, he suggested she reach out to his old college friend who ran an advertising agency. When Emma got around to calling later in the week, an interview was set for the next morning. It was not a surprise when she was offered a job.

The agency employed a little over 100 workers with another location in Los Angeles. There were several departments representing marketing in real estate, entertainment, automotive, government, and non-profit. Emma was excited when she saw the possibility of working on entertainment projects, but when human resources phoned to offer her the position, they happily informed her that she would be working exclusively in the government and non-profit sector. Her face went flat when she heard the news but then became enthusiastic when her father and Orion were pleased.

On her first day of work, Emma was ushered to a desk in the research department. The position consisted of gathering information for initiatives in human rights, homeless outreach, and environmental improvements. Her first assignment was to partner with a co-worker, Naomi, who researched materials on a public education campaign for a new policy, which has now become known as DACA (Deferred Action for Childhood Arrivals).

Emma was intrigued after learning that the program was an American immigration policy that allowed some individuals who entered the country as minors to receive a two-year renewable period of deferred action from deportation, and to be eligible for a work permit. As a participant of this program, Naomi and others like her were referred to as 'Dreamers.' Emma noted her co-worker's passion as she pursued a cause that served a higher purpose.

The year elapsed between Emma and Orion's continued dates on Thursday and Friday nights, and her Monday thru Friday work schedule. Saturday mornings were saved for retail therapy, but Saturday nights were special. Emma was able to maintain some acquaintances she was introduced to by Tamar the previous year. She liked to hang around and strike up conversations with the actors, and the other entertainers. They sipped on drinks, puffed cigarettes, and talked about successes, failures, and current projects.

On one of those nights, Emma was offered to attend as a guest only. Then, if interested, she would need to practice before going on her first audition. On Sunday afternoon, she attended her first dance session. The energy at the dance studio was familiarly infectious. Pointed toes on top of smooth vinyl floors; elongated silhouettes clad in leotards and leggings reflected in ceiling-to-floor mirrors.

The atmosphere made Emma feel nostalgic, reminding her of younger days when her only nightmare was nervousness over forgotten moves for an upcoming recital. Dancers entered with smiling eyes that transformed to fierce glares when the music began; their kindness swallowed by a competitive drive to be the best and nothing less.

Emma enrolled in professional sessions on Sundays, Wednesdays, and Thursdays, with the intention of fast-tracking her dancing career to increase performance opportunities. After two months of showing up for auditions and not getting a slot, she realized the need for an agent.

Tamar phoned on a Wednesday as Emma waited to see if her name would be called for an audition. Fixed glares and upturned noses let her know she was in the wrong place for cell phone conversations. Declining the call, she sent a text message instead:

Can't talk right now what's up?

**Tamar: Really need to talk to you, when are you free?**

**Emma: Tomorrow after 5.**

Tamar was at her front door before Emma arrived, flawless as usual, and noticeably giddy. She flashed her fantastic smile, then produced a brilliant diamond ring.

"I'm getting married," she squealed before Emma could fully connect the smile with the ring to the news.

"Married?" said Emma.

"Drinks on me," said Tamar with intentions of celebrating.

"But I already have plans tonight, Orion's coming over."

"No problem, we'll make it a double date, it'll be fun."

This was Tamar's way, when she wanted something, she went after it. Emma heard her cell phone ringing in the kitchen where she had left it.

"This is her sister, sure come over, I'd like to meet you anyway."

Then she gave instructions for Orion to meet them at a bar.

The conversation was light-hearted. Emma silently judged Tamar's fiancé, and Tamar returned the favor. When Emma excused herself to use the restroom, Tamar recognized the cue.

"I'll follow you, somethings in my eye," she said.

Once in the bathroom, they took turns giving their full analysis. Tamar found Orion to be handsome, a sharp dresser, and very educated. A little on the arrogant side, but that was easily overlooked due to his selfless acts in community service. Emma shared that Beaumont, though somewhat thuggish, had a promising future if he continued his education and earned his medical degree. They both agreed that the guys got along well, and this would make it easier for them to spend more time together, and for that reason, the evening was a success.

As the time grew closer to Tamar's wedding, chaos increased to utter madness. Tamar was irritable; she didn't like the color choices, the cake wasn't her favorite, the dress was just "alright," and she couldn't get the guest list down to where it needed to be. Something and everything seemed wrong, and when Emma asked if she was sure about getting married, Tamar accused her of being jealous and immature. Then Emma claimed that Tamar was not being truthful about having doubts. When Tamar suggested that she not be in the wedding, Emma agreed.

Working full-time and spending the evenings at the dance studio turned out to be more work then she could've imagined. The schedule was affecting her sleep, which caused her to lie awake with thoughts she wished to erase. One night she made the mistake of calling Orion in the middle of the night, but never again.

"If you interfere with my sleep, that puts me behind, and if I'm behind, that cuts into our planned time," he informed her politely, but sternly.

Under normal circumstances, Tamar wouldn't mind a late-night call. In fact, Emma had done so over the past two years, when the nightmares returned. After several nights of racing thoughts that robbed her sleep, Emma abandoned her bed for the living room sofa. Still restless, she reached for the remote control and something else to anesthetize her body. A stiff cocktail at 10 p.m. and then another at midnight knocked her out enough to sleep until the alarm clock buzzed at 6:00 a.m. for work.

# EIGHTEEN

AFTER TAMAR'S WEDDING, the shift in their relationship continued. Tamar's time and attention were rightfully on her spouse and starting a family. The phone calls were frequent enough that they could still depend on one another, at least once a week. On each conversation, they'd picked up where the last left off usually. Tamar was ever ready to take advantage of Emma's listening ear. She shared the joy of her new role as wife, the hope for expanding her family and plans for their future. Emma was more than happy to listen.

There came a day when Emma realized that her friend had gone silent. She wasn't returning phone calls and didn't respond to text messages either. At first, Emma was offended, then her feelings were hurt, and finally, anger turned to concern. Something wasn't right, she needed to track Tamar down - see her face – to make sure she was safe. Emma went to her office and demanded to know why the distance?

Tamar broke down in the women's restroom; it was now eight months after their wedding, and she still wasn't pregnant. She overheard a conversation between Beau and his mother discussing the fact that he couldn't father children. Secretly concealing her knowledge, she became distraught over the news.

Tamar cried, and Emma listened.

"There's always a way," she offered her friend hope.

"No matter what, I will have babies," Tamar agreed.

"Of course, you will," Emma informed her, with modern technology anything was possible.

It was because of Tamar's talks about wanting to be pregnant that Emma almost broke her silence. The words bubbled on her tongue, then pressed up against her closed lips. *I was pregnant once; I had a baby girl.*

Never knowing how to tell one part of her story without disclosing the other, she pinched her lips tighter. It was Tamar's fault she questioned herself now; she insisted on getting married, and now she wanted a baby.

Emma hardly remembered traveling back from Tamar's office to her own. She stood in the break room before the sink, the faucet had been left running as she attempted to rinse out a coffee mug. For the first time in three years, she thought about Shelly. How were they managing? Shelly lived a simple life before, but a baby required stability. What about their finances? Emma had more than enough money; although the adoption freed her of any responsibility, shouldn't she send something for the child? No, things were better this way, denying that it ever happened was far better than admitting to what had occurred. That was it. It never happened.

A tap on her shoulder caused Emma to drop the coffee mug with a thump to the ground that caused a sizeable portion of the cup to break off.

"I'm sorry I scared you, are you alright?" Naomi asked, bending to retrieve the broken pieces.

Emma saw her lips moving but couldn't comprehend the words. She was a petite Latina with gentle brown eyes. When she smiled, dimples accented her round face.

"I'm so sorry I scared you—I'll replace the mug," she enunciated. "Who is in a better place?" she asked.

When Emma failed to respond, Naomi guided her to a nearby chair.

"My friend, she's having a hard time right now," said Emma, as she retrieved her hand from Naomi's.

"I pray your friend has peace in the midst of the storm," she said.

Emma thought Naomi to be peculiar before, now her words had confirmed the impression. "Thanks for helping with the mess," she said and left the break room without saying another word.

'Peace in the storm.' The words repeated back to Emma as she walked down the hallway to her desk.

'Peace in the storm.'

Those words comforted her throughout the rest of the workday.

'Peace in the the storm.'

Whispering it at bedtime, and then wrapping herself in a warm blanket, Emma slept through the night. By morning she woke in a lighter mood and hummed to an unfamiliar tune that came to her as she slept. During her shower, the phrase returned,

"Peace in the storm," she repeated the phrase aloud as she looked for her outfit of the day.

Resonating deep within, peace unlocked a hope she'd lost years ago while running down a road afraid to look back for Biscuit.

Before now, she had no use for hope; in her opinion, things

always seemed to go from bad to worse. Hope was for the lazy, who didn't want to get out there and take matters into their own hands. And yet, here she was with these unusual words, "Peace in the midst of the storm," that somehow restored her hope again.

Three months later, Tamar showed up on her doorstep with yet more news—she was two months pregnant.

"It's a miracle from God," she said.

This time, her grocery bags were missing the usual bottle of wine. Emma donned a fake smile.

"How did that happen, I thought he…"

"There's always a way, come sit down and close your mouth," Tamar said, whisking past her, with a bowl of fruit and a spoon in hand. She patted the sofa seeing Emma was still standing. Tamar was right, her mouth had been hanging wide open. Last time they spoke, her friend was a wreck. Now without explanation, besides a miracle from God, she was pregnant.

"Were you wrong about his condition?" asked Emma.

Tamar grinned and rubbed her tummy. Emma took a deep breath and sat down beside her.

"Congratulations," she remembered this was good news, and forced a smile. "I know what it feels like," she began, hoping to share her deepest secret with her friend, but Tamar jumped up and went to the window.

"That will be me some-day," she pointed to a couple walking with a stroller. "I'm going to be the best Mommy…well, I wanted you to be the first to know. I must get going, I'm in between apartment showings." She kissed Emma on the cheek and was gone.

Tamar's in and out - dropping news - and then off in the wind, was getting old. Emma wanted to have fun—be young, explore her dancing career, and hang out with her boyfriend…then have more fun. Tamar and her constant changes annoyed Emma. What she was beginning to feel toward her friend was envy and jealousy; envious because Tamar seemed to be getting all the things she desired, jealous because this was another circumstance that would further separate them. Tamar had to have known their relationship was affected, but she was content, and that's all that seemed to matter.

Nevertheless, the pregnancy went smoothly, and when the time drew close for Tamar to have the baby, she asked that Emma be the Godmother. Emma not knowing what being a Godparent meant requested time to consider before giving her answer. Tamar wasn't offended, saying the offer would remain open for Emma to decide.

One evening while on a date with Orion, she received the text message that Tamar was in labor. Expecting him to be thrilled, she asked if they could go to the hospital.

"I can drop you off and come back later?" he said.

Emma pouted as he drove, and by the time they arrived, she had coerced him from the car and up to Tamar's room.

Beaumont was standing in the hallway, and as they approached, he pulled out his cell phone to showcase delivery pictures. Not one baby, but two—a girl and a boy. As the men walked off to the nursery, Emma went in to congratulate Tamar.

"You are full of surprises these days," said Emma.

Tamar was lying in bed, and despite no makeup and disheveled hair, she looked just as good.

"You couldn't handle my news of one baby, I would've lost you for sure if I told you there were two," she said, then reached for Emma's hand. "I miss you," she said.

"I see you opted for the drugs," Emma teased, noting her friend's unusual display of sentiment.

When Beaumont and Orion returned to the room, they were

distracted by a debate over baby names and would've missed Tamar's meltdown completely had she not yelled at them.

"NO, get him out of here!" Tamar gasped upon seeing Orion, insisting that she was not up for company.

Emma understood, Orion did look handsome in his fitted black top, and jeans; and he always smelled like he just stepped out of the shower. Emma pushed him out of the room, remembering the day she lay helpless after giving birth and wanted everyone in the world to disappear. The women took good care of her, made sure she was comfortable, and most of all, kept the men out of the room.

In the hallway, Orion sulked and then told Emma he'd be waiting in the car after she kissed him and apologized for the outburst.

"How could you," Tamar fussed when she returned to the room.

"Well, that was interesting," said Beaumont.

"I'm sorry, but he's the one that let him in," she pointed at Beaumont, who shrugged.

"Let's give her some space, she needs to rest," he said, then walked Emma to the nursery to see the babies.

After the twins were born, Emma was surprised at how often they sought to include her. When Tamar begged for relief, she relented and would spend the night at their home to babysit. She changed dirty diapers and rocked crying babies until her head spun. How did Tamar do this? Why would she choose vomiting babies over adults who could at least clean up after themselves? This is what Shelly wanted, and Emma ran from. Gone were the nights of dancing until three in the morning with a drink in one hand, while the other fist pumped in the air.

One night while babysitting, Emma threw a bottle in the

trashcan and placed a dirty diaper in the microwave. At first, Emma thought this was karma for dodging out on her own responsibility, but then she realized the reason Tamar called more frequently than she ever had before; they were out having a good time, and Emma was left to tend to their crying babies.

"Sorry, I have an audition," she said, the next Tamar called for a sitter.

"Me and Orion are going out tonight, it's too late to cancel," next it was, "My Dad's in town," and finally, "I think I'm going to be sick for a while."

# NINETEEN

I T STARTED OFF as an uneventful workday, as far as Wednesday's go. Emma recalled the gloom that lingered with her throughout that day. She dreaded the files on her desk that required attention; research for an advertisement bringing awareness to human trafficking.

After her mind went numb, Emma sought out the office Romeo - Alex – a man with jet black hair that he combed to one side in the front and let fall over the rim of his glasses. He craved attention and loved when women in the office stroked his ego. On her way to find Alex, Emma bypassed Naomi's desk. Her head was down, either reading something hidden or maybe even praying. After circling the office twice, Emma approached Naomi's desk.

"Have you seen Alex?"

As she waited a response Emma took notice of the calendar Naomi had before her. That's when she saw the date, March 24th.

"I don't think you'll ever find him hanging out around my desk," she answered, and chuckled.

Emma continued to stare at the date, trying to remember its

significance.

"He avoids me, doesn't like what I have to say…your friend is she alright?" asked Naomi.

"No, I just remembered something I forgot to do," Emma shook her head, then turned to walk away. Her breathing slowed as the room seemed to stand still. Why was she always freaking when Naomi was around?

"Hey, if you need to talk, I'm here," Naomi called out as Emma retreated.

There was an unfinished project on her desk that needed to be done by tomorrow, was the excuse she gave. When Emma returned to her chair, she typed the name, Shelly Duvall, in the search engine.

Looking back over time now, Emma should've known the audition wasn't going to go well. A year ago, on that date, she sat in a birthing tub and pushed out the remains from her abuse. When she left Maine, Emma tried to deny the incident ever happened; but the memories never went away. No matter how much alcohol she drank or how hard she danced, the past couldn't be erased.

When Emma opened the door to her apartment, she groaned first, then kicked off her shoes. Afterward, she went to the cabinet and poured herself a shot from the first bottle in sight. Mad at herself for trying to locate Shelly, she had become annoyed once her search proved futile.

Shelly planned to live off the grid, so it wasn't a surprise that she had no digital footprint. Emma thought of the promise she'd made to come back and check on them. Now the very thing she vowed against, was the very thing she yearned for. If she could see a picture of them, it would ease her curiosity, but there was nothing— not a trace of Shelly anywhere.

Emma considered taking a flight to Maine. She wouldn't have

to see them; maybe leave a note in the mailbox letting Shelly know she was alright. She could leave her phone number in case Shelly wanted to talk. Emma poured another drink, then allowed her thoughts to wander into places where questions demanded answers.

Why would she want to reach out? Because it was the right thing to do. But the adoption, was it even legal? Maybe it was time to tell her Father or Orion? Someone who could give her sound advice, but mostly listen without being judgmental, if that was possible. What she wanted made no sense, but if anyone had walked in her shoes and experienced what she'd gone through, they would understand. But they hadn't, and that was the reason she refused to open up to anyone.

Emma sought out her own answers until she became paranoid. Orion knew…that was the reason he was always 'busy.' Tamar for sure knew…that was the reason she'd been guilted into babysitting duty, the reason she conveniently cut Emma off whenever she came close to confessing. Her Father knew…she saw his pity every time he looked in her eyes and the reason his visits were now less often. Everyone knew—they all secretly talked behind her back, waiting for her to break.

Emma's dread trailed in and out of secret places where her guilt hid.

"Am I being punished?" She probed but still found no answers.

"Nothing can be done about it now." She left one question unanswered, then the next.

"Is there someone I should tell?"

In and out of her internal inquisition, she poured drink after drink. Each time there was no answer, she took another sip from her cup in exchange for the truth. Emma stretched across the sofa and then blacked out, grateful for the sleep that erased conscious thoughts and pulled curtains over unwanted memories.

There was a melody playing—quiet at first, then progressing in tempo. Leaving her unconscious world of sleep, Emma realized that the song was not in her head but instead the ringtone on her cell phone. After checking the Caller ID, she realized her mistake.

"I'm on my way," was her plea for mercy.

"EMMA, WHAT HAPPENED?" his voice boomed like thunder. "You were supposed to audition at 7, it's almost quarter past!" said Lance, her agent. Although his tone lowered an octave, there was a loud demand on his question. His anger was justified. She had prepared for this audition for weeks up until this very day.

"What time is it?" she asked, dreading the question as soon as it left her mouth.

'Stupid, stupid Emma,' the voice scolded her within.

Springing to action, Emma bolted from her couch, whisked down the hallway and into her closet. Without taking a breath, she slid into her dance gear. While clutching a screaming cell phone in one hand and her keys in the other, she made a dash for the front door.

"ARE YOU SLEEPING?" asked Lance, taking deep breaths. "Please, tell me this isn't happening?" he continued. There was nothing she could say at this point to make the situation better.

"Tell me you are not still at home, ASLEEP?" he demanded, and she heard him take another deep breath. Emma knew this was unforgivable, after the weeks of pleading with Lance to get her more auditions.

"I'm here making excuses for you, come to find out sleeping beauty…" he continued ranting on the other end. She pictured him pacing outside the building to blow off steam, talking more to himself than to her.

"Be right there," she stammered and ended the call so she could focus enough to drive.

She wasn't a good driver and still hadn't mastered the art of driving through city traffic. Emma was more upset with herself than he could ever be. It was her dream on the line; Her opportunity, possibly the last shot considering how fierce the competition was in this town.

"Stupid, stupid, stupid Emma," she verbally assaulted herself as she buckled the seat belt and then lurched out of her parking space. How could she have forgotten the most important thing going for her in the world right now? She berated herself over and over at every grueling red light. Glancing at herself in the rearview mirror, she swiped at hair strands and cleaned her smudged mascara.

"You're so close Emma, don't get sloppy," she fussed at her reflection in the mirror, as she disregarded intolerant honking horns and her poor driving maneuvers.

It was Naomi's fault…she had that calendar out that reminded Emma of the date. Shelly was also to blame…if she had been visible on social media then Emma could've spied on them and put her concerns to rest. And Orion, why didn't he call to wish her luck? He knew she had this big audition today. Plus, she didn't eat all day, and she knew better to drink on an empty stomach. Yes, that was part of the reason; whenever she was upset and sipped on an empty stomach, she made mistakes.

When Emma arrived at the studio, Lance was pacing out front with bulging eyes and flared nostrils. Pulling into the parking space, Emma closed her eyes and took a deep breath.

"Don't come over here with your mess, Lance," she chimed, watching him through the rearview mirror as she rechecked the lipstick she smeared on while driving.

"Ugh, God help me," she whispered before exiting the car. Lance was in her face within seconds.

Emma didn't want to seem aloof, but she had to set her mind to perform well, to make up for the error.

"Okay, I made it, let's get the show—" she said, feigning a smile.

"If you want me to start losing faith in you, then keep doing what you're doing," he barked at her while avoiding eye contact.

She was wise enough to keep silent. Lance had good enough reason to boil over. It wasn't just her reputation on the line, but his as well. Emma purposely tuned his drivel out to concentrate on the inner peace she needed for the audition.

Once inside, her face was set, and her stance was sure. This was her element, late or not. She knew that when the music started nothing was going to take this moment from her. It was all she had to give, her expression to the world; pain and brokenness, strength, and endurance.

When the roar from her theme song cued, she closed her eyes and poured out regret with a stretch and drunk gratification on lifted toes in the first position. Then the room blurred around her until the final note faded.

Emma didn't see their faces, there was no need. She felt every move and knew her turns and jumps were perfect. Her dance spoke the secret that wanted to be told, whether they appreciated it or not. Chest rising and falling, she smiled when the music came to an end. The room smiled back at her, then she bowed and left the floor. Lance stopped her at the door and shook her hand, signifying his delight with her performance.

Still pumped with adrenaline, Emma stood in the hallway after the audition feeling victorious for overcoming her fear of driving, and for pulling off an impressive first audition. This was going to be the start to doors opening in her career, she smiled at herself in a corner mirror. As she wiped perspiration from her forehead and cleaned the smudged mascara from her eyes the voice returned.

"Stupid, stupid, Emma, you almost blew it," she thought.

Maybe the performance was enough to make the judging panel forget her tardiness, she rationalized while dabbing at her face with the edge of her shirt. After taking a sip of water, she noticed someone had been watching her. Emma smacked her lips and stared back.

"Can I help you?" she asked the woman who grinned like she had a secret.

"You don't recognize me?" the woman asked.

With hands on her hips, she turned so Emma could get a better look. There was something familiar about the way she spoke, and her eyes, the way they looked like she was saying, 'I have a knife behind my back, and when you're not looking, I'm going to use it.' Her fake smile used as a lure could draw the unsuspecting in for a closer look until it was too late.

"Vickey?" asked Emma.

Of all the people she longed for to be here tonight, the one person she never imagined seeing again stood defiantly before her.

"It's Victoria to you," she declared while looking Emma over, "Well, well, well, it's a small world after all," she continued.

Standing a few inches taller, it seemed she glared down at Emma. She could tell by the flicker in her eyes that Victoria had plans to live up to her name that evening. Then she must've remembered that she still hadn't auditioned yet because her muscles relaxed.

Emma was grateful to see Victoria step away. She couldn't

imagine having to get into a physical brawl after the exhausting performance she just gave. Looking into her eyes, Emma saw the face of hate. Head throbbing and stomach cramped, she locked her knees in position, balled her fist, and prepared to throw the first blow. When Victoria saw Emma's stance, she rolled her eyes.

"You're not worth my energy," she said.

Emma wondered if a truce between them could be possible. Maybe if she gave Victoria a compliment, or wished her well on her audition? She looked amazing; her hair neatly clipped into a high-bun, and her gold-tone eyeshadow complemented her eyes. Instead, jealousy got the better of her.

"Wow, you sure cleaned up well," Emma spat the words, then braced herself for hair pulling and a tussle on the ground. If this was going to end in a fight, she wanted to get at it while some of her energy lingered.

"Yes, I have turned my life around," said Victoria without an argument. She then picked up her duffel bag and pranced away. Emma watched as she retreated, chin in the air, leaping as she stepped. Something was different, her confidence was unnerving. There was no need for Victoria to fight because she'd already won.

Emma seethed on the drive back home, tightening her grip on the steering wheel as she envisioned Victoria center stage, wearing that smug smile aimed directly at Emma. She imagined seeing the billing, The Scene, lead dancer, Victoria. When she was safe in her apartment, Emma shut the door behind her and then screamed until the voice in her head stopped calling her stupid. After an hour, when she feared the neighbors had called 911 to report a crime in progress, she left her apartment.

Emma entered the first bar she could find. That next morning when sunlight seeped through the blinds, she was relieved to be in her own bed, although she had narrowly made it home after 3 a.m. The set alarm on her phone buzzed, and when she reached to turn it off, the room began to spin. Lying in bed with covers pulled over her head, Emma groaned, as she replayed the events of the previous day. She didn't need to wait on Lance's phone call to know that her best wasn't good enough. She rolled over and smashed a pillow over her ears. That must've been when she fell back to sleep.

*In a dream, she saw herself driving a car, fast and reckless. Watching as she dodged a few corners, barely missing concrete objects, she began to lose control. The vehicle careened headfirst into a brick wall, and just before impact.*

When she awoke the time was 9 a.m. Another mad dash through the apartment commenced. "I was in an accident," she thought of the excuse she'd give her supervisor while showering. No, saying it would bring bad karma. It was one thing to be late for work, but then what if she did get in a car accident?

And that dream, it was a warning and confirmation that she shouldn't be driving. Even though she was late, the office was just a few blocks over, and she was quick enough on her feet to make it there in less time than it would take to get in the car, maneuver through traffic, park, and hustle through the building.

While she dressed for work, Emma shivered as the vision of impact replayed in her head. Down the elevator then out the front entrance, her hands trembled. Once out on the sidewalk, she tried to keep pace with the frantic morning rush of New Yorkers in a race to start their day. Eventually, her wobbly legs steadied, as she focused on anything else besides the replay of the nightmare. Otherwise, the stack of unfinished work on her desk had zero chance of being completed today.

By the time Emma made it to the office, it had occurred to her, she never called to say she was running late. When she saw a small group of the office staff huddled around her desk, her face went clammy as her heartbeat quickened.

"Are you ok?" Naomi was the first one to speak.

"Sorry guys, I'm not feeling well," she said.

It was a safe excuse giving that her hands were still trembling, and her stomach was in knots.

"You really don't look good," she heard another concerned coworker say.

"I'll be fine," she said. But before Emma could herd them away, a voice called out.

"In my office, please."

Farid the office manager gestured with his hands for Emma to follow. He was the kind of man who was only interested in the end result, and typically said what was on his mind without looking you in the eyes.

"Please, take a seat," he waved toward a pair of burgundy leather winged chairs.

Emma's knees knocked, which caused her to stumble over her step. When the door thumped closed behind them, she flinched. 'He is going to fire me,' she thought.

"I've meant to have this conversation with you sooner," he began.

It was the last thing she heard. The room grew darker, which caused her to blink to focus on his face, maybe even his desk would be better. She remembered wanting to speak, or yell, but there was a knot in her throat which barely allowed her to breathe—let alone talk. With her shaking hands, Emma managed to rub beads of sweat from her forehead. The next thing she recalled was the sight of

Farid's nose closer to her face than it should've been.

"What are you doing?" She shoved him back as she jumped on her feet.

"Calm down, please," Farid was shushing her. "You fainted, you're not well," he said. "Go home for the rest of the day, we'll talk about the project next week—just go home," he said.

"I'm so sorry, please continue," she stammered.

But it was too late, Farid shifted to his computer and some papers on his desk. "Did I faint?" she asked.

With the wave of his hand he dismissed her, excusing her for the remainder of the day. It was true, she didn't feel well.

# TWENTY

AFTER THAT DREADFUL audition, Emma avoided the studio for two months out of shame. The other dancers were sure to be talking about how their performance had gone, and how unprofessional Emma was—at least that's the story she told herself.

To satisfy her desire for dancing, every party within city limits became her stage. The nightlife replaced Tamar and Orion's absence. She settled into a crew of like-minded people who dreamed of show business, but for whatever reason success was stalled.

Struggling bands, singers, dancers, and actors - everyone who had a talent waiting to be discovered became her companion. They fed on each other's hopes and dreams, pretended to be the other's biggest fan, then secretly preyed on the next person's spotlight.

Emma had heard the talks in the bathroom, as small cliques secretly gathered and gossiped while their target awaited their return. Distasteful pictures posted on social media under the guise of "fun" were guaranteed viral fame. Emma realized it wasn't so hard to be discovered after all.

The problem had become more about controlling what the

world had access to, and less about showcasing talent. Grandma Rose had no idea what the world had evolved into since they'd last seen each other. In her day, the only threat to the Veteran's Hall gossip was a slim possibility of a misquoted mention in the local gazette.

Social media was a rogue beast that devoured everything the eyes could behold. In a day, your career was launched, and then the very next week, with one mishap you could be ruined. Emma learned to trust no one and watch their every move. She was not going to be caught slipping; especially knowing that Victoria was lurking about.

Her girls uploaded more pictures of her in the club. Emma thought she was making a name for herself by creating a following. She arrived early and left late into the next morning. They looked for her to be first through the doors and were elated when Emma already had the table set with drinks.

No one ever asked directly, but occasionally made snide comments about her lovely apartment and ease with money. Emma was dancing less and drinking more and more. She would start at home -just a shot to help while getting dressed - and wouldn't stop until the next morning at 4 a.m. Emma went in and out of the days, hardly giving any thought to Orion's unavailability or Tamar's infrequent phone calls.

It was a Friday evening, and Emma prepared for her usual night out. She had to find the right look for the pictures that would be taken that night. Pulling a red dress out of her closet, she decided it wasn't tight enough. Reaching for a black strapless dress, she figured it would do.

The music blared on her speakers as she set her mind to the evening's festivities. A knock at the front door interrupted her routine. Emma blushed when she saw Orion through the peephole.

There was no phone call or text message, so his visit caught her off guard. When she opened the door, he flashed that smile that knocked down her defenses. She had an urge to throw herself in his arms, but a voice within stopped her. 'Don't you dare give in so easy, do you realize what you just went through to get over him?'

"Is it ok if I come in?" he asked when she failed to step aside.

'Yes,' she thought. 'You may come in and take my heart, stomp it on the ground then toss it out the window.' She denied her smile.

"Why, what do you want?" she said flatly, holding the door partly closed.

"So, you're not going to let me in?"

He raised his eyebrows and leaned closer.

"Actually, I was on my way out—" she started, but he pushed past her and made himself comfortable on the sofa. "Can I help you?" she asked after the door was closed. She remained standing, blinked her eyes, and tried to appear annoyed as best she could.

"I just want to talk," he patted the cushion for her to take a seat. His timing was terrible, barging in unannounced expecting her world to pause at his command. Emma sighed, grabbed her phone to text her girls saying she would be late.

"Ok, what's up?" she asked, refusing to look at him for fear he'd flash that smile she loved, and those eyes would hypnotize her for sure.

"It's been a long time since we've talked," he started.

Emma made a deliberate attempt to recheck her cell phone and read a text message.

"I need to tell you something," he said and leaned forward to make eye contact with her.

She allowed herself to look at him once, then placed the phone closer to block her view. Hearing his request, she wanted no part of his confessional that was sure to ruin her night. Emma had spent months adjusting to Orion's predetermined schedule, never available when she needed him the most.

Finally, she made peace with his inability to be present, and then he shows up like this with some new story. What, that he was married after all? This wasn't part of the plan for the evening. She had her friends now. They didn't expect anything but a good time. Nothing serious; laughs, drinks, loud music, then at the end of the night or morning, they parted ways.

"You know, this is not how I was planning to spend my evening," she said, then stopped when he moved closer.

"I need to tell you something," he tried again, but Emma rolled her eyes to show her annoyance.

"Ok, so you're married," she blurted at him.

"I've never been married," he shook his head. Orion cleared his throat. "I'm not seeing anyone else." He stood and went to the kitchen, "Do you have anything to drink?"

"It's in the cabinet," she huffed.

"How about a drink?"

He returned with two glasses and a bottle. He raised the bottle and half-filled their glasses. She watched as he struggled. She shifted in her seat when she noticed a familiar look on his face. On the night she wrestled with telling her father the truth about her kidnapping, she donned that mask and felt its heaviness as she sought to free herself. Emma took the glass from Orion and drank it fast. When he saw her glass empty, he sipped from his own.

Two weeks? No, that was when she was invited to open mic on a Thursday, he didn't show that night. Three weeks…it had been weeks since she'd seen him last. Although he did text, which was nice of him to let her know he was still alive. His text messages were short; Busy, in a meeting, or, call you back, but taking several days to call her back - and then saying he was still busy. She had finally gotten strong enough to move forward, and here he was, holding her hostage, and she wasn't too thrilled about it.

"So, what is it? And why now?" she demanded.

When she asked him the question, and their eyes finally connected, Orion flashed that smile she loved. His ego had been bruised by her rejection, but when she slipped and looked at him, he lit up like Times Square on New Year's Eve.

"Don't smile at me," she said. With each passing moment, his charm melted her anger.

"I have something I want to tell you, and it's tough," he said.

Emma left the sofa to find something frivolous to busy her hands. There was a cobweb in a corner, so she went for the broom and swept around edges, then checked behind furniture.

"I told you I have plans for tonight," she interjected. "If you're seeing someone else, that's cool, but I'm really busy tonight," she finished.

"I'm not seeing anyone else!" he said, raising his voice and stepping closer.

"Then are you sick?" she asked.

"No," he shook his head again.

"I hope you can say what you need to say in five minutes because I really need to go," she said, then went to put the broom back in the kitchen.

Emma decided that if he wasn't seeing another woman, and he wasn't sick, then whatever guilt he carried was his alone. She was already overburdened with her own baggage, unless…was he trying to tell her that he found out? Did he know about her secret? That had to be it. He was studying law, and attorneys are trained to dig and search for evidence.

"It's getting late, and I have people waiting on me."

She hurried to her bedroom, closing the door behind her. She wracked her brain for an explanation of her past. For a moment, she imagined jumping out of the window. It didn't make any sense, that couldn't have been her thought. But to escape, she needed to get out of there.

"Are you ok?" Orion asked.

He walked down the hall and stood outside her bedroom door.

"Yes, I…cut my finger," she lied.

Then ran to the bathroom for a band-aid to wrap on a dry, uncut finger.

"Ok, when can you make time for me then?" he sighed.

She heard him lean against the wall, waiting for her response.

"How about you call me tomorrow and take me on a date?" she said, then opened the door and walked him back to the living room.

He smiled at her, then agreed to call her first thing in the morning to arrange a date. When he was gone, she exhaled and checked the mirror to make sure her hair and face were on point before leaving the apartment. Emma planned to stay out late that night, but Orion's intrusion earlier soured her mood.

By 12 a.m., she couldn't take another toothy grin or worthless conversation. How was she going to respond to his questions once he told her what he knew?

"Girl, the nights just getting started," someone objected when she asked for the bill and reached for her purse.

"One more dance?" asked a guy, as she waved him off.

"You're not leaving without setting us up?" was their primary concern, but she couldn't help them tonight. Emma needed a quiet place to process her thoughts. This was a conversation she wished to never have with anyone, but maybe it was time. Making her way to the exit, she left with no explanations. ⌒

At home, the noise in her head was just as chaotic as the party she'd just left. Why hadn't she gone to the cops? She couldn't think of a good excuse, at least one that would make sense to Orion. Deep down inside, she knew the real reason. It was because of Gray. He would tell a different story if he was brought in and questioned; one where she complied and even conspired. They had made a deal, one she failed to uphold. Part of his story was the truth, but her side would be the whole truth, and shouldn't that be enough?

After hours of strategizing, she decided to admit only to what Orion uncovered - nothing more, and nothing less. If he knew she had once been reported as a missing person—that was true ...the argument with Reba. Yes, that's what she told her Dad. Emma left after a fight between them.

If by some chance he dug up more information about a baby born, maybe papers signed, then that was different. That's where the roadblock formed in her mind, preventing her from maneuvering around the facts. Spinning out of one bogus excuse to another, there was no explanation past the truth. She hated the truth that insisted on being told.

By morning she had slept all but three hours, if that. No matter how much foundation and eyeshadow she applied, nothing could erase sleep deprivation and her weariness. When Orion called and asked if they could meet for lunch, she smothered a yawn and concealed her exhaustion. Somehow Emma managed to get in another hour of sleep before he showed at noon. To her surprise, the brief nap helped to calm her anxieties and rekindled a spark in her eyes.

He arrived wearing his usual charm and winning smile. The

man always smelled like fresh soap, and that was a bonus. He kissed her on the cheek and handed her a bouquet of roses before they left the apartment.

Emma talked more than she usual, filling him in on the details of restarting dance class, auditions, and trying to maintain work. He listened, mostly, nodded his head at the right moments, encouraging her to keep speaking. The flow of the conversation was natural, and she considered telling him about her past then, but not wanting to sour the mood, she held back. The only time he took his eyes off her was to take a bite of his hamburger. She couldn't deny there was something different about him that seemed somewhat somber.

"I had an encounter with someone you know," he blurted, as she contemplated his health.

Emma raised her eyebrows and then squinted, trying to comprehend the news. What did he mean by an encounter? Had he seen someone she knew? Bumped into someone from her past who possibly knew about—what did he know? They sat looking at each other for a moment. Emma imagined that he waited for her to question him further.

"What did they say about me?" she said, rubbing crumbs from the tabletop, trying to remain calm.

"I don't think you understand what I'm saying," he shook his head, "this has nothing to do with you, I need to confess something," he admitted.

Emma almost snickered, how she kept inadvertently dodging the truth, allowing her secret to stay hidden was a wonder. As discreet as possible she sighed her relief before clearing her throat to speak.

"What's done is done," she said, to both their surprise.

Orion blinked a few times then fumbled with the dinnerware.

"What? But this thing happened," he began.

Emma held up a hand to stop him.

"No need, what's done is done." she repeated.

Emma flashed him a smile then diverted her eyes to a couple in the next booth before commenting on their matching outfits. When turned back to face him, his eyes questioned her calm.

"You're a free man, what you do on your time is your business—what do you want from me?" she asked.

"I miss us, I'd like to make more time for you," he said, lost in the conversation, so he decided to follow her lead.

Emma suggested that they start their relationship from this day forward, forget the past, and whatever encounter happened. He was happy to comply. One of the reasons she didn't mind having the set days with Orion was because…well, it was easier to do what she liked to do. He didn't care to drink, sometimes wine on special occasions. Orion avoided fast-food or staying up late at night, which he considered a waste of time. He was the type that prepped meals for the week and rarely deviated from the planned menu. He worked long hours and still managed to attend law school in the evenings and volunteer on weekends. He was health-conscious and worked out three times a week. At first, his comments about her drinking were out of concern for the empty calories she was consuming. Then after a few months into their reunion, his interest turned more judgmental.

"Wow, seems like you picked up some bad habits while I was gone," he said one night.

Emma didn't think much of her drinking. She liked a cocktail right after work; another before they went out for dinner…and while they ate. "I'm a social drinker," was her response. It was a good defense in her opinion if he was going to act as the prosecutor.

"I don't like to drink, and maybe you should cut down some too?" he said.

After a few more dates and his full account of how many drinks she'd had, Emma resorted to drinking when he wasn't around. The problem was, now he was around quite a bit—thanks to his guilty conscience that wanted to make up for his unnamed encounter.

# TWENTY-ONE

*The Garden*

IN THE GARDEN, Emma lay with her head in Grandma Rose's lap. As she rested her perception gave way to full knowledge and understanding. Visions of a wounded girl trying to cope with life by surrounding herself with partygoers, senseless conversations and superficial laughter, then when alone at night, she cried. Scenes from her life played out like a movie. She now acknowledged the confusion of the masquerade; as her mask was lifted, a reckless existence built around a frenzy for survival was exposed.

Fearing that Grandma Rose could somehow sense, or see the life Emma had created, she tried to shift her thoughts on happier times from her childhood. Then she heard the beeps in the distance. The flowers, was a good distraction—or Grandpa, didn't she want to know how he was doing without her?

"There's nothing you could do that will change my mind about you!" Grandma Rose stroked her hair, tightening her embrace.

Supported by her love and comforted by her presence, Emma relaxed and freed herself to continue a journey of self-awareness. It was hopelessness that caused her to reject the truth. Emma had been so absorbed with the things she couldn't control, she never stopped to acknowledge the answered prayers along the way; the first being how she escaped human trafficking. She was a survivor despite the residue she tirelessly struggled with. Despite the trauma from the incident, she had been strong enough to withstand nine months of pregnancy and then deliver …a healthy baby, complication-free. Neither Reba nor Ogre had been heard from since she fled, and Emma knew full well that some victims in the same situation don't make it home.

Unfortunate cases made headlines of victims who had to fight back, resulting in their captor's death - which led to criminal charges for the survivor. As a teenager, Emma spoke with the women personally during her time at PAHST. She remembered the day she knelt in that room and prayed for a way out, there was no time to rejoice. She lost Biscuit during the escape. Some would call it survivor's guilt; for Emma, retribution was owed.

The story she told herself was the world owed her far more than money could repay. Emma had enough income to see the best therapist in town, but what good would that do. Talking about what happened and how she should work through it...maybe it helped, she'd never given it a try, but like Shelly said, what about the takers?

This was the kind of thinking that led to Shelly's madness. There were never answers, only the voices. So, she drank to forget...to silence the noise...to numb emotions…and to calm her nerves. Grandma Rose wanted to know why her dancing wasn't good enough, well Emma knew the reason.

"I might be an alcoholic!" she finally admitted.

As cliché as it sounds, admitting she had a problem really was the first step towards being free. Once she addressed the severity of her actions, then Emma could face the major calamities that awaited her return behind that beeping door. If not for the peace of the garden and the comfort of seeing people she loved, her admission would not have been possible. Lying across her Grandma's lap, with the cool breeze and smell of lavender, she gently drifted into those painful places in her mind recalling more unfavorable events; all of which she could no longer refute.

•  •  •  •  •  •  •  •  •  •  •

A distinct vision of Tamar sitting across the table during one of their meetings came to mind. She sternly suggested that Emma join an Alcoholics Anonymous group, due to concerns about her appearance, which was "sloppy." Tamar had made comments throughout the years about Emma's 'high tolerance' for alcohol; at the time she mistook the observation for a compliment. Tamar and Orion had every right to be concerned about how much she drank, after all, they were the closest people to her. If they hadn't noticed the problem, then that would be a shame. If it wasn't too late to make things right, she was going to choose to do better. First on the list: stop drinking altogether.

Tamar was as determined to get help for Emma, as she was about any other project she undertook. Emma received daily text messages; Here's an AA meeting not too far from you, going on tonight, with address and phone number included. After receiving about five of those messages, Emma finally caved; Only one meeting! Tamar was so happy she showed up at her front door.

"I'm so happy you agreed to go to a meeting, I'll go with you!"

she said.

Her dazzling smile stretched from ear to ear, as her blue maxi dress swished with the wind created by her strides. Emma recalled the usual bottle of wine was replaced by soda pop and a bag of potato chips.

"Cola?" She asked.

"What's on Lifetime?" she said then clicked the remote control.

Tamar purposely avoided looking back at her. Emma, frustrated with Tamar's meddling, flung the cabinet door open and searched for the ugliest mug she could find. 'Life Sucks Scotch Helps!' declared the crabby lady printed on the mug.

"Interesting choice," said Tamar.

She held the cup out to be filled, exchanging looks they each understood. Tamar grinned as she sipped her soda. Emma sat on the sofa, rolled her eyes, and turned to a music station.

"So why are you pestering me about this group?" Emma frowned.

"We both know the answer to that question."

When Tamar barely flinched, Emma knew Tamar had carefully planned the so-called intervention.

"No, WE both don't know the answer, or I wouldn't have asked the question!" she turned to Tamar, ready for a face-off.

"Don't you think you've been drinking a lot lately?"

It was a direct and straightforward question, but Emma refused to answer; wasn't Tamar the one who used to drink with her all those nights before she decided to get married and start a family? Now that she seemed to have her life together, what gave her the right to pry into Emma's affairs? Seemingly out of left field, Tamar was insisting that she attend AA meetings.

"You're telling me that no one else around you noticed how

much you drink?" Tamar asked.

Emma couldn't answer her then but sitting here now she understood. Orion had noticed she was drinking at every excuse she could come up with.

'Motivation to get up!' She had told him that morning he stayed over. 'One more drink to get the night started!' She announced, the night he agreed to go dancing with her. 'I'm bored, there's nothing else to do!' Another excuse she gave on a Thursday evening. Her co-workers noticed it for sure. Even Alex pointed out, 'You don't seem as on point as you usually are!'

But no one else said anything. They were all drinking right alongside her, just as much in fact. Emma recalled Tamar's puzzled expression when she told her so.

"You don't seem to put the care in what you're wearing anymore!" Tamar complained.

Emma found herself adjusting and tugging at her blouse, then brushed her hair with a free hand.

"Your eyes are puffy," she said.

They had come to know each other so well, Tamar could almost predict what Emma would say next, and Emma knew what Tamar was really thinking; she was disgusted. It was all about self-image and branding with Tamar.

"What'd you do, bring a checklist?" Emma asked, before pulling a mirror out of her handbag to give herself a look-over. They both sighed in unison. Tamar loved Emma like a sister, so the conversation was crucial.

"You work for one of the most prestigious advertising companies in the city!" she exclaimed as if Emma needed to be reminded. She knew who she worked for, and what image the agency expected of her.

"I make that place look better every time I show up!" Emma teased.

They both had to agree she had a wardrobe to turn heads on a fashion runway. Tamar's intervention was as unpleasant as a cross-examination, but Emma knew the only way out was to surrender.

"I'll go to one meeting like I said I would!"

She opted at the time not to tell Tamar that she felt judged.

"Alone!" she said, which satisfied Tamar for the moment.

Approximately two weeks later, Emma attended her first AA meeting, the only meeting, she planned to ever visit. 'I don't belong here!' She thought while the small group convened in a circle. They took turns and introduced themselves one by one. Some spoke their name, others said whatever else they felt comfortable enough to share. All eyes were on Emma at once as she twiddled her fingers. Noticing their blank stares, she worried if her inward scrutiny had slipped out her mouth by accident.

It was Emma's turn to introduce herself. She only needed to give her name, but that seemed to be more information than she cared to offer. "Lynn," she finally said, feeling little guilt for snubbing their kindness. She noticed their smiles and concluded they were a happy bunch for a group of recovering alcoholics. The meeting was ridiculous, in her opinion. Emma's assessment of the others was that they had a problem...she, on the other hand, did not.

She sat in a chair beside Buzz, a husky Hungarian man. His yellowish-stained beard reeked of tobacco, and he seemed to be a somewhat emotional man. Buzz explained to the small group that he came from a long line of alcoholics.

"Nemzedek utan nemzedek...after generation," he explained, "It's hereditary for me and my folks!" he rattled off his excuse.

Nobody seemed to be buying into his plea. So, Buzz sat placidly in his seat, sulking as he explored the rooms' cracks and chipped paint. A question was asked, and before she knew it, Emma was back in the hot seat.

"Well…" she started carefully, unsure of how to respond because she wasn't paying attention. Not caring enough to ask for the question to be repeated, she spoke whatever came to mind, "I don't see it as a problem—I mean, everyone drinks, I have it under control." She gave her defense.

"Come on Hun, who ya think you're fooling?" Roxy, a tall woman grilled.

Emma was upset when no one bothered to bail her out. She imagined the rest of the group was probably used to the antics. Roxy fired away at Emma like a sitting duck. When she spoke, her hands flew about dramatically.

"I used to be the same way, but I finally had to get real with myself," she snapped.

There was something different about this woman, Emma noticed whenever Roxy said "I," her voice was more baritone. She sat on the very edge of her seat, and with each exaggerated gesture, her snug body-con dress was about to reveal some very detailed information to the group.

"The sooner you admit there's a problem, the sooner you'll be on your way to recovery," mumbled James, who said he was an English Professor. "I've been attending AA meetings for the past 5 months." He held up five stubby fingers, as he spoke specifically to Emma. "And let me tell you," he continued nervously, "I still don't want to admit that I have a drinking problem." He paused briefly before continuing, "But the truth is I do!"

Emma observed that James spoke gently as if trying to get a

two-year-old to understand why it was dangerous to play with fire. The room had become uncomfortably silent, enough that she considered leaving. She thought about excusing herself to use the bathroom, then ditch out from there, but before she could execute the plan, James was speaking again.

"The truth is a roomful of students watched as I carried on in a drunken performance—" He managed to finally admit to the group.

"If ya wanted a performance honey, all ya had to do was call Ms. Roxy!"

The group laughed, some tried to hide their smiles.

"Go on, joke all you want!" James blurted out defensively. "My career is on the line, it's no laughing matter for me!"

The room fell silent again.

A frail blonde-haired woman introduced herself as Debra. She sat between Buzz and Roxy and appeared captivated entirely by the circles' increased drama. Debra seemed to be the group-mommy, eager to jump in and cater to any one of their needs. Turning to Emma, Debra shared that she wasn't ashamed to admit she had a "concrete problem." Her attending the meetings was solely for her baby. Debra shared with Emma that her husband was threatening divorce, but that didn't matter much to her.

"If not for my precious baby boy I would've never sought help," she said.

A young girl sat near James, the professor, and alongside the group facilitator. She introduced herself as "Jenny, a 19-year old college student." It was apparent to everyone that the teen was not fully invested. Emma observed that she frequently pulled out her cell phone and mashed buttons, at which the group facilitator would remind everyone.

"No Cell Phones while in the circle, it's a group rule!"

Jenny rolled her eyes and stuffed the phone in her purse.

"I'm only here because my parents aren't going to pay for my classes if I don't!" she reminded the group.

Emma noted how the others took it easy on Jenny. Roxy hardly glanced in her direction, as if boycotting her presence in the group. After sitting and listening for what turned out to be 40 minutes, Emma wondered why two shots of liquor and several drinks on an evening out with friends landed her in a place like this. In her opinion, it was hardly grounds for categorizing her with a drinking problem and seeking treatment for alcohol abuse. But Tamar was threatening to have nothing more to do with her until she did something quick about her "problem." Squirming in her seat, lip turned down in protest, Emma decided that enough was enough.

"I hate to be a party-pooper," she stood and reached for her purse, "But I've got to go!" She was kind enough to take the pamphlet that was given to her when she arrived. All five feet, eight inches of her frame was at the door within four quick strides. When her hand touched the doorknob, she heard someone smirk, and another gently protest. Then the door shut behind her.

"You can run Boo, but ya can't hide," Roxy called out.

Emma could still hear her banter behind the closed door.

"The genie in the bottle will find you, and when it does, we'll be right here waiting on you!"

Once on the street, Emma breathed in the early evening air and began to feel the tension release from her shoulders. That room, she thought, made her feel low and somehow dirty. Now back on the sidewalk, she felt cleaner. Glancing in a storefront window, Emma caught a reflection of herself. Her jeans and blouse fit perfectly, hair pulled back, she didn't look like a woman that had a problem. The many years of dance lessons had given her a straight posture and graceful steps.

A man sat on the sidewalk and held a brown paper bag to his lips. She didn't expect he'd catch her staring, but before she could look away, he saw her.

"Have a drink?" He held the brown paper bag up.

"No, thank you," Emma replied, quickening her steps to a jog.

"Yes, I do need a drink!"

She calculated the distance home to include a stop by the liquor mart. When she entered the store, she remembered Roxy, wagging a finger taunting about the genie in the bottle. Then Tamar, what she would say about her leaving the meeting and getting a bottle. Mostly she thought of what she'd feel like once at home and after she poured herself the first drink. Emma couldn't make it in the door quick enough before she heard her cell phone beep. It was a text message, but she hoped it was from Orion. Throwing her bag on the counter, she rushed to the kitchen to find herself a glass before reading her text message.

**Tamar: How was your meeting :-)**

For a split second, she felt guilty for having a drink, but then reminded herself that she never promised to stop drinking, only to attend one meeting.

**Emma: Interesting group of people!**

Taking the first sip from her glass, she downed the drink in one full swallow. **Tamar: Details**

Emma reached for the bottle and poured another drink.

**Emma:** It was enlightening, I'm cured!

**Tamar:** ???  She probed for more details.

Emma searched the internet for a picture of a nun.

**Tamar:** LOL, in your dreams!

The tension from the evening was beginning to wane, but what came in its place was far worse. Emma didn't want to admit feeling depressed, but for some reason, she just felt 'blah.' If she could get through another glass or two, she'd pass out and not have to deal with the unwanted emotions.

"Not tonight!" she spoke out loud, trying as best she could to reject her unwelcomed guest. Guilt wanted to attend her party for one. Emma sighed when the voice began to speak.

"You gave up too easily."

It said in the most detestable voice she'd ever heard.

"Like you always do!"

The voice continued to antagonize her. Emma didn't know it then, but she understood now, the ugly voice was birthed from her own anxieties. If she had the insight then, maybe she wouldn't have drunk so much that night. Emma recalled the last conversation with.

"I'm tired of making excuses for you to the kids and to Beaumont…"

Emma frowned. So, this was coming from Beaumont? He didn't like her from the start, she thought. Now that he had her friend and the babies, he wanted to squeeze Emma out of the picture entirely. She couldn't stop herself from what happened next. She dialed Tamar's phone number and gave her a sloppy piece of her mind. Anything and everything she wanted to get off her chest were unloaded. By morning Emma faintly recalled the conversation, but whatever she told Tamar warranted a face-to-face meeting at her job that next day.

"Drunk or sober, don't you ever put your mouth on my babies again!" she said sternly.

Because she cared for Emma like a sister, she gave her a warning. Then, when she got home from work, there were several messages from her Father on the answering machine. He was coming out for the weekend, just because he was thinking of her. Emma knew Tamar was behind his impromptu visit. She promised him years ago that she'd let him know if anything happened to his princess. Tamar kept her word.

Her Father gave an excuse that he had been invited to Tamar's twins' birthday party, which Emma forgot all about. Tamar hadn't uninvited her, so whether she liked it or not, she and her Dad were going together. He wasted no time booking a flight and arrived by the end of that week. When her father arrived in town, Emma noticed how he watched over her.

"How are you eating?" he wanted to know.

"And work?" he questioned, "What about continuing your education?"

Work was good, eating three meals a day, and haven't started school yet. I'm fine, don't worry, she assured him. At the birthday party, Tamar conveniently found herself alone with him in the kitchen. Emma saw them talking but refrained from joining the conversation. At first due to not wanting to appear guilty, then deciding that what Tamar had to tell him didn't matter. There was nothing she could say to change the way her Daddy cared for her. His role was to keep her finances in order, and he did that well.

# TWENTY-TWO

HAIR IN A ponytail, very little makeup, and an oversized blouse over her leggings, Emma barely pulled it together for work. She was tired, dehydrated, and could feel tightness in her forehead as a headache slowly built up momentum. Remembering that a report waited on her desk unfinished and was due by 5pm, she shrank into her chair. There was no way it'd be done with her in this condition. Standing, she decided that coffee and chocolate… lots of chocolate, was her only hope.

Naomi stood at the vending machine when she entered the break room. Typically, Emma would run in the opposite direction, steal a peak from behind a corner, then wait until she saw the coast was clear. Thanks to her throbbing head and semi-inebriated state, she lacked the agility to quickly move out of sight. Emma figured if she kept silent and avoided eye contact, then Naomi would take the hint and give her some space.

That was the plan, just get the goods and get out unnoticed. When she caught a glimpse of Naomi her defenses weakened.

"Hi," she mumbled then looked away.

Naomi patted her on the arm as she walked by to sit at a table in the corner. She didn't speak a word, not even to ask how Emma was doing.

As she bent down to retrieve her goods from the bottom of the vending machine, Emma watched her through the glass. Moving to the coffee machine, she continued to secretly spy on Naomi, who was engrossed in reading something. It was a thick book, and Emma could see by the frayed edges that it was well read. When Naomi lifted her head momentarily, Emma turned away then pretended to read a notice on the bulletin board. She looked once more, Naomi's head was down again, unaware that she was being stalked.

Meaning to take a step in the direction to leave the break room, Emma turned around just before she reached the door; then marched over in Naomi's direction. Maybe she wasn't feeling well and wanted Emma to comfort her this time. She was always kind and quick to offer words of encouragement to others when they were down, it wouldn't hurt for Emma to try and return the kindness.

"How's it going?" asked Emma, the coffee hot in her hands, she frowned and set the mug on the tabletop.

"All is well," Naomi answered.

A peculiar response in Emma's opinion, but she was familiar with Naomi's odd way of speaking.

"Must be a good book!" she sat down without an invitation.

"It is," Naomi smiled.

Taking a sip from her coffee, she continued to observe Naomi, who would occasionally write something down in the margin of her page or highlight some words. She thought to ask for help with her report and wondered how to phrase the question. When Naomi finally looked at her, Emma seized the opportunity.

"I have a report due by 5," She poked her lips out, looked down and sighed hoping to portray helplessness.⌒

"Are you asking for help?" said Naomi, she twisted her lips.

"If you don't mind?" Emma whined. Of course, she didn't, Emma knew Naomi was a helper, it came naturally for her.

Grabbing what was left of her coffee and chocolate, she tried to stand but instead remained seated. Taking another sip of the java, she watched as Naomi continued to read; highlighter in hand, she marked through a paragraph.

"What are you reading?" she asked, her curiosity growing.

"The Bible," said Naomi.

Emma gasped, blinked a few times while her mouth hung open. She couldn't conceal her shock, on purpose. Naomi chuckled and kept reading. Emma wanted to know why she was sitting in a break room, at work, on a Tuesday for that matter, reading The Bible?

"Did you lose a bet?" she teased.

Naomi closed her Bible, looked Emma in the eyes and spoke gently.

"Food for the soul," she said.

"Oh, you're religious!"

"I'm a believer—" said Naomi, then paused seeing Emma's confused expression. "—In Jesus…you know, the Way, the Truth, the Light!"

Emma didn't understand what she was getting at, but she did believe in Jesus. She remembered Grandma Rose told her to pray in hard times; call on Jesus, if she didn't know what to pray. There was a Bible at her Grandparents' house, but she had never heard of anyone reading it outside of Church. Emma slid her hand across the table and grasped hold of the Bible, then turned it over for further inspection.

"It's like a history book," Emma frowned. She wasn't fond of History. Naomi nodded her agreement.

"Except it tells of the past, present and the future," she clarified.

Emma opened her mouth but then decided some things were better left unsaid. Looking from Naomi to the Bible, and then back to Naomi, she had more questions but wasn't sure how to put them into words. She was more surprised at her growing interest in Naomi and wanted to know what was her problem that she needed to read the Bible on her own time. Emma scrutinized Naomi carefully, trying to discern if she too had a secret.

"How old are you?" Emma asked.

Naomi giggled before she answered, "Twenty-five."

Emma judged her business suit, minimal makeup if any, and a pendant hung from around her neck. She was pretty in the face but was more modest than most women her age. Emma wondered who were her friends and where she hung out? They had worked together for over three years now, and it never crossed Emma's mind before now that Naomi could be lonely and yearning for friendship, if so, she had an awkward way of showing it. From her first day on the job, Emma noticed how different Naomi was from the others; keeping to herself mostly, placing little thought or energy into what others were doing in the office. She stayed in her own lane and seemed content.

Emma decided to make more of an effort to include Naomi in conversations whenever possible. She even considered inviting Naomi out on a Friday or Saturday evening. Her crew at the nightclub might find her odd at first, but they were a self-absorbed group that probably wouldn't notice the extra person until they already saw double after too many shots anyway.

"Emma?" she rapped on the table to get her attention. "Have you ever read the Bible?" asked Naomi.

"I've never known anyone to read it!" said Emma, defensively.

She ran her fingers across the leather binding, then flipped through some pages, glancing at the many words before stopping on a random page, John.

"Jesus answered and said unto him, Verily, verily, I say unto thee, except a man be born again, he cannot see the kingdom of God." She shut the book then slid it back across the table to Naomi.

"Who is John, why is it written like that?" she wrinkled her nose, "sounds ancient, verily, I say unto thee." She waved a hand in the air and dismissed her own questions. There was still the report waiting at her desk, no need to complicate the day further.

"It means you; He's referring to you, and me." Naomi smiled, pushed her Bible to the side, and pulled a sandwich out of her lunch bag.

Emma was more confused now than ever, the words, her questions, Naomi writing and highlighting in her book—the Bible.

"Why were you writing in there? Isn't it supposed to be holy or something like that?" she asked.

Naomi nodded her head as she swallowed a bite of her sandwich.

"It is the Word of God," she mumbled.

"I don't think you should be marking up the Bible like that!" Emma frowned admonishing her, Naomi chuckled. "I'll let you finish your lunch—will you still be able to help me with that report?" She feared her words had offended Naomi.

"Absolutely!" she said.

Alex entered the break room, and Emma excused herself before he caught them together. When she walked past him, he winked, expecting her to respond in the usual manner. Not sure if Naomi was watching, she ignored his advance.

Emma replayed the discussion as she walked down the hallway. She remembered the words on the page, "♪ Verily, verily, ♪" repeated in her mind. By the time she reached her desk, she had hummed a tune with the words.

"♪ Verily, verily ♪" she sang then turned on her desktop monitor.

"♪ Verily, verily ♪" repeating, as she typed. Grandma Rose had talked about this Jesus. The one she understood to be a good man, whether you believed in him or not, he didn't deserve to be beaten like that, and hung on a cross!

Emma pulled out her files, then opened an excel spreadsheet, and continued her song. She tapped her feet, then clicked on her keyboard, "♪ Verily, verily," all while singing a song she had never heard before. By the time Naomi stopped by her desk - forty minutes later - they were both surprised that Emma had completed her project.

"After our conversation, I marched back to my desk…you saw I had to avoid that Alex—well, never mind that, but before I knew what happened I was finished!" she said, throwing her hands in the air excitedly. Naomi laughed with her until a male's voice joined them. Turning around, she saw it was Alex.

"Great job, Emma!" repeated Naomi, then excused herself quickly.

Emma observed Naomi's behavior as she left. She stepped away, making sure none of her touched any part of him. Most of the women in the office flocked to Alex, Naomi was not like the rest. To her surprise, Emma was disappointed when Naomi was gone. They had shared a moment just before Alex's intrusion. It was the first time she had laughed in some time, and it reminded her of the days she and Tamar shared together before everything changed.

The group she hung around in the night liked to joke and laugh at one another. There communication centered around who could be the most sarcastic, the funniest, and draw the most attention. The exchange with Naomi was genuine and calm, which made Emma feel like she could let her defenses down. In some ways, she reminded Emma of Shelly except Naomi was more at peace with herself. Naomi was hope, and Emma found that part of her refreshing. She wanted to call her back, convince her to stay so they could continue their conversation.

Alex sat in the seat intended for Naomi. His smile revealed most of his teeth, grinning like a hyena in pursuit of exhausted prey. Her imagination ran wild, and strangely, she envisioned blood smeared across his lips, barely dry, from devouring his last victim. His dark eyes, hollow and menacing searched over her, sized her up. He was a tad bulky around the middle and strutted like a juvenile male lion, whose only goal was to eat and mate with every female that crossed his path.

On days when she was feeling low, Emma sought him out, for a confidence boost. She liked it when he'd point out how beautiful her eyes were, and how gorgeous she looked with her hair curled, flowing around her face! She'd smile back at him and say, "I know!" winking, as she walked away. Today, she didn't want or need his affirmations. Alex's cologne sat down before he did, and Emma inhaled more than she wanted to, then frowned.

"Can I help you?" she uttered while holding her breath, turning her back to him hoping to appear busy.

"Have you thought about my offer?"

Emma bit her lip, remembering his offer to take her on a date.

He leaned forward and rested an arm around the back of her chair.

"Uh, can I get back to you tomorrow? I really need to get this done by the end of the day." She said over her shoulders, refusing to face him.

Alex had a reputation around the office of dating girls and then breaking up with them. She had devised a plan to turn the tables on him when she was ready and on her terms.

"Alright, get at me when you can!" were his parting words.

She cringed when he leaned in and whispered in her ear. Once he was gone she scolded herself for not telling him she already had a boyfriend.

"Hold that elevator!" he called out, as he disappeared around a corner.

She released a breath after he entered, and the doors closed behind him.

"Verily, verily I say unto thee."

The tune returned once her space resumed to quiet. She meditated on the words that reminded her of old-world literature, Shakespeare perhaps. Emma remembered reading Othello and Julius Caesar in high school.

"Et tu, Brute?" the famous last words of Caesar, after he was betrayed and stabbed to death came to mind. Emma had little knowledge of Jesus but knew like Caesar, Jesus had been betrayed by someone close to him.

"What was his name?"

She typed the question into her search engine, 'Judas Iscariot.' There was a picture of a man kissing another on the cheek.

"Judas is known for the kiss and betrayal of Jesus to the Sanhedrin for thirty silver coins."

The article discussed who Judas was, his role as one of the

original 12 disciples, his betrayal of Jesus, and his gruesome death in the field of blood. It was an interesting article with colorful 16th-century paintings included.

"Old world literature, like I thought!" She shook her head and closed the search.

It was 5:10pm, and she was still at her desk. Shutting down the computer and overhead lights, Emma's mind was consumed with thoughts of a new friendship. Usually, she'd be one of the first at the elevator by 4:45 trying to beat the mad rush out of the building and onto 16th street. Otherwise, she'd be caught amongst the workers turned zombie-like, with tunnel vision and memorized steps, marching in unison to blaring taxicabs, speeding subways, and screeching city buses. One too many briefcases had jutted into her legs and thighs during the people stampede, threatening to dislocate her kneecaps and leaving a bruise for over a week.

Today, she'd plan to stay back ten minutes, timing her departure to coincide with Naomi's. Emma was aware of the shift in her thoughts that centered around a small spark ignited after her conversation with Naomi. Their brief encounter had aroused a hunger for answers to questions she never had before. Emma waited by the elevator, hoping to ride down with Naomi, then sulked out the building realizing she had miscalculated Naomi's departure. Strolling through Central Park, she considered each of her current associations.

Who would be the Judas in her circle? Initially, there was a circle of seven, herself and Tamar included. Tamar was now enjoying her bliss with Beaumont, which narrowed it down to the six of them. "Out of the five, is there anyone that I can trust?" She searched for an answer while making a careful inspection of each friend… Gianna, Tamia, Sofia, Kaylee, and Faith.

Gianna was one that she clicked with the most. She was a soft-spoken young lady from London, with dark hair and eyes. Gianna loved to talk and befriended everyone she met, which is why she and Emma were the closest.

Tamia and Sofia were twins, not only sisters but also best friends; they enjoyed one another's company and shared a secret language between them. They had an impressive social media following which centered on their fashion sense and hairstyles where they posted weekly blogs that demonstrated how to look good on a modest budget. Tamia and Sofia tended to discount Emma's input because of her noticeable deep pockets. Nonetheless, Emma enjoyed watching their videos, which gave her a few pointers on how to better style her over-priced threads.

Kaylee was a talented actress and dancer. She had a headful of ginger-colored curls and a fiery personality to match. She found minimal success as a model, doing print work for a local agency. In very little time she landed a part in two commercials and was now auditioning for movie roles.

"Anyone standing in between me and that door to success, is a target!" She would often announce to anyone within earshot. Kaylee was set on a course for stardom and was strategic about where she was seen and the company she kept.

Then there was Faith, the protector of the group.

"Making sure my girls are straight!" was her only concern.

She knew the streets; what to avoid and who not to get caught up with. Faith liked to intimidate her opponents and would quickly remind them that a "serious dude in the Bronx" owed her a favor. No one wanted to know if she could make good on the threat or dared ask why someone obviously dangerous owed her a favor?

Most people left Faith alone; when she inserted herself into a debate Tamar, Mia and Sofia had over natural vs. permed hair, they knew not to question her. She was black and a Latina, and let it be known that she was a woman of color, no matter which way you sliced her. Besides, she knew a "serious dude from the Bronx" that owed her a favor. They were a colorful group of young women, but for all that variety, talent and gift for gab, none of them had stirred Emma in the way that Naomi had.

Emma was home by 7:00pm, after stopping by the corner deli for bottled water and a roast beef sandwich for dinner. Tossing aside the letters she'd just retrieved from her mailbox, she flipped on the television, kicked off her shoes, and pushed the power button on her laptop, practically on autopilot. Next, she checked her cell phone for any missed phone calls or messages. There was a text from Tamar, wanting to know if she would be attending a meeting that evening? After taking two bites from her sandwich, Emma went into her bedroom and changed into jogging pants for a quick run through the park.

Head high, shoulders low, Emma took deep breaths as she ran. Her mind filled with thoughts of Naomi, and what a friendship with her would be like. It could work, the girls would like her too. She didn't talk much but wouldn't need to, and it was more likely that she wouldn't get the chance to speak between herself and Gianna. After about a quarter of a mile into her run, Emma came to her senses and realized that taking Naomi to a bar was complete nonsense.

The location would need to be quiet, where she and Naomi could have an intimate conversation. Naomi would need to be comfortable enough to disclose her secrets. Then, maybe Emma could share how her demons haunted her in the night and threatened to give her no waking peace. By a mile into her run, Emma figured that a person who sat around in the middle of the day with a Bible and markers in hand had to know something! Naomi would be able to shed light on what it meant to be 'born again.' After all, isn't that what it would take to be free of her past? And then there was the tune that replayed in her head.

♪ Verily, verily ♪

Emma turned the volume up on her earbuds, replacing her inner debate with pop tunes. "I wonder if Naomi has a boyfriend." Was one of her final question before the music drowned out her racing thoughts. Emma amused herself with an image of Naomi and a mystery man. It wasn't that Naomi was unattractive, but if she could fix herself up a bit. Add some makeup, raise the hemline on her skirt, maybe a pair of skin-tight jeans. She had beautiful round eyes, and deep-set dimples, with the right outfit, Naomi could turn heads… Perhaps she would like to hang out sometime! They could find other things to do, like shopping and get a bite to eat.

Emma's foot hit the pavement hard, sending a pinch from her heel and up her shin. Ignoring the pain, she ran faster, but when the ache spread, she slowed to a brisk walk. She hoped this would be the night she broke her personal record of making it around the 6.1-mile loop in under 60 minutes. Anything under that would be an accomplishment, as it had taken her a whole year to advance from two hours to 60 minutes. She was hoping for 45 minutes someday, but tonight she limped back to her apartment.

When her cell phone beeped, Emma was happy for the distraction.

**Orion: Can you meet me at community center,**

**coaching tonight, would love you to be there.**

**Emma: Sorry babe, washing my hair stop by after
if you can.**

Watching a bunch of men fall over themselves in pursuit of a ball was not on the agenda for her evening.

"Great, now I'll have to wash my hair, just in case he decides to show up!" she pouted and limped to her bedroom.

# TWENTY-THREE

EMMA SEARCHED FOR Naomi everywhere when she arrived at work the next day. She wasn't at her desk, not in the restroom, nor in the break room or the supply room…she was nowhere to be found. Every time someone walked by her desk, she jumped, hoping to catch Naomi. Why were the words written in old English? And what did it mean, "Except you be born again?"

She needed to know if Naomi understood what it meant to be born again. Was that the reason she highlighted the text? She disappeared so suddenly after their conversation, as if she had found the answers, and was now born again into a new person, maybe someone Emma wouldn't recognize altogether. Not possible, people don't just disappear and reappear as someone else. Jesus was resurrected after death, unless Naomi had—No, not likely!

Mostly Emma wanted to know if Grandma Rose made it to the Kingdom of Heaven. If so, Emma had to make sure to get there as well. That was what she needed to know; was Grandma Rose there, and what was required to get her there too? She needed to speak with Naomi. If I can just make it to Heaven, that'll be good enough for me! She thought, and if her past decisions and actions had separated her from eternal happiness; that would be tragic. After living a life of tragedy, peace in the afterlife was her only hope.

Emma was now on her third search around the office, she scoped out the bathroom, went back to the break- room, then to the conference room. She left the office, got on the elevator, searched on the floor below, then out on the sidewalk in front of the building. The air was chilly as the season showed signs of autumns approach. Emma shivered and went back inside. Instead of the elevator, she walked the stairs, slowly focusing her attention on breathing to calm her nerves. By lunchtime, it was apparent that Naomi was out for the day.

It was not by coincidence that she ended up at Naomi's desk first chance that following morning. Hoping to catch her before the start of the day, Emma skipped her morning coffee and left her apartment 30 minutes earlier than usual. Investigating Naomi's desk; sticky notes affixed to files, pens out of place, stacks of papers shoved in binders. It gave the impression that she had left in a rush.

"Good morning!" she appeared suddenly then dumped another stack of papers on her desk.

"Hey, uh, I see you're really busy, don't mean to disturb you, but what're you doing for lunch today?"

Emma reached over and adjusted the folders filled with papers into a neat pile. Then she moved to the tossed pens and placed them in a pencil holder. Naomi watched her and scratched her head.

"Sorry for my mess, I'm headed out to LaGuardia to wrap up a project in Los Angeles. I won't be back until Monday!" she said, then shuffled on her feet. Emma had rehearsed her questions all morning but now blindsided by Naomi's news, she felt selfish for her intrusion.

"Oh, cool, maybe next week sometime when you're back? When you want, that is we could have lunch. Or coffee? You like Coffee?" she asked.

If there was a word to describe her disappointment after learning that Naomi would be gone for a week, leaving her with those questions, it was panic. It was cruel to give someone enough information to provoke their curiosity and then disappear before their questions were answered.

"Sure, I'd like that," she replied, "Are you ok?" she asked when Emma remained standing at her desk.

Emma nodded her response, then said next week would be excellent, but her mind said, 'there are tiny hairline fractures in this painted mask I wear.' Emma felt if she breathed too hard her world would shatter. She calmed her breathing to a slow rhythm, bunched a wad of material in her hand, then left Naomi's desk. She didn't think to ask for a phone number until after Naomi had left for her trip, so there was nothing more Emma could do but carry on as she'd always done before. That week, Orion must've asked her a dozen times if she was alright.

"Yes," she replied, "just thinking about life."

He was satisfied with her answer. If he sensed that she wasn't truthful, he kept that to himself. When her father called, she asked him what he thought about Heaven?

"Can't wait to get there!" He said with confidence as if he knew by default that's where he was going.

Emma speculated as to whether everyone had a free pass to Heaven by default. No need to question it, just know that's where people go. Or maybe it was where good people go. That's where all people go? Just when she thought she had it figured out; more questions surfaced.

By that following Monday morning, Naomi was not at her desk. Emma, who was sleep-deprived and jittery from one too many javas, wore sunglasses into the office hoping to mask her bugged eyes. She moped throughout the day and ate no food accept an apple left on her desk from the previous week. Nothing was enjoyable, and she knew nothing would be until after she spoke with Naomi. Out of desperation, she turned to the internet, 'What does born again mean,' she typed into the search engine.

Converted to a personal faith in Christ, is what one website reported. Wasn't that what she was, Emma thought. It made her happy, for the moment, as she closed the search and went back to work. Then by midday, confusion set in again. Converted? That didn't sound like a default ticket into Heaven, no it most certainly did not. By the time Emma left work, she had to call her Dad. Either he knew something he forgot to tell her, or she was overthinking this by a long shot. When his voice message came on, Emma threw her own little tantrum.

"Dad, call me, we need to talk about Heaven," she breathed into the receiver. "I don't think you've told me the whole story, or maybe Grandma Rose forgot, but I'm sure you know what we need to talk about by now," she said then ended the call.

It was another sleepless night; this time, Emma avoided her morning cup of coffee. She walked slow, arrived fifteen minutes late, and sulked at her desk. By now, she concluded that everyone was avoiding the talk about Heaven with her because they all knew she was doomed to hell. How did they know this? Some people always knew these things…they all knew, and she had missed the memo.

The morning flew by, but by 12:30 it was her stiff joints, not food, that led Emma to the breakroom.

"There you are!" she said, more exasperated than excited to see

Naomi. "I have searched for you everywhere, these questions—am I going to Heaven or not? Tell me, Naomi, am I going to Hell? I don't want to go there; my Grandma Rose is waiting for me in Heaven!" She couldn't control herself. "Is that why you read the bible? Did you want me to know, too?" she continued.

Naomi took a deep breath and waited for Emma to finish.

"I understand your concerns, let's meet after work," she offered.

Emma was satisfied once some of the questions were out of her head, even though still unanswered. They met on a park bench, and Emma came prepared with a dozen questions.

"I can't give you the answers," Naomi said.

"Why? Why wouldn't you?" Emma wanted to know.

"You have to read the Bible, and seek God for the answers," she told her.

"How do I seek a God that can't be seen and doesn't speak?" Emma questioned.

"Oh, He speaks, you're not listening with spiritually tuned ears," said Naomi.

"Are you sure about that?" Emma questioned Naomi's insanity for a moment.

"Don't freak out, I know this is beyond your understanding, but there's a reason why you have questions, it's time you get some answers!" she said.

Emma nodded her head, then was embarrassed after her eyes welled with tears. She hardly knew Naomi, and here again, was showing her vulnerability. If she wanted to win her over as a friend, she was doing a lousy job thus far.

"Money isn't a problem; I could pay you. Is there something I can do for you; do you need anything?"

Feeling desperate, and at her wits ends, she all but begged for Naomi's time. Five years had passed since her arrival in New York, and what she had to show past her fancy apartment were a meaningless job and superficial friendships.

"How about you meet me here, no need to pay me, just come," she wrote down an address to a Church.

"I've never been, is this necessary?" Emma took the sheet of paper and said she'd think about it.

"What could it hurt, sounds like it's time you gave something else a try!" she suggested.

"Maybe…maybe just one time," said Emma.

It took two full days for Emma to conclude that going to bible study with Naomi on Thursday evening was a harmless gesture. This would be the first time she set foot in a Church as an adult, and she expected to be singled out as a sinner. When she arrived, the others greeted her with open arms and smiles. They were kind, like Naomi, and focused on prayer and reading the bible, like Naomi. Emma didn't return their smiles because she had nothing to be excited about.

They apparently were satisfied with their eternal fate, she, on the other hand, didn't have the contentment of knowing. With her questions still unanswered, Emma needed more than a friendly greeting and kind words to convince her of where she would end up.

"What must I do to be born again?" she asked the minister when he approached.

"You're in the right place, just so happens to be the topic tonight," he informed her before everyone was seated.

"A wise woman asked, what must I do to be born again?" he spoke into the microphone.

Emma sat on her seat and hung on his every word.

"Born of water and Spirit" he informed the small crowd.

He then went on to explain the baptism by water and by the Spirit. How the indwelling of the Holy Spirit took place. Emma believed he was speaking directly to her. The message didn't answer every question she sought but gave her some valuable information to consider. Two hours later when the service ended, Emma was surprised at her desire to visit one day soon.

There was a song in her heart that night while she slept, and it was there in the morning when she opened her eyes. She found out that God was concerned about what had happened to her in the past, and He was concerned with her future. She learned that He already knew everything that happened, and what she had done. The secrets that she worked so hard to conceal; this God knew all about it. That was a huge load off her shoulders since the burden of hiding was beginning to drive her insane. It was going to take a little work—not work, but faith on her part, to believe that she was forgiven, then get baptized of water and Spirit. The baptism was the part that would be her responsibility.

By the time Emma reached the office, fueled with hope, she had greeted her coworkers. The first thing she planned to do was thank Naomi for the invitation to Bible study.

"How's that working for you?" said Alex, pointing to the pamphlets on her desk from the Church service.

"Can I help you with something?" she asked and snatched the paper out of his hand.

"No judgment here," he raised his hands in surrender, "just be warned, you're either in it or you're not with those people."

To her surprise, she nodded in agreement. It would have to be all in or continue falling for Emma to have results. Her drunkenness had changed nothing besides her looks and reputation. She still heard voices, her nightmares had increased, and her confidence had been stripped away in pieces starting from her backyard in Cherry Creek, and when she left Sebec Lake. Emma figured she had nothing more to lose and everything to gain by accepting Jesus as her Lord and Savior. Orion would be pleased, and so would her Dad. Tamar could finally chill out and stop pushing the alcoholic's support group. And if the ugly voices could be silenced, that would be a welcome bonus.

The next time Naomi invited her to Church, it was for a Sunday morning service. Emma said yes without hesitation. The music was soft, then changed to an up-tempo song. The choir lifted their voices and sang hallelujah to a God they loved. The people rejoiced freely, unashamed of what they looked like or how they sounded to the next person. The atmosphere felt alive, charged with an unseen force that soared through the room and aimed straight at Emma's heart.

"What is this feeling?" she asked when her insides quickened, and a tear rolled out of her eyes.

"This is that, which was spoken of by the prophet Joel," said the evangelist before he laid hands on her. Then she did the strangest thing…raising her arms, Emma joined the others as they sang together in unison.

Later that afternoon, she called Orion to share her news.

"I'm getting baptized!" she declared to him.

"You?" He didn't hide his surprise. They had never discussed religion or beliefs. "No offense, that's a good thing," he told her, it was just that the topic never came up, but he was excited. "Let's talk about this more over dinner," he replied.

Next, she needed to inform Tamar, who wasn't answering her phone calls. What she did do was continue sending weekly reminders to encourage AA attendance. Tamar was hard to read and skeptic.

*Tamar: Does this mean you're not going to AA meetings anymore? Don't use this as an excuse to avoid your problems.*

Was Tamar's response to Emma's text message. She tried to convince herself that her friend was not jealous, maybe just a little bit, of her freedom. Tamar was married with children, tied down with a noose and a whip. It had been her own choosing. If Emma stayed out all night and drank herself into debt, she had every right to do so. Not that she wanted to, but she didn't have a husband to run home to, or children whining at her heels.

# PART IV

# *THE ACCIDENT*

*2017*

# TWENTY-FOUR

*The Corridor*

EMMA FELT THE breeze before she saw Him. The Gentleman stood at the opposite end of the fountain. He looked away, then staring at the door, gestured for her to come closer. Without hesitation, she left the bench and walked over to Him.

"Did you know she'd be here?" she asked.

It didn't matter that Grandma Rose had left her, again; Emma knew what needed to be done going forward. She offered Him the flower crown after plucking a bud from the ring.

"What do you see?" He asked.

"The flowers," she said, waving the bud in the air, His silence an indication that she hadn't answered correctly. Closing her eyes, Emma exhaled, then inhaled, "Rows and rows of Lavender fields." When she opened her eyes, she was holding a lavender bud instead of the orange blossom.

"What you choose to see becomes what you believe."

He walked, then came near the door leading back into the corridor, she felt flutters in her stomach, as she went near the entryway. When she turned away from the door, her stomach settled. The Gentleman now following her lead, waited until she was ready to speak.

"Why do some people get away with so much?" she asked.

He held his silence, knowing there was more she wanted to say. With hands on her hips, she looked Him straight in the eyes, "they not only take, but they also leave behind a mess that can't be cleaned or fixed!" she said.

"There's nothing in your past that you can't be saved from. Just say the word," The Gentleman gave her a comforting look.

Emma heard a silent voice within saying, *"Repent."*

Her nostrils flared as she labored with her defiance. Refusing to surrender her desires for revenge to God's will of forgiveness. Again, it came down to what she needed to do and what the others could get away with.

It was Reba who should repent! And Ogre deserved to burn in the eternal lake of fire. Gray hadn't offered to help past his own lusts, shouldn't he repent? Victoria she was a foe long before Emma stole her boyfriend. Tamar AND Orion both needed to repent for their betrayal. She had a growing list of people that had wronged her.

*"What about the babies?"* The silent voice questioned. She swallowed hard, the muscles in her neck stiffened.

"What do you see?" He asked again.

Clamping her mouth shut, a tear fell from her eye.

"The answers to your questions can only be found in truth, when you're ready." He raised his eyebrows and waited to see if she'd taken the bait; instead, Emma sat on the ground, folded her hands behind her head, and laid back in the grass. She wanted nothing to do with the truth if it meant she was the one who'd have to repent. Maybe if she hung around long enough, He'd come up with another solution, one that didn't involve her suffering yet again.

It was comforting to see that He hadn't given up on her, despite her defiance. The Gentleman stood by and waited; she believed He'd wait for as long as needed for her to see things His way.

"I can tell you about truth, that so-called Mother, Reba, abandoned my Dad and me long before she finally moved out."

He shifted on his feet and folded His arms as she explained her position. When Emma saw that she had His attention, she sat up then continued.

"Do you know what that woman and her boyfriend did to me? If my Grandma had been around, they would've never gotten away with it!"

She expected to get a reaction from Him, after all, she was now yelling, and He nor the tranquil garden deserved this treatment. What she wanted Him to understand was that her Mother was a cruel-hearted parent, and because of it, Emma feared she was turning out to be just as heartless.

"People sometimes repeat what they are shown, and yet some make better choices because of it," He spoke.

Emma liked it when He read her thoughts because it gave her a chance to cool down.

"You get to choose, to be better for it or worse?"

His words reminded her of the day she chose to get baptized. Things had gotten better; Emma recalled the days after reading scripture in the Bible before taking a shower, she hid the Word in her heart, then called it to mind throughout her day until the Spirit of God gave her understanding.

There were two paths before her; follow in the way Grandma Rose had instructed or continue the crooked road Reba had shown her. If one stood in judgment of her, Emma appeared to prefer her Mother's ways. Hanging her head down, she continued her discourse toward truth: The very things she hated most in life she was becoming. Like her mother, there was no responsibility for the fragile life she delivered into this world. Though her circumstances had been different, unlike Reba, she didn't have a say in the matter.

No one could fault her for giving up the child and walking away. Still, there was no denying the pain she felt in her soul, stronger than the one she'd felt from her Grandmother's early demise…or even her Dad's. If it was the right thing to do, why was she left with so much grief after her decision?

"Sometimes the loneliness is so great!" she said, refusing to let her tears break free.

"You've held on to it far too long," He reminded her.

*"The Secret."* The voice whispered in the wind.

Emma looked to the Gentleman who knew about everything she hid in her tightly sealed jar. It was His wisdom that spoke to her, bringing forth knowledge and revealed understanding. He nodded, encouraging her to talk.

"Loneliness is comfortable for me, it's what I know."

She had never admitted her friendship with loneliness before, not to Grandma Rose or Tamar. That sometimes when she was happy, she'd search out a place in her mind that gave her permission to feel lonely. "When I'm by myself there are no casualties, it's better this way," she said. He extended His hand when she attempted to stand up.

"What do you see?" he asked yet again.

Emma tightened her throat, knowing He wanted to

provoke her to see what awaited beyond the door. "Behind every act of mankind is a hidden desire." He said, waving one hand in a circular motion. An image of Reba appeared.

*A confused young girl, who packed a tattered suitcase and snuck out of a window, past dark shadows and propositioning men. Leaving Louisiana, she left behind a world of drugs and prostitution in search of a better life than the one she'd been shown from her mother and other relatives. Reba landed in Denver, enrolled in college and not too long after she met an optimistic young man who confessed his love and proposed marriage.*

*Reba was happy to embrace her new life, abandoning her dreams of becoming an actress and singer to support her husband and prepare for motherhood. Then she stood at a door, devastated when her two uncles, the toughest pimps known in the South, tracked her down. Fresh off her honeymoon, they gave her an ultimatum, continue bringing money into the family 'business,' and her new husband lives. Otherwise become a young widow, with any luck she'd get a payout from an insurance policy.*

Speechless, Emma watched as the wave of His hand demolished the stone wall built-up against her Mother. Reba was reacting out of fear; like Emma had done, determined to keep her secrets concealed. More than that, this was her love. She tried to protect them the only way she knew how, by leaving. When she could take the distance no longer, she returned for Emma.

"Aren't you glad you weren't successful?" He said.

Emma bit her lip and looked back towards the pond.

"Back in the room, you and Gray, that was the name you gave

him, right?" He continued, "she was to take your place in the room…you promised to be his if he made sure she—"

"Got a pure dose that took her out." Emma's cheeks flushed, as she finished his sentence, then hung her head in shame. "I've held on to that secret for so long, I don't know if she's dead or alive…did he—did he really do it?" her eyes soaked with the tears she could no longer contain.

"Everything man does good or evil, it is based on hidden desires in the heart," The Gentleman restated, bending to lift Emma's chin up, "Gray—Vulkan McLaughlin, is a lonely businessman, with a family in Iceland who depends on him for their survival back home."

Emma was relieved to know his real name. If only the dilemma surrounding her encounter with Vulkan ended there. No matter where she ran or who she pretended to be, she would always be the girl who was supposed to advocate for survivors of human trafficking, then wound up becoming a victim herself. Emma wanted to put the incident behind her, but it would never leave her, only lying dormant at times to keep her from going completely mad. The events would always be waiting for an opportune moment to threaten the stability of her existence. The only solution Emma saw fitting was—

"Revenge is a misplaced desire; it seeks retribution for a wrong that can't be undone!" He cautioned.

She snorted back tears, wiped her nose with her sleeve, then accepted the fact that the past was gone, and it was time to move on. Thinking that she was free after her secret had been exposed, Emma attempted to think of something positive. There wasn't a Broadway stage built, a nightclub, or a drink that could've given her the relief the Gentleman had just gifted her with. Looking around the garden, to the place where she sat with her Grandma Rose, the flower crown, Lavender, and the spot where she met with her Dad, what made her the happiest was seeing the pond.

"I see the water!"

# TWENTY- FIVE

THE MORNING OF her baptism, Emma awoke from a peculiar dream. She had been in a car wreck, and though the impact was jarring, she walked away unscathed. *Emma saw herself strolling along a roadside that was surrounded by towering mountains. She began to run, slowly at first, then her pace quickened to a sprint. There was a smile on her face, as she continued to run, somehow, knowing that just around the bend of the road something she had been searching for waited; She ran faster, and faster, running still as she awoke.*

The dream left her feeling unsettled and questioning if it was an omen, she grabbed her cell phone and sent Naomi a text message.

**Emma: Hey, I'm feeling weird about today.**

She pressed the button to send her message then pulled the covers over her chest. Clicking on the television, she heard her cell phone alert the response.

**Naomi: What part?**

**Emma: Not feeling well, maybe another time.**

**Naomi: Sorry to hear you're not feeling well, praying for you!**

She planned to get a little more sleep before heading out to shop for groceries. Turning up the volume on her television she sought after a feel-good movie; a woman looking for love pretended to be a Christian to attract a guy she was crushing on...somehow, she ended up truly seeking a relationship with God and got baptized for herself and forgot about her interest in the guy.

Emma turned the channel and found another movie; a man jokingly told another he needed a 'come to Jesus' talk. Annoyed, she turned to the music channel, "♪ Wade in the Water, God's gonna trouble the water ♪" the updated version of an old gospel sang out into her room. Emma reached for her cell phone.

**Emma: I'm feeling better, what time will you be here?**

**Naomi: Glad you're feeling better, I prayed!**

The pews were packed when Naomi and Emma arrived at Church. She was hesitant because of the crowd but then took comfort when the Pastor announced there would be three baptisms that morning.

"Praise God," the congregation clapped.

"Hallelujah!" others shouted.

Naomi gave Emma the thumbs up. Emma was relieved that she didn't have to stand in the spotlight alone. The message that morning was on how Jesus was God manifest in the flesh.

"He did it for love," said the Pastor, "To save the lost and set the captives free."

He explained that the "lost" wasn't merely in location, it was also a mindset; the same as being captive was. People can be lost and enslaved in their thinking, which dictates their behaviors. There was hope, though. Jesus was the Way the Truth and the Light. Through Him, all men could have redemption, be free from a life of sin, and become a new person in Christ. The way to receive this new hope was baptism in Jesus' name.

The congregation lifted their voices and hands, then cheered at hearing this news. They believed in this way, it was their hope. Emma was tired of suffering loss, feeling alone, and being angry at everyone who aided in sending her life into a tailspin of chaos. She wanted her pain to end, the voices to shut up, and the nightmares to stop. Emma wanted what all the people standing around her were excited about.

By the time the Preacher called for the ones who were ready to be baptized, her footsteps were swift in approaching the front of the line. The water was warm and clear, a reflection of the life she hoped to begin after this day. She was instructed to gently pinch her nose, close her mouth, then the Pastor dipped her under. Swaddled in a watery embrace, she imagined the grime and dirt from that room in Breaux Bridge scrubbed off her body, claws from the monster detaching from her soul.

When she came back up, the water falling from her face and torso rinsed away the remaining residue from her mind. It would be left here in the water. Neglect, abandonment, abuse, and shame. Grief from her Grandmother's passing and poor decisions that led to more problems. They could throw the filth out when they dumped the water. Emma was ready to embrace a walk with the One who would never leave her or forsake her; though she couldn't see Him, she felt his presence.

Her heart never beat like this before. There was no drug, or alcohol, no amount of sex, not a song, or extreme sport that could replicate this feeling. Sheer ecstasy and complete nirvana were dull in comparison to this experience. This was what Shelly searched for in the vast universe, chanting to gods under the moonlit sky. These people spoke to God in an unknown tongue, they called it a Holy language that helped them pray with power and believe for a change. When the service ended, Emma craved more.

"How do you feel?" asked Naomi when she was finally able to get a word in between Emma's excitement as she recounted the day's event.

If she had to be honest, it was on the drive home that she began to feel the pull. In between her joy and singing, she heard the voice.

'What about the baby?'

She viewed it as an inopportune time to discuss guilt. The water was supposed to wash away all her negative feelings over giving away the innocent life she considered to be the very spawn of darkness.

"I feel like everything in me is alive, like I hear clearer, I can see much better…" she searched for a deeper meaning or a fancier word to describe her emotions. "Joy, I got this joy in my heart, it's unexplainable!" said Emma.

It was how she felt, but she also had an imaginary fly that buzzed at her ear. Still, her newfound joy was greater than her guilt. This is what Grandma Rose tried to explain as her secret to success, a life of prayer, and a relationship with God. If Emma could describe what she experienced, she would tell everyone about the hope she discovered.

Her Dad would understand, she'd call him later, but first, she needed to tell Tamar, Orion, and anyone else who would listen just five minutes to what she had to say. This feeling was with her, living inside her; hope caused her to see everything around her as life potential. Emma was not alone in this world anymore. She had a God in Heaven that had her on His mind, enough so that He came in the form of man to bring her out of a life of death and into His marvelous light.

The first thing she did was call Tamar, and to her surprise, she answered the phone. It was easier to talk in person, they both agreed; besides, Tamar needed a break from the twins and wanted to discuss a problem between her and Beaumont. By 6:30 that evening, she arrived, bags in hand customarily to their old routine.

"I'm so glad you came, I wish you had been there…it was unexplainable, I'm—I'm at a loss for words, I mean, it feels so good, it is good, right?" she said.

Tamar nodded her head while she hunted through the cabinets, and then the dishwasher.

"Mm-hmm, why aren't your dishes put away?" she asked.

"The message was about living in Christ, that old things would be passed away and all things new, My God, I wish you were there with me!" said Emma.

She began to walk around the living room putting away shoes and papers, knowing Tamar would make her way around to fussing about the mess.

"Cheers!" said Tamar.

She handed Emma a glass after she poured them both a drink from the bottle she had brought. Emma's expression remained the same, but inside, her heart raced. Should she have the drink to memorialize the moment with a toast? One drink wasn't the problem… what it would lead to after was what she feared.

This one drink would lead to another, that would end her back on the hamster wheel again with her existence continually spinning and going nowhere. This wasn't what she envisioned her life to be after getting baptized, she had an expectation for change. Still filled with the excitement from her baptism earlier that day, she observed Tamar raise her glass to her mouth.

"What's wrong, did Naomi tell you it wasn't okay for you to drink?" said Tamar, her hands propped her hip as she smacked her lips.

Emma held her breath, stared at the glass in her hands, and wished she could speak in a Holy language that would call down Heaven, and change wine to water. Then she could drink and be sober without offending her friend. When Tamar saw that Emma wouldn't budge, she pouted, then poured herself another glassful.

"Come on, we need this…besides you're gonna want to drink first before I tell you he latest develops in my world," she poured herself another glass then sat on the sofa.

Emma raised the glass to her lips, took a small sip, then placed the glass on a coaster. Fifteen minutes was all it took for Emma to realize she'd made a mistake in inviting Tamar over that day. In mere moments, a friendship disintegrated into smoke and embers, as one felt disregarded and the other unheard.

Emma figured out Tamar's reason for stopping by had nothing to do with her good news at all. She needed a shoulder to cry on. Why this was a surprise was the real question - she should've known better. Tamar had been unavailable for months, making brief appearances only to scold Emma for drinking too much and hanging out at indecent hours. When she finally started coming back around, it was for her own selfish reasons. She even had the nerve to bring a bottle—after all the complaints about Emma's drinking problem.

Tamar poured her third glass, going into a lengthy reason of how she was feeling different about Beaumont lately, and how she had something eating at her that she needed to get off her chest.

"You know, this was a very special day for me, you were the first person I thought of, I sent you a text message yesterday, you never responded, you don't pick up my calls...now you're here going on and on about your drama," she explained.

Tamar rolled her eyes, knowing Emma was upset by the way she paced back and forth, hands darting in the air as if she was conducting the crescendo in Bohemian Rhapsody.

"Oh, did Naomi tell you to say that?" Tamar rolled her eyes once more, afterward she waved a dismissive hand.

When Emma stood by the front door, Tamar's claws came out.

"All this time I've pleaded with you to check yourself; this chick shows up and the heavens part, give me a break!" she argued, then stormed to the kitchen and crammed her bottle and the other items back in the tote-bag. For Emma, there was nothing more that needed to be said. She held the front door open.

"Call me when you're through being brainwashed!" said Tamar as she made her exit.

Her words were sharp as a snake bite and left a sting long after her departure. Emma felt the venom coursing through her veins and immobilize her heart. After she recovered from the shock, she continued her march around the apartment, picking up clothes and reorganizing papers, emptied the trash and then scrubbed down the counters and mopped the floor. Vexed by the argument, she replayed their words line for line, trying to analyze what went wrong. Tamar wanted her friend back; she wanted Emma to drink with her, listen as she spoke about her troubles, and share in her pain like she always had before.

Emma was willing to be there for Tamar, but first, she needed her friend to share in her good news. Why did Tamar have to be so hot-headed? No, she was jealous. Emma had someone else to confide in now, and that didn't sit well with Tamar, who was now having troubles and wanted her friend back temporarily. She wouldn't have minded if the new friend was shallow like Gianna, but Naomi was a threat because she introduced Emma to a new lifestyle, one that didn't involve her reliance on man alone, but on a living God that knew all things.

These are the things she wished to share with Tamar. If she could have a retake, she'd handle the conversation differently. She'd start by thanking her friend, it was because of her that Emma wanted to change her ways initially. She was proud of the wife, and Mother Tamar was. This new way of living gave her the strength to do what Tamar had been asking her to do all along. If she were still here, sitting on the sofa, minus the drink, Emma would tell her, "When you're ready, come and go with me." She wanted to show her the place where she found freedom from the ghosts that taunted her in dreams and screamed obscenities in her head.

That first week of the rest of her life was bittersweet. On the one hand, she found comfort in studying the Bible at night and discussing what she read with Naomi. On the other, she grieved for Tamar and wished she could share this too with her sister. She was grateful for Naomi, Dear sweet Naomi. She was equally excited with Emma, rejoicing with her when she discovered new revelation.

"What does it mean that man is fallen?" she asked.

"What is sin exactly?"

"Is it ok to drink, do I have to stop listening to my favorite songs now?" She questioned every aspect of her life because nothing she'd done up to this point felt like she was on the right path.

"What does the Bible say about it?" Naomi refused to give her an answer. Telling her she could find to answers to all her questions there. Because of her desperation, Emma downloaded a Bible app on her cell phone, glancing at it whenever she could spare a few moments.

Naomi was attentive, making herself available whenever Emma asked for a moment; meet me in the breakroom, she replied without hesitation. Their discussion was endless, each new revelation led to another question. Lunch break conversations carried over to evening phone calls, then continued the next day.

By Friday evening, Emma and Naomi made plans to hang out at her apartment to conclude a week-long debate. What does it mean to be a new creation? Specifically, how was she going to be 'new,' when she was haunted by past circumstances? Move forward and never look back—If only things were that easy. Emma needed reassurance that her past wouldn't catch up to her present or future. No matter how hard she tried, the threat of Reba was around every corner, hidden amongst every crowded block. One day she'd see her mother again, and she was going to have to extend forgiveness.

"Sounds like you're struggling with condemnation," said Naomi, "like you have guilt or shame for something in your past!"

Compelled by the love Naomi had shown her over the past weeks, she considered having the talk she dreaded for years. Naomi never pried, only offered an outstretched hand to lift her up. This was a woman that could be trusted with her horrid secret.

"Well, there is something—"

Her cell phone beeped before she could confess. Checking the text message allowed her time to think about what, or how much, she should disclose.

The message was from Orion, who was in the neighborhood and wanted to know if he could stop in briefly. Emma debated inwardly, she wanted to see him but was nervous because Naomi was there. Then she considered his smile that turned her stomach to mush and decided it was safer for him to visit while she had a back-up, with Naomi around he would be less of a temptation.

This was apart of her other dilemma, expectations of dating as a newly converted Christian. She didn't need to read the Bible to know abstinence was preferred, until marriage. At least that's what Grandma Rose told her when she entered junior high school and noticed Emma blushing at a boy.

"Is everything ok?" asked Naomi.

Emma held on to her cell phone, the silence growing between them.

"This guy I'm dating, he wants to stop by, this will be my first time seeing him since my baptism," said Emma, she looked to Naomi then tried to gage her approval or at least that she understood Emma's confusion.

"Oh, I can leave if you'd like some privacy…or I could stay?" she said, after reading the conflict in Emma's eyes.

"I think you better stay; he smells really good!" said Emma, she blushed after the words were spoken.

Naomi raised her eyelids and nodded her head, indicating that she understood. They'd never discussed the topic of men and dating beforehand, Emma assumed that Naomi was inexperienced, now she wondered if she'd had her own struggles, possibly some fails, with men. Overcome with curiosity, she set her mind to probe, that's when the doorbell buzzed.

When she opened the door, her first response was to act unhappy with him for showing up without waiting for her answer, but his smile made her forget what it was she had been upset about.

"Baby girl, you are looking good!" he said, then pulled her closer.

When he squeezed her in his arms, she inhaled his scent, then melted when he kissed her.

"Come in, I want you to meet my friend," she said, then pried herself from out of his arms sooner then she wanted to.

She introduced Orion to Naomi and told him about the day she got baptized and how she had a new perspective on life and was hopeful about her future. He listened to every word, asked Naomi how long she'd been in Church, then shared how his father had once been a minister at the very Church she attended. He had never told Emma this before, nor had she known that his parents were ministers.

"Well, Evangelists actually, I was born in Ghana while my parents were missionaries" he told them.

She noticed how comfortable he had been talking about his religious beliefs with Naomi. He shared memories of his childhood, watching as his parents prayed for other and expressed their burden to lead people to Christ. After hearing of his upbringing Orion's passion for serving other's made sense.

When she got around to calling her Father, it was a week later. He apologized for not being there for her, and she assured him it wasn't his fault because she failed to inform him in advance.

"Still, I would've liked to have been there for you, I should've been there."

Emma felt like there was something more he wanted to share.

"If anything should ever happen to me, there's a safe deposit box, the keys are in my desk drawer, the one in my home office—"

"Did something happen?" Emma interrupted, she stopped listening past 'should ever happen to me,'

"No, but if something were to happen, you are my beneficiary—"

"Where's Reba, did you see her?" she asked.

"Reba moved away a long time ago, she's somewhere in Louisiana," he assured her.

"When are you coming to see me?"

"Soon as I can, keep up the good work and while you're at it, enroll in school!" he said, before ending the call.

There was an unnerving tone to the phone call, and an unsettled feeling in the pit of her stomach, if it wasn't Reba, then something or someone else had upset him. It was her first time praying for another person, she asked the Lord to give her Dad peace about whatever was troubling him and fill him with a love that replaced Reba's betrayal.

# TWENTY-SIX

GUILT AND SHAME, Emma had come to learn were constant irritants. They served as reminders of past mistakes that needed to be avoided. When she saw an advertisement with a baby, she cringed, then a silent voice spoke to her.

"This is love."

Emma was incapable of raising the child born from her body, but she was sure the girl was happy and thriving with a mommy that showered her with love and affection.

Emma imagined the child growing, being taught healthy eating habits, and a passion for nature and life. If she could speak with Shelly now, she'd share all the beautiful things she'd learned on her journey. Not everyone was a "taker" as Shelly called them. Some people found strength in unity and love in fellowship. If Shelly could only believe, she could have this peace too.

Emma considered trying another search for her friend and even thought about hiring a private investigator. Before she turned on her laptop, her cell phone rang. Gianna wanted Emma to know they were having a surprise birthday party for the twins, Tamia and Sofia.

Emma had to be there.

"Hey, I forgot to tell you I got baptized two weeks ago, it was the most amazing experience of my life—"

"That's good, we'll see you at 7 on Friday!" she said, then hung up the phone.

It seemed as though every time she attempted to take another step forward, someone either stood in her way, or sent her reeling two steps backward. Just when she was getting over the loss of Tamar's friendship, it was now time to face Gianna and the rest of the squad. Emma wondered if they'd consider her brainwashed like Tamar. Of course, she could decline the offer, but that would lead to a continual stream of excuses.

"I'm a Christian now!" she practiced saying to her friends.

"Yeah, so am I," someone was bound to point out. Or she imagined them asking if she'd gotten herself mixed in with a cult. Why couldn't she tell them she hadn't felt this good since the days spent with her Grandma Rose in Castle Rock, or even the times running across her lawn with Biscuit. It was a restless sleep that night as she pondered her decision.

"What's wrong?" asked Naomi when they met for lunch that next day.

"I was invited to a birthday party on Friday, and I'm feeling conflicted about going," she said, hoping her facial expression matched her grief.

"That's a tough one, what's this group like?"

Emma saw the concern in Naomi's eyes when she described them one by one. "What if you told them beforehand that you had to leave at a certain time?" said Naomi.

"That's an idea, but I'd rather not go…I'm nervous about it," Emma said. If she went, she'd face them all at once, tell them about her change, and be done with it. Naomi asked for a check-in after the party. She was sure it was going to turn out well.

When Friday came, Naomi informed Emma that she wanted to attend the party with her and if she thought her friends would mind.

"Not this crowd," said Emma, "the more, the merrier."

It was her first answered prayer since getting baptized, a way of escape from the temptation that lay ahead.

To her surprise, Naomi wore a modest but appealing black dress and gold embellished heels. A classy ensemble that said this woman was sure of herself. The party was held on a rooftop lounge, and Emma could hear the music before they opened the door. When Gianna spotted Emma, she waved her to their table.

"Who's your friend?" She looked Naomi over, then smelled for weakness. Before Emma could respond, Naomi introduced herself.

"I'm Naomi, nice to meet you."

"I don't think you'll find anyone to your liking around here," said Gianna.

"Oh, among all these faces there's not one lost soul?" Naomi questioned.

Her eyes scanned the crowd. Emma gasped when Gianna hurried out of their presence.

"Don't look so shocked, I've witnessed to much tougher crowds than this!"

Emma was relieved to know Naomi could hold her own, until she saw Gianna whisper in Faith and Kaylee's ear, and then point in their direction.

"What's good? Is she with you?" asked Faith, being the toughest of them all, approached ahead of the rest.

"I'm just passing through, but I wanted to wish Tamia and Sophia a happy birthday before I head out," said Emma. She failed to introduce Naomi.

"And who do we have here?" she asked.

When Naomi extended her hand, Faith glared at her.

"Oh, I'm just a nobody, trying to tell—"

"EVERYBODY ABOUT SOMEBODY WHO CAN SAVE ANYBODY!" Faith and Naomi said in unison.

"That's my momma's favorite song. She used to sing it to me all the time when I was a kid," said Faith.

When Faith and Naomi sang a few bars of the song, Gianna and Kaylee frowned behind her back. This was Emma's second answered prayer since being saved. After the birthday ladies arrived, the attention shifted. Emma and Naomi were left in a corner while the others joined the celebration.

"How do you do it, you're different from the others our age, and yet you're comfortable with it," said Emma.

"I haven't always been, and sometimes I'm not—you learn to pray through it all," she said. "I have a few years on you, in age and in my Christian walk. It doesn't make it easier, but you learn quickly; the only way to survive is by having a prayer life," Naomi explained.

What was this prayer life Emma wanted to know? Naomi explained it was in all things, and in every situation, praying. The hardest was to pray when it seemed like prayers were going unanswered, and the more you prayed, the more things appeared to get worse. This was the time, Naomi explained, "where faith is stretched, and trust in God is tested." By the time Emma's preset alarm beeped, they had become so engrossed in conversation that it seemed a disappointment to leave.

"To be continued," they'd learn to say to one another.

Emma said goodbye to her old squad, who hugged them both and invited Naomi to hang out with them sometimes if she wanted.

"This isn't something I usually do, but thanks for the invite," she said politely.

"It's all good girl, look we cut up when we get together—drinking and some other stuff going down, but much love and respect, come through when you want," said Faith, as Emma and Naomi made their exit.

Two months into her new life, Emma was now attending church services on Sunday and Bible study midweek. She was surprised that her father had not visited since hearing her news. When she called him, he was brief, told her everything was fine and as soon as he could, he'd be there. Three months later her suspicions were confirmed by a phone call from an unknown woman, a lady friend of her father's. She was more than a friend, and they'd been seeing each other for a few years now.

This wasn't the way she wanted to introduce herself to Emma, but her Dad was not getting better. He was in the hospital; there was no need for her to come now, but to be on standby should his symptoms get worse. Emma felt sick to her stomach. Not only could she not bear having to return to Denver, but the thought of losing her Dad made her nauseous. If ever she needed another prayer answered, she thought, now Lord is a perfect time for a miracle. Emma searched for Naomi at work everywhere that next day.

**Emma: Meet me in the conference room.**

She sent the text message around 10 a.m. Encouraged by her plan, Emma was eager to begin praying and decided to start alone at her desk silently, until they could meet. By lunch, she still hadn't heard from Naomi, and finally, a reply came while Emma sat alone eating her sandwich.

**Tamar: I'm sure this was intended for your new bestie.**

In her excitement, she sent the text message to the wrong person. But it wasn't the wrong person really. Not so long-ago Tamar would be the one Emma confided in, and she knew had even been close to Emma's father. Tamar should know about his condition, no matter what their differences were.

**Emma: Sorry about that, my Dad's not doing well.**

Tamar's response took a while, though Emma imagined she contemplated whether to act like she cared or continue their previous disagreement.

**Tamar: Sorry to hear that I hope he gets better.**

It wasn't much, but enough to give Emma hope that someday they could reconcile. When Emma returned from lunch, she was filled with hope because of her silent prayers. Before returning to her desk, she entered the breakroom to fill her water bottle and bumped into Naomi.

When Emma told Naomi about her Father's illness, her response was quick and genuine.

"Let's join hands now," she said, then nodded for Emma to start the prayer. Emma thought she'd faint dead on the floor.

"Your prayers are just as good as mine," said Naomi.

Emma felt like her first time praying out loud was nothing more than babble. First, she closed her eyes tight, hoping to block out her surroundings, and then she peeped one eye open, to watch in case Alex disrupted them.

Afterward she relieved of two things, no one had walked in on them, and she didn't die of humiliation. At her desk she powered through assignments and completed unfinished tasks that threatened her peace the day before. With earbuds on, she selected a gospel track, "♪ You make all things new… ♪" She hummed along with the artist. A tap on her shoulder caused Emma to jump. Expecting to see her friend's smile, she softened her eyes and smiled.

"Yeah, that's how I like to be greeted," said Alex.

His eyes trailed from her lips down the length of her body. Emma followed him and noticed where his eyes stopped. Immediately, her hands tugged at her top. Pulling at the tail-end, she hoped the front of her shirt would shift upward. Not too long ago, his attention flattered her. She wore tight clothes intended to leave an impression. Now she shifted and tugged at fabric not designed to stretch. The more she fumbled with her blouse, the longer he leered. Emma silently prayed for him to leave.

"Woah, I'm not making you nervous, am I?" Alex said, taking a step back. The frown lines on his forehead showing his confusion.

"Hey, nice to see you," she said, not wanting to be rude.

He hadn't been around much these days. The rumor was his last office romance ended with charges and a pending court date. Alex waited for a cue that it was okay to give her a hug, but there was none. Right now, Emma would refuse to blink if an eyelash fell into her eyes, and she made sure not to touch her hair. Finally, she folded her arms across her chest, and when she looked up, he winked at her.

'Lord, please get this man away from me!' she prayed silently, taking her seat. He stood for a moment, unsure of his next move.

"I'll talk to you later when you're in a better mood." He turned to walk away, but not before running his hand along her back. Emma flinched, with an urge to correct him with some colorful verbiage, but he was gone. Leaving her seething at the memory of his touch.

# TWENTY- SEVEN

ON THE MORNING Emma lost total and complete interest in life, she rejected Naomi's phone calls, ignored her text messages, and avoided the doorbell—and the knocks at her front door. On the second evening of her seclusion, a dog barking outside her door restored hope. In her delusion, she believed it was Biscuit. She even rushed to the door to search for him, but there was no dog. Instead, Naomi was there, sitting with her legs folded and eyes closed. Emma nudged at her and then instructed her to come inside.

She told Naomi to lay down in her spare bedroom and placed a cover over her. After closing her own bedroom door, a Bible verse came to mind.

A man who has friends must himself be friendly, but there is a friend who sticks closer than a brother.

Naomi was that friend. Her friendship filled in the empty space and erased Emma's fear of abandonment. And Naomi was there as she prepared to face disappointment while she cried out for answers.

When Emma wanted to pray, Naomi made herself available for prayer.

When Emma cried, Naomi wept with her.

When grief kept her from Church and work, Naomi covered for her and even brought her lunch. Then when Emma shut down and refused to speak, Naomi sat in silence with her and refused to leave her side.

Emma prayed one last prayer for her daddy.

God, take away my dad's pain.

Naomi was with her when she received the phone call from her Uncle Eli, who lived in Florida. Though he struggled with his words, she already knew.

"My brother's not in pain anymore," he said.

Emma could still hear him breathing on the other end, though nothing more was said. After a moment of silence, his wife took over the conversation. She wanted to know how soon Emma could get to Denver, and what help she could offer?

One year to the date of that first phone call from the unknown woman, Emma's Dad was gone. She spent a year praying fervently, searching through the Bible cover to cover, for every instance of healing, and even resurrections from death. If it was done before, Emma hoped for a miracle. She attended every church service, went to prayer meetings, and placed his name, Emanuel St. Roman, on every prayer list she came across. She joined an online prayer group and followed more apostles, preachers, and evangelists then she could remember; making sure to request prayer for her Dad whenever she saw an opportunity.

There was no help anyone outside of Heaven could offer. Emma had more than enough money; her Dad had begun depositing large amounts of money into her savings account shortly after their discussion about the security deposit box. Emma was a wealthy woman, though at the time she had little understanding of what it meant to have that type of financial freedom.

Emma told no one about her millionaire status and continued living as if her bank account hadn't placed her in a position to start her own business and create job opportunities for others. She considered a discussion with Orion about a business venture but thought to put the conversation on hold until after her trip to Denver. For now, she needed an excuse to give her Uncle Eli, and Naomi, as to why she didn't want to attend the funeral.

"I can go with you," said Naomi, when Emma gave her the news.

"I'm not going," she said, without an explanation.

Her friend said nothing more as she dusted in corners, opened the blinds, and then put several drops of essential oil into a diffuser, the way Emma liked.

"I'm not going back there," she said again, throwing the covers over her head and turning away from the open blinds. Naomi left the room briefly and then returned with a towel in hand.

"You like this one, right," she held up a bottle of lavender foam bath. When Naomi left the room again, Emma sniffed the air, delighted with the vanilla aroma that wafted through the apartment from diffusers.

"Your bath's hot and ready," Naomi announced when she returned. Without an argument, Emma took the towel she'd placed on the foot of her bed and went into the bathroom.

"Do you mind looking up airline tickets for both of us?" Emma asked from behind the closed door.

"No problem," said Naomi.

The next morning Emma stared out of an airplane window, watching as darkness gave way to morning light, and seagulls squawked at the rising sun. By the time the plane lifted off she had turned to Naomi and told her it was because of their friendship that she was strong enough to return to Denver.

"No," Naomi corrected, "it is the grace of God" that allowed them to support one another. During the plane ride, Naomi mentioned a troubled past with her family, particularly her ex, that prevented her from going home. Emma wanted to pry for more information, and would have, if not for the trouble she sensed awaited when they landed.

By the time she exited the plane, Emma had clutched her stomach and struggled to breathe. Naomi handed her a bottle of water and then demonstrated a breathing technique to help Emma relax. Despite her inner turmoil, she was ready to see her old bedroom and the front yard where she used to play with Biscuit for hours it seemed.

Emma froze when she saw a man wave to her who resembled her Dad. If not for the difference in eye color, she would've thought someone had played a cruel joke on her. Uncle Eli and his wife greeted them with flat expressions that begged to fake a smile. When his wife asked if she would stay at the house or at the ranch with the rest of the family, Emma couldn't give an answer. The idea of staying at a nearby hotel now seemed cold, and Naomi gave her those puppy dog eyes, so she agreed to stay at the ranch.

On the drive, Naomi chattered about how much she loved horses. She missed being in the country and shared that someday she had plans to leave the city and settle down with land to watch over, and fresh air to breath. Emma closed her eyes, then imagined younger days where on this very drive from Denver to Castle Rock, Grandma Rose fed her wisdom and enough love to sustain her through adolescence. She smiled when the car turned down the driveway, and several hoses stood beyond the fence with a setting sun behind them.

When they awoke the next morning, Uncle Eli and his wife, Miranda, made the decision that the house in Cherry Creek should be emptied while they were all together. Especially since Emma vowed to never live there again. Her Uncle Eli had created a spreadsheet and explained how his brother's possessions should be examined, inventoried, and what should be donated.

Emma would have to decide what should be kept, things to store for future use, and which mementos to hold onto. As he spoke, Emma's stomach curled in knots, and she broke a sweat. It wasn't the work of the day that troubled her but returning to the spot in the backyard where she confronted Reba.

When they arrived at her childhood home, the woman who approached them greeted Emma first. She apologized for the phone call last year of bad news and said how proud her Dad had been of her. After she exchanged words with Uncle Eli about matters of the house, she gave him the house key. Before she left, the woman reached for Emma and embraced her as a mother would a daughter, and then whispered in her ear, so the others wouldn't hear. Afterward, she slid an envelope and a key to the safety deposit box into Emma's hands.

"He wanted to make sure you had this," she said, then gave Emma another hug before leaving.

When Uncle Eli eyed the contents, Emma slid both into her purse and said nothing of it.

"He knew," is what the woman whispered in her ear.

He knew about Breaux Bridge. He knew about Maine, and he knew about the baby.

Emma swallowed the lump in her throat and then tried to study her hands as she opened the front door to let everyone inside. The décor had changed, but the pictures of her youth remained on the mantle. Emma took her time and walked the length of each room, marking places with memories she thought long forgotten.

Uncle Eli took the others and began to pack and mark boxes. Within seven hours, they'd gone through every inch of the house, and designated the things to be donated, shipped to Florida, or moved to the Ranch. Naomi helped Emma while she packed away her old bedroom and looked over the forgotten memoirs.

"You look so happy," said Naomi, gushing at a picture of Emma and Biscuit. "You should take these things, in case you get another dog," she said, placing the dog bed, leash, and hygiene products into a box.

"There'll never be another Biscuit," said Emma.

She stood at the window and remembered the night noise outside her bedroom window that drew her into the backyard. With the blinds removed, she could see straight through to the spot where Reba stood and shivered under the moonlight. Emma remembered the moment she felt compassion for her Mother, a weakness Reba and Ogre took advantage of.

"Is there something out back you want?" asked Naomi.

"Me and Biscuit used to race out there…from that side of the yard, and way over there. He always let me win," she smiled.

"You need to keep these."

She placed a handful of pictures in Emma's hands. She decided to hold onto the box since most of her items, including clothes, were marked to be donated, there was no room for them at her apartment in Manhattan. When they were finished, Emma turned her back to the window, and then closed the door of her old bedroom.

When she returned to the living room, her Uncle Eli insisted on keeping Biscuits things. He would hold on to them and placed the box marked Biscuit into a moving truck headed for Florida. The household furniture went into a separate truck to be unloaded at the Ranch. As her Uncle continued to bark orders at the movers, Emma sat in the car and said goodbye to her Daddy's home. In her hands, she held onto two small boxes of disposable items.

The handler at the ranch lived on the premises with his wife; he cared for the horses, and she kept the house cobweb free. Though her Grandpa now lived in Florida with Uncle Eli, his one wish was for the maintenance of the ranch to continue while he was alive. "People in town relied on the stable," he reminded them. When they returned, Uncle Eli sat her Grandpa out by the fence, and each day during their two-week stay. He spent hours watching as the horses strutted and whinnied at the helpers' care.

Naomi went out to sit with him on one of those days, and after thirty minutes, said she'd like to ride a mare. When she asked, Emma and her Uncle Eli noticed a flicker of light in Grandpa's eyes. Naomi walked away with the horse handler, and then returned with a beautiful red horse with a spot-free coat that shimmered in the sunlight. Grandpa tried to stand on his feet when Naomi saddled and hopped on the horse like a pro.

Emma felt a pinch of jealousy, as she remembered her dream to one day ride a horse. The red horse galloped at Naomi's command and then sprinted across the field like a firebolt. To everyone's amazement, Grandpa smiled and waved after them.

When Naomi returned, she walked the horse over to Emma, motioning for her to come closer.

"I can't, I've never—" she stammered, eyes wide and mouth open.

"You can, I'll show you how," said Naomi.

She guided Emma closer with a free hand while keeping the

horse steady. With a great deal of persuasion and Grandpa clapping his hands, Emma rode a horse for the first time that day. Though she didn't sprint off in the wind like Naomi had, in her mind, she looked just as majestic as Grandpa had when he rose Misty, back in the days when she felt like a small haystack, and they hovered over her like giants. If this were her horse, Emma thought, she'd name her Elektra.

As far as Emma was concerned, her trip home could've ended at the horse stables. But reality kicked in when Uncle Eli announced they had to be at the mortuary by 6:30 p.m. Emma didn't want to go, but there was no excuse she could give for skipping out except, I don't want to do this. Would any of them understand how hard it would be for her to see her Dad this way? She preferred to remember him the way he was the last time he visited; alive, hard-working, and always looking out for his princess.

His goal was to start a reputable law firm, a legacy to leave for generations to come. From Emma's perspective, he had found success, but he was the only one who could've known for sure. At the viewing, his close friends and business partners had said he was a visionary. They said kind words to comfort, but confirm, he had accomplished his dream. They told stories that explained his absence on days she needed a buffer to Reba's temperament. As a criminal lawyer, he specialized in child endangerment cases, and fought for children's rights, while assuming his own daughter was safe at home. As the guests spoke, Emma scanned the room for Reba.

The next day the funeral was held. Through her tears, Emma continued to watch the door. When it was her Uncle Eli's turn to offer words about his brother, he gave her a puzzled look. Uncle Eli spoke about his proud memories of the two of them, watching as his younger brother built his career, and how he wished for a little more time to take that tour of Europe, together.

During his speech, Uncle Eli kept eyes on Emma, who remained with eyes fixed on the entrance. When she caught him staring, Emma wondered if he thought she had gone mad, or maybe she would make a wild dash for the door she kept watch over. Emma nodded her head, signaling to him that she was okay.

Emma would be able to hold it together. Her Dad was the one who visited her in their posh Manhattan apartment. She believed he would visit again, in spring—after he wrapped up his last case—just as he promised. This time, he would stay with her, that's the reason she told Uncle Eli to sell the house; her Dad was going to leave Denver for good, move to New York, and take walks through Central Park whenever he pleased.

"Who are you looking for?" Uncle Eli asked her when there was no longer a door but the open sky.

He stood beside her at the gravesite and watched as she looked over her shoulders, and through shadows behind trees.

"She didn't come!" Emma snapped and shook her head in disgust.

Reba owed it to her father to be there at his funeral. If she would've shown, Emma planned to point-out Ogre and tell them all how he and Reba first kidnapped and then destroyed her life. They were cowards, the two of them. One day Emma would make them pay for having her stand alone at her Father's grave, holding a secret she never got around to discuss with him.

He knew!

# TWENTY- EIGHT

EMMA REMAINED SILENT for most of the flight back to New York. When they landed, Naomi hugged her and then held on for longer than usual. There was something different about the look in Naomi's eyes, but being overcome with grief, she forgot to question her friend. Nothing unkind had been spoken between them. In fact, Naomi had been her usual encouraging self from start to finish. As Emma reflected over the past days, she realized there was a point when Naomi became less talkative. After the horseback ride, she said reminded her of a place where she grew up.

"I'm always a phone call away," she said, after dropping Emma off at her apartment.

Naomi kissed her friend on the cheek and left. It was at work two days later when Emma received a text message from Naomi saying she had taken an extended leave from work and would be back in a month, or two.

**Naomi: Emma, seeing you tie up loose ends at home, gave me the strength to face my own family. You're stronger than you know and Brave. Pray for me, as**

**where I'm going will be a great challenge.**

After she read Naomi's message, Emma put her head down and wished Naomi would've taken her along for the trip.

One month without her friend and Emma realized her weekly call for a ride was absurd. She was a terrible driver, so it would take prayer, and every ounce of courage she could muster to drive her Mercedes to church. Emma took several deep breaths, and with clenched knuckles tight around the steering wheel, she turned the key and started the engine. When she pulled out of her tight parking space, Emma inched into the roadway, pressing hard on the brakes as pedestrians jaywalked.

By the time Emma arrived at church an hour late, she had gone straight to the altar and cried, asked the Lord to make her brave enough to drive so she could get to church on time. On the drive back home, she sang a gospel hymn to relax. And when Emma pulled into her parking space, though her fingers ached, and her back needed to be cracked, she felt a sense of accomplishment. Driving on Sunday morning was doable, but that was as far as she willed herself to go.

Emma prayed for Naomi's return. After she was inside, alive but shaken, Emma pulled out her cell phone and dialed Naomi's phone number. The call went straight to voicemail, so Emma sent a text message.

**Emma: I drove myself to Church this morning, I can do all things through Christ who strengthens me!**

Naomi replied with a smiley emoji, and then clapping hands.

**Emma: When are you coming back?**

When there was no response, Emma busied herself with lunch

and then prepared for an early evening run through the park. Three hours later, Naomi still hadn't responded. ∩

Two months had gone by, and Naomi still hadn't returned. What was worse, she had stopped taking phone calls or responding to text messages—it was as if her phone had been disconnected. Orion was kind enough to spend more time with Emma during Naomi's absence, but still, he was stretched beyond his schedule, and Emma didn't want to burden him.

Of all the men in New York to fall in love with, she had to find one who wanted to practice law. Emma knew the sacrifice required of Orion, so she tried to show support, although knowing each day she was falling into the same routine Reba had with her Dad. He appreciated Emma's patience, which made their time together special.

Emma's birthday fell on a Thursday, and that morning Orion was at her door by 7 a.m. In his hand were a dozen roses and a promise to celebrate on Friday evening. Pleased with his gesture, Emma left for work with a happy countenance and light heart. The day would be perfect if she found Naomi at her desk, but there was still no trace of her friend. A missed call from Kaylee came first that morning, and when Faith phoned later, Emma knew they had hoped to celebrate her birthday. This was her second warning to heed the slippery slope ahead.

Her first warning had come before Orion's visit that morning. The ugly voice had woken her up, threatening to expose her as a fraud. It mocked her for thinking her Dad hadn't known—

He Knew!

Inside the envelope had been an account set up for his grandchild, and in the security deposit box were pictures of the baby with copies of the agreement she signed for the adoption.

He knew and did the right thing, the voice taunted her. No matter how hard she tried, she couldn't get the ugly voice to shut up.

Emma had been having a hard time with sleep. When Orion noticed her struggle, he mentioned the importance of allowing herself to grieve the loss. Aware of Naomi's absence, his phone calls increased in the mornings, to remind her that she wasn't alone, and at night when he couldn't be there. Orion mentioned more than once that he cared about what she was going through, and he loved her. Even though he couldn't offer more time, things would improve after he graduated. He was working hard to secure a future for them. Emma understood because she knew the routine.

Why would God take Him? She questioned this when she bypassed the portrait of her Dad hanging in her apartment. The more she sought answers, the angrier the voice became, growing louder until it drowned out the gentler whisper of her prayers. Until finally, she could stand it no more. By the time Kaylee called, Emma was already sipping on her first drink.

No, she didn't have plans for her birthday. Sure, she'd meet her at the lounge around the corner at 6 p.m.? Yes, she'd be there. They cheered for her when she walked into the dimly lit lounge. Emma imagined their relief when they noticed she had come alone. It was Gianna's remark that confirmed her suspicion.

"Glad to see you came without your bodyguard, have a drink," she said and handed Emma a shot glass. She drank the first shot.

"You can't keep pretending!" The ugly voice whispered.

Then another said, "it's only a matter of time before everyone knows!"

Next, the voice in her head threatened, "Drink now, because tomorrow your perfect little world will come crashing down!"

And, finally quiet when the bumping beats and girls that

screeched to their favorite song silenced the voice. It was around four in the morning when Emma made it back to her apartment. To her surprise, there was a note stuck to front door.

**Sorry I missed you, hope you enjoyed your twenty-fifth,
Love Orion.**

Emma checked her cell phone for the missed call and then realized her phone had died because she forgot to charge the battery before leaving home. After she connected the phone to the charger, she saw six missed phone calls from him, and two text messages:

**Naomi: I hope you enjoyed your special day.**

And the other surprise.
**Tamar: Thinking of you my Irish Twin on our day, enjoy
and let's get together soon.**

Emma slept in that following morning and then dragged herself to work at noon. When she arrived at her desk, there were balloons, a gift box, flowers and a card signed by Orion, Dinner at Seven. To her surprise, the gift box had been from Naomi, and inside a picture of Emma sitting on the red horse, in a frame that read, "I Can Do All Things Through Christ Who Strengthens Me, Philippians 4:13." She smiled at the photo which Naomi had secretly snapped. Emma put the frame on her desk and sent Naomi a text message.

**Emma: Thank you for the gift.
Naomi: Meet me in the conference room.**

She winced after sending the text message, a pain in her forehead reminded her of the hangover that needed to nurse.

**Emma: Sorry, I have a migraine today.**

She had every intention of calling Naomi after work, but a phone call from her Uncle Eli came first. He wanted to assure Emma of her financial stability, and his plan to oversee her portfolio so she could remain living the lifestyle she had grown accustomed to. The phone call lasted sixty-four minutes, and the only way she was able to get him off the line was to tell him she'd visit him soon in Florida.

By the time it was over, she had rushed to dress for plans with Orion. Naomi called as Emma was about to step into the shower, so it wasn't a lie when she said, "I'm sorry, I can't talk right now—late for a dinner date with Orion." But it may have been untrue when she said, "I'll call you first thing in the morning."

The weekend had gone by before Emma found the time to return Naomi's phone call or respond to Tamar's text message. When Naomi caught up to her on Wednesday afternoon, Emma understood what her Mother must have felt like those years ago, standing in the backyard when the moonlight exposed her secrets. When their eyes met, Naomi's silence spoke, I know you're struggling, Emma's blank stare replied Give me time to work this out—on my own. The two friends left the break room with few words spoken, and yet they had shared a conversation that left nothing more to be said.

A week after their encounter, Emma decided it was time to use her resources and pursue her passions. It was Kaylee who inspired her to take the risk, which involved nothing more than a sacrifice of her time. The night before, they had met at the lounge to celebrate Kaylee's news. Because of her diligence, she had landed her first movie role. Everyone knew how much time Kaylee had invested in getting the part. Her big break was always just an audition away. That was the day Emma decided it was time to put her dancing shoes back on and set out to accomplish what she came to New York to do.

She had nothing to lose by quitting her day job. In fact, she decided that night, her time had been wasted eight hours a day, which left her no time to focus on her dream. When Emma announced to Kaylee and the others that she was going to step out on faith and pursue a career as a dancer and choreographer, she heard a familiar voice. It spoke so loudly it caused her to look around to see if Reba, Ogre, or Shelly had caught up to her.

*FRAUD!*

When she could find no familiar face from her past, Emma clinked glasses and pumped her fist in the air.

"Why haven't you returned any of my phone calls," someone said over her shoulder.

Emma choked on her drink as her knees knocked together. When she regained her composure, Tamar took the glass from her hand and finished it off. Emma ordered them both another round, and then they danced together, like before, when husbands and boyfriends didn't exist, and best friends were forever. Faith and Gianna spotted them together on the dance floor, and they all danced until their feet throbbed.

"I get it, you lost your Dad, and your Mom split when you were young," Tamar was the first to speak after they had walked to Emma's apartment.

Emma wanted to tell her the rest, but then remembered Tamar had lost that place in her heart four years ago when she got married. She bit her lip, refused to say anything to ruin their reunion.

"I was bounced from home to home in foster care. If anyone gets you, baby it's me." Tamar rested her feet on the sofa, then laid her head upon the armrest. "Naomi hasn't walked in our shoes, so she can't relate to the way we are," Tamar said.

Emma nodded her agreement. For a moment, Tamar's hand-crafted deception had blinded her judgment. Then she remembered the woman who labored with her through the most painful of days and gave her a promise for a better future.

"I buried my Dad eight months ago," Emma had curled herself in a ball on the opposite end of the sofa. "I quit my job today, and I don't need you," she said. If anyone knew that Emma came from money, it was Tamar.

Tamar was the one who showed them property around the five boroughs of New York. She watched as Emma's Dad made decisions like money wasn't a problem. If she didn't believe he had the resources, his actions proved so.

"Wait a minute, this isn't about your money," Tamar defended. "I just want my sister back, the way we were before SHE—"

"Before Beaumont," Emma held up a hand to stop her friend's tantrum. Tamar grunted and laid her head back on the throw pillow.

# TWENTY- NINE

SIX MONTHS AFTER Emma's public declaration, and she was over the hype. It wasn't that she no longer had desires of becoming a dancer, or choreographer, but she was tired. Sleep had become her comforter. The music had become too loud, and her favorite songs had lost their meaning—still she forged ahead because they were all waiting for her breakout performance.

During the day, she attended dance classes to brush up on her skill. At home, she practiced in her guest bedroom which had been converted into a dance studio, complete with a barre and mirrors on the wall. On the weekends, Emma met with Gianna and the others at the lounge, and when her feet ached from the repetitive impact, she made time for Orion.

Now that Emma was the one with less availability, Orion answered her phone calls quickly, or else it could be another week or so before they were able to meet.

"I love you. I can see us married with miniature Orion's and Emma's in a big house," he said.

Emma smiled because she liked his vision for them.

"It's time we start thinking about our future together."

His conversation reminded Emma that her Dad wouldn't be there to meet her husband-to-be or walk her down the aisle. She considered making good on her promise to visit Uncle Eli over a year ago. Maybe if Orion continued with his sweet talk about their future together, she'd invite him to Florida. For now, her feet ached from blisters that needed time to heel, and her body was flat-out tired. Emma stared at him, the man she loved as he massaged her feet.

"You should take it easy for a few weeks," he said before placing her feet into a bath of Epsom salt.

"Sounds like wise counsel, Attorney Stone," she said, leaning her head against the sofa cushion.

"I've meant to ask you what happened to your nice friend, the one you went to church with," Orion said, handing Emma a glass of water with an Ibuprofen. The pill was harsh on her empty stomach, so she gagged and ran for a nearby trash pail.

"I haven't had much time to eat," she said when her stomach calmed.

"Like I said, you should take a break from dancing. You're working harder now than you ever did at the firm," he said. Then he gave her a sympathetic look and sat down beside her. "Let me take care of you today…I'll cook," he offered, setting her feet back into the footbath. Then he went off into the kitchen.

"So, about that friend…Naomi is her name, right? I thought we could invite her over for dinner," he said and peeked his head around the corner when he got no response. Emma closed her eyes and pretended to be asleep.

Two weeks after that discussion, Emma's feet swelled, and nothing she did seemed to help. To make matters worse, she slept throughout the day, and when she awoke, another nap was a yawn away. Emma was groggy after her morning coffee, exhausted after a short walk through the park, and pooped hours before her usual bedtime.

On Saturday afternoon, she was still in her nightclothes when her phone beeped with messages that she was too weak to answer. She sucked her teeth when the doorbell rang and despised the walk from her bedroom to the front door. Tamar flashed her pearly whites at the peephole, and when Emma opened the door, she greeted her with hands on hips and twisted lip.

"Where were you last night?" Tamar asked.

She entered with her clickety-clack heels.

"I'm holding up my end of the bargain, what's up with your slack end?" It was nice having Tamar around again, but something didn't feel right. For a married woman with two small children, her night outings were uncomfortably frequent.

"I'm nursing the flu…why aren't you home with your family?" Emma said, wrapping herself in a blanket to corroborate her story.

"Flu? Eww," she said, and then took a few steps back. "Where's your cough medicine, and your napkins?" Tamar glanced around the room and then made a full inspection as she always did.

"Never mind that, what's going on with you and Beau?" Emma patted the cushion for Tamar to sit.

There was a time when Emma didn't have to pry anything out of Tamar. She was confident, unashamed of anything she did, and basically cared zero percent about anyone else's opinion of her. Emma thought about asking Tamar if she wanted to pray. After all, that's what Naomi would do when Emma came to her with a problem. To keep from agitating their strained friendship, Emma said a silent prayer.

Father, please give my friend the courage to unload this heavy burden.

"I've been living a lie these past few years," Tamar said after the silence. "Ever since Dilan and Dalani were born."

Emma wrinkled her forehead and then tried to conceal her bewilderment.

"Don't give me that look, I know I was hard on you," Tamar shrugged. "I tried to play the perfect part, but nothing ever goes as planned." She continued, wiping her face with a sleeve. They sat in quiet for a moment, long enough for Emma to hear a small, gentle voice she hadn't heard since her return from Castle Rock.

'Tell her I Love her,' Emma heard a voice say within.

After everything she'd done this past year, the wild nights of partying until daybreak, drinking and indulging in activities she knew would lead to destruction, she finally came back to what she had learned. The soft, silent voice had returned to comfort her, urging her to offer this love to a friend, even after she had closed the Bible on her nightstand and deleted the Bible app on her cell phone.

She had long stopped attending church, and although Naomi continued to text words of encouragement, Emma ignored them all and turned back to old ways that brought her pleasure in the night and headaches by morning.

"I have to tell you something," said Emma.

She turned to her friend and braced herself. Then she said, "Jesus loves you!" She waited for Tamar to yell or slap her back to reality. But Tamar didn't say a word—she blinked her eyes a few times, but her mouth was glued shut. Emma was going to ask if they could pray together, but her queasy stomach was a distraction.

"The twins…they're not my husband's children," Tamar admitted, and no sooner had her confession come out Emma had leaped from the couch and barely made it to the trash can.

"The flu?" Tamar asked. "That flu reminds me of when I was pregnant," she said when Emma returned to the sofa.

They looked at each other, one held her breath, the other gasped. Even though she protested, Tamar left the apartment abruptly and found the closest pharmacy. When she returned, Emma already knew the bag contained a pregnancy test. Now in the bathroom, she groaned.

It was as if time reversed and she was back in the cabin with moose and fish décor. Seven years had gone by since her time in Maine, and Emma wished this scenario would have an alternate ending. When Tamar tapped on the door, she dropped the stick on the floor just before she dipped it in toilet water. When she retrieved it from the floor, she felt guilty for trying to fool Tamar.

After she had added her sample to the collection window, Emma set the stick on the marble-top vanity. This time she would be the first to see the results; hoping all the while that she was right about having the flu, and Tamar had been wrong.

"You're going to be a Mommy," Tamar said flatly.

She had run into the bathroom as soon as Emma opened the door. The first thing Emma did this time around was pick up the phone and call Orion. If he were a man of his word, he'd need to fast-track his plans to include Emma and their offspring sooner than either of them anticipated.

Tamar said she had to leave before Orion arrived, but promised to finish their discussion later. As she left, Tamar said it didn't matter now who her twin's biological father was. Beaumont raised them, and he would always be their daddy. Then she swore Emma to secrecy and cautioned that the news would destroy Beau if he ever found out the truth.

Now alone, Emma had time to process her thoughts before Orion arrived. She was going to have a baby. Emma could feel her nerves tying in knots from the pit of her stomach all the way up through her scalp. Orion's reaction was a comfort as she heard his muffled yelp on the other end of the line.

This pregnancy would be different, not hidden in a cabin, but out in the open for all her friends to see. And this child would be born in a hospital, with its Father excitedly beside her. But wouldn't the Doctor be able to tell she'd given birth before? If so, Orion would be in for a big surprise. She was sure he would ask about the first baby…and the father. No way would she ever tell him or another living soul about the details of the other pregnancy.

Orion's smile revealed dimples she'd forgotten were there. He sat her on the couch, soft-like, so she didn't break or accidentally poke something that shouldn't be poked. Then he put her feet on an ottoman, propped a pillow behind her back and reached for her hands.

"You have my word. We'll be married before our baby is born," he said and kissed the back of both her hands.

At that moment she believed he would. He only asked for Emma to give him until the end of summer. Then his internship would end, and they could have whatever kind of wedding she desired. Orion stayed with her that night, and though his offer was promising, Emma had an unsettled feeling growing in the back of her mind.

The roles felt eerily like her parents. She imagined Reba must've felt this way when she had become pregnant. Maybe their outcome could be different? If she managed to set her own goals and not give up on herself, as her mother had apparently done, she might succeed. But the baby would come before her career, so her choices felt slim.

With each day that passed, the ugly voice grew. It screamed threats until Emma could have no peace. Most days, it called out, Fraud! And at other times it accused her of being a hypocrite. What hurt her the most is when she heard the voice say, 'Reba incarnate!' Then proceeded to tell her she would be the same failure her Mom had been. Finally, it convinced her that her best hope was to cling to Orion's Mom, so the child could at least have the same chance at normalcy, the same as Grandma Rose had provided her.

When the voice told her that the child would someday grow up and plot her murder, something snapped, and that's when she brought the first bottle of wine home - four bottles, in fact. One in the refrigerator, another in the cabinet, one in her bedroom closet and the last one in the guest bedroom. If Orion became indignant and demanded she toss out the bottle in the refrigerator, the others were her backup.

Orion stopped by on a Tuesday with plans for dinner. When he went to put leftovers in the refrigerator, he returned with a puzzled expression.

"Tamar left it, in case I needed something for my company to drink," she lied with a straight face.

"Oh, okay well we'll just pour this down the drain then," he said as he tilted the bottle. Emma watched as the sink guzzled the wine intended for her nightcap. "Have you seen Naomi?" he asked. When she shot him an unpleasant look, he didn't blink. Then he told her that he had questions about his baptism.

"One baptism's just as good as any other," said Emma, hoping to change the subject. But he continued.

"If that's true, why was I baptized in the name of the Father, the Son, and the Holy Ghost? You and Naomi said you were baptized in the name of Jesus," he said.

"I can answer that question for you, Jesus is the name of the Father, the Son, and the Holy Ghost," she said, happy to have remembered.

"But there was something different about you when you got baptized, you were happier, almost radiant," he said.

He continued questioning his salvation until Emma had no choice but to promise she'd call Naomi. On Friday morning when Orion would show for their standing date, she made the call at a time she thought Naomi would be busy.

"Praise the Lord, I've been praying that you would reach out," said Naomi after the first ring. Emma asked when she would be free for dinner? "Any night," she would clear her schedule on any night to see her friend again.

"How about Sunday?" asked Emma, knowing Orion wouldn't be free that day.

"I sure can, what time?" she asked.

Orion was disappointed upon hearing he'd miss seeing Naomi but felt better when Emma agreed to ask the questions for him if he wrote them down. Satisfied with herself, she contemplated canceling their meeting altogether. Instead, Emma sent a text message that asked if Naomi would be free at 5 p.m. on Sunday? Of course, she replied.

When Sunday came, Emma had bitten all her nails down to nubs and finished the bottle of wine in the cabinet. Naomi was due in another hour, and Emma wondered if she should call off their dinner plan. She had been terrified since morning, by an awful voice that had a wicked laugh. When she tried to pray it away the voice snapped at her.

'You're better off dead like the rest of your uppity family!'

By the time Naomi arrived, Emma had become hysterical.

"This voice in my head, it won't shut up!"

At first, Naomi said nothing. She simply guided Emma to the sofa and rocked her until she was calm.

"And the dead babies in my dreams, they're scared—I'm a terrible mother," she said and wept some more.

Naomi showed the same compassion as she always had. Sitting beside Emma, she pulled out her cell phone and pressed her playlist of gospel music. Then Naomi went to find a washcloth and ran it under warm water before she wiped Emma's face and hands. When the cloth turned cold, she warmed it again, wiped Emma's face once more, and brought her a cup of chamomile tea. "This too shall pass," she said, and then sang along with the singer. Before long, Emma fell asleep to the soft hum of Naomi's voice.

The light breaking through her living room window woke Emma. She panicked at first, unsure if she'd passed out from boozing the night before.

"Good morning, are you feeling better?" Naomi asked, turning over on the floor.

"Why'd you sleep down there?" asked Emma.

"I've slept in worse places than this," she replied, and when she giggled, Emma remembered how nice it was to have Naomi around.

Tamar was fun, but there was a side to her that always made Emma feel like she couldn't do anything right. Naomi was an encourager. She made Emma believe she could be better, and no matter what life threw at her, with God, she could be an overcomer. It was Naomi's walk that made her a consistent friend; her faith gave her enough joy to hold and to spread around.

Emma knew what needed to be done to be free again. Like Orion said, there was something different about her before. The difference was what Naomi had continued to exemplify in her daily life. Praying and studying the Bible were her lifeline to heaven. Grandma Rose called it her secret to success, and Naomi said it had been food for her soul. Emma longed for a deeper understanding of this God they both held on to with locked claws.

Emma dreaded the hour because she knew Naomi would need to leave for work. Instead, she called out, saying there had been a family emergency. Then she told Emma to get dressed so they could take a drive into North Jersey to visit a friend who had just returned from missionary work in Guatemala. On the way, Naomi asked if Emma had considered coming back to church?

"Do you remember our one Bible study…it was about idle time?" Naomi asked.

"Yes," Emma answered, "idle time is the devil's playground, I know, I'll go back soon."

"Well, let me remind you, you're in the perfect environment for that devil to wreak havoc on your mind," Naomi said.

Emma didn't argue with her, because she felt like the devil had twisted her mind like a wrung hand towel. As she thought about the last days living with a talking, angry voice inside her head, Emma wondered if her sanity or the devil had been to blame? And now Naomi wanted to know what her plans were? A straight jacket would help her for starters.

"We're getting married at the end of summer, just before my baby is born. I'll go back to church then," said Emma.

Why would she wait until then, Naomi wanted to know? What stopped her from making a change now? Emma wouldn't tell Naomi then, but it was because that angry voice inside her head had said she was the biggest hypocrite to have ever walked into a church. Emma believed if she cleaned up her act first, then she could go back. Otherwise, that accusing voice wasn't going to shut up.

Eighteen weeks into her pregnancy, and there was a new round of bottles hidden in closets and pantries. Emma drank when Orion or Naomi was not around. It wasn't like she couldn't stop drinking, more like she wasn't quite ready. It was on a Monday afternoon when an ultrasound revealed that her baby would be another girl that Emma knew she had to quit drinking.

Next Monday she'd stop cold turkey, she said after sipping a drink from the bottle in her closet. Tamar was the only one who knew Emma drank while pregnant. She even reasoned that wine was good for the blood.

"Some women drink wine throughout their whole pregnancy," said Tamar, as she poured them both a glass. But there was a different voice in her head now, not the one that called her derogatory names and branded her as a hypocrite, this softer voice asked.

"Have you counted the cost?"

It was a logical question that provoked an honest answer. And when Tamar had left, she contemplated her behavior. No matter what anyone else wished for her, what Emma wanted above anything else was the courage to live without outside influence that sought to derail her path. Whatever she did from this day forward, it had to be her decision alone; and what she wanted was to be sober.

Emma remembered the twelve-step meeting from several years back. It was the face of the woman, Debra, who said she was there for her baby, and no one else mattered. Emma remembered the notebook she held onto that night. It had been shoved to the back of her nightstand because she wanted to hide it from guests. When she pulled the drawer free, Emma was shocked to find the crumpled brochure with faded letters.

Fueled by hope, Emma ran to her laptop and searched for the

group's contact information online. There was a class held every Monday evening for three months, just the amount of time left before Emma's baby was due. The website explained how each week would focus on a different twelve-step principle that outlined addiction and compulsive behaviors. At the end of the program, members would learn their internal and external triggers.

Monday's were the typical days when Naomi and Orion were tied up, and Emma was alone. One class a week, for twelve Mondays, and Emma would be alcohol-free. She placed a copy of her ultrasound in the nightstand with the flyer for motivation.

# THIRTY

*The Garden*

EMMA HELD HER breath while feeling around her now flat stomach. She looked for the Gentleman who had walked back to the entryway leading into the corridor.

"Where is she—where's my baby?" she moaned, staring at him with eyes that showed her readiness for truth.

"Your baby is well, by now she's being monitored in neonatal intensive care. Orion is with her, he'll keep a close eye on her, and you also," He said, waiting for the news to register with Emma.

"I'm leaving now, unless you're thinking of holding me against my will?" she asked.

But He didn't say anything, nor would he stand in her way if she was serious about leaving. Emma took a step toward the door and then looked for him to follow. When He didn't move, she knew there was more about her situation that needed to be said.

"You're free to go, you were never here against your will," He said, holding His hand up pointing in the direction of the door. But Emma couldn't move. She stood looking to the garden then back at the door.

"Aren't you coming?" she asked.

The Gentleman shook his head.

"No, but we'll meet again," He said, "but before you go, will you answer this one final question—did you complete the twelve classes?" He bent and then sat in the grass.

Emma thought carefully about the question. Then she turned and walked over to the Gentleman and took her seat beside him. "I went to four of them, the first was difficult. I was happy that Roxy wasn't there to welcome me back," she answered, and then looked to him knowing what his next question would be.

"And why not all twelve?" He asked, only as a reminder to her because if Emma was going to go back, she had to accept her full truth. If not, once she walked through that door, she would not only face prison time for attempted murder…or worse. She might possibly end up in a vegetative state for the rest of her life.

This was mercy. The Gentleman was offering to help Emma, but only if she admitted what she had done—and all of it. She looked to him, unsure of where to start, and his silent wisdom told her; start from the class you never attended.

Emma began, "On that fourth Monday, I woke up groggy and because my growing belly kept me from sleep, I went into the living room, turned on the morning news, and then went into the kitchen to start my coffee pot. That's when I heard her name mentioned— the reporter said Michelle Venable was petitioning the court to appeal her sentence of involuntary manslaughter."

The Gentleman nodded his head, encouraging Emma to continue.

"I saw her face in the corner of the screen, it was Shelly…then a clip from the trial three years prior, she spoke to the camera saying, 'I would never intentionally hurt another person, especially not my daughter!'" Emma mimicked Shelly's plea.

"Yes, I remember the incident." He said and finished the story, "The DA argued that the girl died from neglect, and lack of medical treatment for a condition that was easily treatable. They reasoned that the problem with alternative lifestyles is the children don't have a say in the matter, and this was a senseless and preventable death."

He repeated the words that caused Emma's jar of secrets to spill over like a boiling pot left too long on the fire. She remembered it all now, standing between the living room and kitchen.

. . . . . . . . . . . . . . . . . .

After hearing Shelly's voice, Emma dropped her coffee mug onto the hardwood floor. She held this secret for far too long, nursing her guilt and shame like they were two unwanted babies someone else had left on her doorstep. After the news went off, Emma's vision went dark, she groped for the couch and then reached for her cell phone. Naomi's phone rang several times and then rolled over to her voicemail.

"Please call me, I—there's something terrible that happened, and I need to tell you about my daughter, the first one!" Emma pleaded.

Her next phone call was to Tamar.

"Well, well, well—funny you should be calling me right now," she teased.

"Please, please come, I just got some awful news, and I—please come," she pleaded with her friend.

"Okay, I'll be there, but not right now, in fact, I need to call you back—I'll take two of those, yes in size 8…," she said, and then hung up the phone.

Emma knew Orion would be busy at this hour. Still, she dialed his number anyway. When his voicemail answered, she hung up without leaving a message. Then she went to the guest room and found the last bottle she'd hidden months ago. Uncorking the top, Emma drank the wine from the bottle, without stopping to take a breath.

"I told you it was only a matter of time," said the angry voice, slow and dreadful—seemingly outside of her head.

"Times up, the fraud is finally exposed," it mocked at her.

Before Emma could steady her trembling hands, she grabbed the keys to her car and ran from her apartment wearing nothing more than a nightshirt, and her bedroom slippers. By the time she pulled the car out into traffic, a torrent of rain had fallen upon the hood. It took several tries before she was able to adjust the windshield wipers to an adequate setting.

The only thing on Emma's mind that morning was to get to North Jersey, where Orion worked, no matter how long it took her. "Drive slow Emma, you can do this," she coached herself as she steadied the wheel and the rain filled the streets and beat heavy on the roof.

She continued onto the Lincoln Tunnel ramp and headed toward New Jersey. Emma's head was dizzy from the drink, so she decreased her speed to 30 miles per hour. She ignored the cars that blared their horns and annoyed drivers who glared at her overly cautious driving. If she had been in her right mind, Emma would've called for a driver.

The rainfall in New Jersey was stronger and caused her car to hydroplane through a puddle in the road. When she saw a shoulder, Emma navigated to the curb, where she heaved from fear and wiped her sticky palms across her sweaty forehead. It was a miracle that she found the building where Orion had been working.

Emma sat in the parking lot across the street, contemplating her next move. She checked her face in the mirror, groaned at her streaked makeup and messy hair, and then picked up the cell phone to inform Orion that she was outside. Her hands were damp and shaking, which caused the cell phone to slip out of her hands. After she bent to retrieve the phone, she sat up and there he was.

Orion came out of the building and walked over to a parked car. He spoke to someone in the car for a moment until a woman walked over to him and interrupted the conversation. When Orion looked up, Emma ducked so she wouldn't be seen. Then, when she thought it was clear, she peeked over the steering wheel, and that's when she saw the woman was Tamar. She was angry and shouted at him. Orion pointed, told her to leave, as the person inside the car approached Tamar with her own fury. When the second person turned in her direction, Emma could see that it was—Victoria.

None of this made sense. Why was Tamar here? What was she mad about and why were Victoria and Tamar now going at each other? Orion broke them apart, but then Tamar threw something in their direction, and after yelling obscenities, she left. When she was gone, Orion reached to pull Victoria closer to him, and that's when Emma's foot pressed on the gas pedal. Keeping them in her sight, the car accelerated forward - faster and faster. She aimed at the two of them. When she heard a loud crash, everything went dark.

This was every bit of Emma's undignified truth. She swore she'd never tell another soul. She had crammed it in a mason jar and sealed it with an airtight lid, and then prayed that no one would ever find out her secret.

Even the sturdiest glass has a breaking point; too much pressure or a hard knock on the ground could crack the jar. The years had produced an intense strain, and the least amount of tension by this point could have aided in the combustion. Emma's breaking point was yesterday, finding out her first child had died and then seeing Orion with another woman. Of all the women in the world, it had to be Victoria.

They stood together on the sidewalk—in the rain—not knowing it was Emma in the parked car who faced opposite them. Neither Orion nor Tamar expected she'd have driven a vehicle that remained parked most of the time. Emma had a fear of driving. When Orion leaned closer to Victoria, Emma didn't wait to see if they shook hands as if concluding a business deal or embraced like lovers.

Emma's lid had popped, sending fragments of herself throughout the cosmos.

. . . . . . . . . . . . . . . .

## The Corridor

It was clear now that she had already been shattered years ago, before Maine and Breaux Bridge. This was an overdue eruption causing all the volatile pieces Emma had concealed throughout the years breaking free. She was the jar that overheated, and now her effervescent particles had made their way to this place beside the Gentleman.

"Orion and Victoria are both fine. They saw the car hurtling toward them and were able to jump to safety," He told her.

When the Gentleman stood and extended His hand, she took hold of it.

"You, on the other hand, have a skull fracture, and some other injuries that are of less concern for now," He said as they walked together.

"When you return, you will be in a Coma."

Emma wasn't concerned about her condition, thinking her punishment was fair. She was ashamed of her behavior and acknowledged that she had acted like a spoiled brat.

"I don't want to live," she said, defeated by the experience.

But the Gentleman continued to guide Emma back down the corridor, and just when the door with the phantom beeps came in to view, there was the little girl in a yellow dress.

Suniva—she remembered Shelly called the baby by name the day Emma was brave enough to ask. Slowing her steps, she thought of that day in Central Park. Suniva Venable was the name on the paperwork, and the name on documents her Dad had left for her inside the envelope.

Suniva, Scandinavian for the gift of the Sun. Emma kneeled before the girl and looked into eyes the same color as her Father's.

"You have hazel eyes just like your Grandpa," Emma said. She cupped the girl's face in her hands.

"You knew all along, you waited here for me. I'm sorry I wasn't there for you."

Suniva lifted the flower crown that was in her hands and then tilted her head forward so Emma could set it on top her head of curls.

"Do I look pretty?" she questioned.

"You are the loveliest, the most beautiful girl I've ever seen," said Emma, kissing her tenderly on the cheek and then along her forehead.

*Beep…Beep…*

Emma looked to the door when she heard the sounds on the other side. Then she remembered the machines working around the clock to keep her stable as she lay in critical condition.

"Your Mommy's here now Suniva, I'm not going anywhere," she whispered, running a hand across the girls' peach-fuzz cheeks, touching her cottony-soft hair. Emma kissed each of her pudgy little fingers. When Suniva giggled, Emma sat in the chair and then placed the girl in her lap.

She saw the shadows in her peripheral view and imagined Grandma Rose and her Dad watching from the entryway of the garden. When she turned to face them, they waved their goodbyes until they became like swirls of wind. For the moment, the beeping machines were silent behind the door. The only sounds Emma could hear were Suniva's tiny breaths, as she fell asleep in her Mother's arms.

# DISCUSSION:

1. What does the "playful" Light represent in the opening scene?

2. Which event had the most impact on Emma's life?

3. Which areas in Emma's life can you relate to the most?

4. How would Emma's life be different had she returned to Denver, instead of traveling to Maine?

5. What were the similarities, and differences in Emma's relationship with Shelly and Tamar? Or Naomi?

6. Assess Emma's reasons for assimilating to the culture of New York?

7. What role do faith and baptism play in Emma's mental and emotional well-being?

8. Are the 'ugly voices' that Emma hears real or imagined?

9. Reflect on moments of restoration and reconciliation throughout various segments of Emma's life.

# About the Author

Laura Caldwell-Gaisie has participated in NaNoWriMo since 2017 and has successfully competed and received certificates for the 2018 and 2019 National Novel Writing Month contest. She looks forward to entering the annual competition where she writes the first draft of a new Novel. Laura has been writing fiction since she was a small girl. She enjoys writing coming of age stories, women's fiction with an inspirational and faith-based message. For further information visit her website at: https://www.lauragaisie.com

# Thanks for reading!

Reviews are extremely important for Authors.

Please add your review on Amazon and/or

Goodreads!

Don't forget to share your review on social media.

#twelvemondays

## I truly appreciate your support!

# Acknowledgments

**My Mom, Juanita,** my biggest cheerleader and number one fan. You always encourage me to aim high and never lose hope. You taught me to pray whether I'm right or wrong, and those words led me on a path of seeking God for myself.

**My husband, Emmanuel,** when my insecurities got the best of me, you encouraged me to believe what God gave me was enough, and never give up until I accomplished my goal.

**My spiritual sisters,** Rosie, Rachelle, Valorie and Regina thank you for your prayers, encouragement and faith-examples.

**Briana and Brian**, thank you for being patient with your mom while I attempted to complete a goal started when I was both your ages now. Whatever you desire to accomplish in life you can achieve, but please, put God first.

**I Love you all.**

# Twelve Hearings excerpt …

During the second week of my hospitalization, something wonderful occurs; I feel a sensation on the tip of my left pointer finger. This miracle happens once, but it's enough to give me hope. Listening to footsteps at my bedside, I await another grim report from the attending physician.

"How about that, can you feel anything?" says Tamar.

Despite our recent troubles, hearing her voice is like achy feet soaking in a steamy hot bath of Epsom salts. When my heartbeat quickens, I imagine her interest turning toward the electrocardiograph machine beside me.

*"Tell me—my once dear friend—What were you doing with my fiancé on the day of my accident?"* She doesn't provide an answer because my question is never spoken.

Tamar's voice is calm, not demanding, as was her usual demeanor. I suppose seeing my mangled body lying in a sterile hospital bed is unnerving. She approaches my bed several times, whispers her request, then walks away.

After each round, she pokes or pinches my finger. I know this because she says, "Did you feel that poke?" or "Can you feel this pinch?" I feel nothing past the first pinch to my fingertip.

"Wake up, Emma, don't make me snatch you up out of this bed," she demands. I almost laugh. This is the Tamar I know. I'm sure she doesn't appreciate being ignored by my unconscious body. If I could answer her, my question would stay the same; why were you arguing with Orion in the rain?

"I want to tell you everything, but not like this," says Tamar. The sound of her short, quick breaths lets me know she's frustrated. She takes a seat, then is up again, moving around the room. "I'm no coward, what I have to say will wait until you're awake," she huffs.

For a moment, she is quiet, and then she moves to the chair beside me and sits. There is nothing but silence upon silence; her calm matching the stillness of my body. When I think she's left the room, she blows wind from her mouth before speaking.

"The twins are doing well; in case you're wondering. Me and Beaumont are separated, but you would know that if you were more concerned with us than spending all that time with Naomi," she says.

Ah, yes! She has expressed her feelings about my new friend before.

"I blame her for this confusion, filling your head with all that hocus pocus. Everything was fine before she stuck her self-righteous nose in other people's affairs," Tamar says. Her opinion is now bordering on jealousy and her argument getting old.

"Did you feel that?" She is back at my side, poking or pinching but only she knows which of the two. Seeing there is still no response from my body, her footsteps leave my hospital room.

*"Don't go yet,"* I imagine myself calling out to stop her. *"What is it you need to tell me?"* After she has gone, I turn my plea toward the dark contraption masquerading as a hospital bed.

*Let me loose, let me be!"*

*Beep…beep…Lub-dub, lub-dub, lub-dub*

The orchestra begins to soothe, or is it to distract me?

I have fallen asleep, and when I awake, the Corridor returns like a recurrent dream. I run toward the Garden in search of Suniva, but it is the Gentleman who greets me this time. Gesturing to me with an outstretched hand, He leads me back to the door.

"Why must I go back there? It's so unkind," I protest, following closely at his heels.

"This is the only way, you must go through the process," He explains while walking ahead of me. When we approach the door, His eyes guide me to the worn doorknob.

"No," I shake my head, backing away. "It's dark there, and I can't feel anything. My mouth doesn't speak, and my body won't move. It's that bed, it won't let me be," I complain.

"The point is to listen; you must hear what needs to be said," He tells me.

"At least help me out of that bed, let me see something. Even Ebenezer Scrooge was able to see, to feel…and move." I debate with the Gentleman to no avail.

"The Scrooge is a fictional character," He laughs.

"Well, I'm not really here, and I'm not really there. I'm not alive, and yet I'm not dead." I tell Him.

"Your heart is still beating; have you not been listening?" He questions me.

I nod, Yes. How could I not hear the concert of my body and the machines. They are like the slow rising horns and shimmering violins of the Blue Danube Waltz. Only my rendition differs from the classical piece, which was beautiful and lively; the version I'm left with is slightly off-key, never quite reaching its triumphant peak.

The Gentleman raises an arm toward the door. Shaking my head, I continue backing away. Forgetting He's able to hear my thoughts, I consider running away from the corridor. Before I can take another step, He touches the door, and the darkness of the hospital bed returns.